Benjamin Manry
and the
Scarlet Stone

BOOK THREE
of

The Adventures of Benjamin Manry

BENJAMIN MANRY
AND THE
Scarlet Stone

Owen Palmiotti

Benjamin Manry and the Scarlet Stone

Copyright © 2013 Owen Palmiotti. All rights reserved. No part of this book may be reproduced or retransmitted in any form or by any means without the written permission of the publisher.

Published by Wheatmark®
1760 East River Road, Tucson, Arizona 85718 U.S.A.
www.wheatmark.com

ISBN: 978-1-60494-977-3 (paperback)
ISBN: 978-1-60494-978-0 (ebook)
LCCN: 2013935288

"I suppose we dream, so that it gives us certain goals to attain, and there is nothing more enjoyable than living the *dream*."

-Benjamin Manry-

To the Cadets, crew, and Officers of the T.S. Empire State,

This may very well be the best of them all... until the fourth comes!

There are a lot of people that help you through writing a book. For me, I'd like to express my gratitude to the memory of my mother, Lorraine Palmiotti. This also goes out to my friends and family for their unending support over the years. To Lynne for doing an excellent job with the editing. Also, I express my utmost thanks to the friendly personnel at Wheatmark for getting my words into print. And lastly, to the readers who make a writer enjoy their job of putting their thoughts down on paper, because after all, without you guys, I wouldn't be writing this dedication.

Enjoy!

Prologue

Modern Day
St. Augustine, Florida

John Manry was humming to himself as he worked under the hood of his classic car, a 1963 Chevrolet Nova. It was one of the first vehicles with a fuel-injected engine. One at a time, he tightened the bolts on the standard six-cylinder engine. With a damp rag, he wiped off the engine block, cleaning his newfound hobby. Things had certainly changed around their household when both his sons went missing.

Several months earlier, Benjamin and Harris Manry, and their best friend, Sal Draben, had discovered the cursed treasure of the famous pirate, Captain Blood Bones. They had been lost to the perils of time, transported back to 1763.

The household was now very quiet—almost too quiet. Oftentimes John and his wife Margie would just sit around and simply wait for their children to come home. After months of this they realized that doing so would be a burden on their hearts and would quickly drive them insane.

It took a while to adjust, but John found something to keep his mind busy—he bought an old and beat-up car and began working on it. It was something he had always wanted to do if he had free time, and now he had plenty of it. John had invested a few thousand dollars on the actual vehicle, and about the same in parts. Now a week into the project, he had just finished cleaning the engine compartment, and refitted the engine block with brand new belts.

He was proud of his work. He closed his eyes and sniffed, basking in the aroma of new rubber and cleaning agents—it was something that calmed him.

A startling noise behind him caused him to jump. John bumped his head on the hood of the car, causing him to curse loudly.

The phone was ringing in the kitchen. He could let it go to the answering machine, but he realized his wife was out running errands and assumed it was her calling. He knew that her car was in definite need of a check-up, so it could be an emergency. It was always better to be prepared for the worst. He left the rag he'd been using on the edge of the car and then made his way through the side entrance to his house. As his feet touched the kitchen floor, he heard a familiar voice.

"Good afternoon, this is Professor Yocklem at the Boston Museum. Um, this is going to sound kind of weird, but um…." He trailed off, leaving a brief moment of silence. "…I'm not really sure how to say this, but I think your children may be alive. There was a break-in this morning in the Pirates and Privateers exhibit. The security guard said there were three males and one female—"

John sprinted across the kitchen at full speed, pushing aside a chair. It toppled over. With a swoop of his hand, he picked up the phone. His heavy breathing interrupted the man's speech.

"—that had entered the museum about an hour before it opened for the day," Professor Yocklem said in a wavering voice. He heard a click and assumed that someone was on the other end of the line. "Hello? Mr. Manry? Mrs. Manry?"

"Sorry, yeah, it's John. I was in the garage when you called. I had to run into the house." He paused. "What happened? Tell me everything!"

The professor heard the father's sudden enthusiasm. There was no easy way to phrase what he was about to say. "Hello, John. I am glad I got in touch with you." He cleared his throat. "Yes, yes. So, as I was saying—I went in to work as usual, and I received a message that there had been a disturbance in the Pirates and Privateers exhibit. I talked with the security guards on duty at the time of the event. They explained that there were three males and one female involved. One of them broke into the glass display, setting off the alarm. On first inspection nothing seemed to be missing, but then I noticed that the three-foot long staff you and your wife sent me a few months back was nowhere to be found." He paused for a moment, gathering himself for the rest of what he had to say.

John remained quiet, not sure if anything he might say would incriminate his family.

"The other thing is that they went missing—again."

"What do you mean, they went missing again?" John asked.

There was a pause, as the professor phrased his words carefully. "Several of the on-duty security guards managed to capture one of the four. The other three escaped. We had local authorities interrogate this man, who calls himself Captain Arthur F. Nelson. He claimed to be from the eighteenth century and said he was an English privateer. He mentioned that they were on a quest to save Benjamin Manry. In any case, he was locked inside a break room for a good portion of the day. The other three managed to sneak back into the museum, which had been guarded, of course." He caught his breath. "They were dressed in business suits, pretending to be nautical relic specialists. The guard let them in without consulting me, and when I arrived to investigate no one was inside. It looked like a violent whirlwind had passed through the room—everything was in complete disarray. We also found counterfeit identification badges, and there were two exact matches to the missing persons from when we last spoke. I believe one of them to be your son—I believe Harris, your oldest."

John closed his eyes, adding up the facts and his heart raced. He remembered seeing the discarded windbreaker inside the cave where his children had disappeared many months ago. There was also something special about the name of the privateer the curator had just mentioned, but there were only two identification matches. Harris, and from what it seemed, Sal. It was not enough for him.

"Is there anything else?" John's voice was aggressive and forceful. "Please. Tell me everything you know or even think you know."

There was a shuffle of paperwork and then the professor's voice filled the phone. "The report of the initial break-in said that the four members were dressed oddly, as if for Halloween costume party or some sort of historical reenactment." The professor paused, allowing for his words to sink in. "We all thought it was a prank at first, but the item stolen is quite magnificent. It is worth a lot of money, and is an invaluable piece for our museum. I remembered your association with the item and I felt obliged to inform you of what had happened, just in case there was more to the story. We are still looking through the surveillance footage to learn as much as we can about what happened, but I'll send you over a copies of the ID badges we found."

John sighed. "Well, thanks for the information. It's a start at least. I appreciate the help. I will pass the story on to my wife and to the Drabens. If anything else develops, please let us know."

"Of course," the professor said. "We are looking over the security tapes as we speak to see if there is anything else we are missing. I'll be in touch the moment we figure out what happened."

"Great, thanks. Have a good day."

John hung up the phone and shook his head, warding off the insane possibility that his children had found a way home, back to modern day. He then smiled, wondering if it was even possible to travel leisurely back and forth through time. He knew that his sons had stumbled upon something behind their wildest imaginations, and as much as the father inside him was upset and worried at their sudden disappearance, there was something else that caused a stir of excitement in their adventures.

"They're smart kids. They'll find a way back home—I'm sure of it." John said to an empty room.

1

June 25, 1763
King's Quarters
Buckingham Palace, London

Just a few days before, King George III had dispatched Captain Arthur F. Nelson and his men on a daring mission to assassinate Prime Minister George Grenville. England was in financial ruin: in debt from the Seven Years' War that had been fought on two different continents. The king had asked his new prime minister to focus his efforts on steadying the nation's finances. He had many ears and eyes throughout his kingdom, and rumor was that the prime minister planned to heavily tax the American colonies. King George was against this strategy for filling the nation's empty coffers, and he had warned George Grenville several times against it. Parliament, however, went along with Grenville's efforts, as they were looking for a quick and easy, temporary solution.

The king was left with only one option—to kill George Grenville.

He anxiously paced back and forth through his study. It seemed that the minutes had turned to hours, and quickly into days while he waited for news of the mission. Sleep had not been on his agenda since he sent his loyal men on the task. Time was insignificant at the moment, he just wanted to hear news of the mission.

There was a light knock on the door, but he was too distracted with his puttering footsteps. The second knock, which was a little louder, brought him out of his reverie.

He made his way slowly to the door and opened it.

"Your majesty," a young uniformed man bowed in greeting. "With all due respect, these men wish to have a moment of your time."

He looked at his guard, and then at the men behind him.

"Well, what is it?" King George said. He scanned the faces closer, focusing on the individuals rather than the group as a whole. Since issuing the orders for the assassination, he had not once slept through an entire night, and he was clearly on edge.

His wondering gaze then stopped on Prime Minster George Grenville, the man he had ordered assassinated. Surprise flashed across his face. *The man should be dead!* He thought.

He hoped no one noticed his expression. His gaze shifted once again, taking in the other faces in the crowd.

Beside the prime minister stood Captain Richard Highmore. His army uniform was neatly pressed, displaying the many awards and medals he had earned over his long career. He had fought with honor in India during the Seven Years' War, winning many battles for king and country. His fiery red hair was tied back in a greasy ponytail and he had a smile on his face that could only mean trouble. His smirk was sinister in every way possible. Several other high officials stood nearby, awaiting counsel.

"My king." He took a deep bow. "There was an assassination attempt on the prime minister in Sherwood Forest. After my spies learned of this, I set a trap to surround the traitors and saved Prime Minister Grenville," Captain Highmore said. In truth, the spy was following his beautiful young wife, Leah. She was young, and in love with Benjamin Manry, a handsome privateer half his age. The spy lurked in the shadows, and learned of the traitorous act, devised by Captain Arthur F. Nelson, Ben's senior officer. Highmore's chest swelled with pride—in one fortunate act, he had served his country as well as ended the romance between his wife and the young sailor. "The miscreants fought back and killed many of our men, but we prevailed. They are locked up now in the dungeons and await your decision for their fate."

This may be the only man who knows of my attachment to the assassination. I must be very careful with my words, King George thought.

"Those woods are haunted and plagued by hooligans and rascals. I am glad you are safe. You can never be too careful in that blasted forest," he said, looking directly at the man he wished dead. "An attack upon you is the same as an attack upon myself, and this attempt must receive the proper attention! Those men you speak of will be hung tomorrow!"

"Thank you for your kind words, sire. I was on my way to my family's estate when our carriage was attacked," Grenville said. "Luckily, Captain Highmore and his men were there to save us. Without his rescue, I would most certainly be dead, or at the very least held for ransom."

Ah, that is too bad, King George thought. He suppressed a chuckle at the irony of what had happened. *I wonder how all of this happened.*

"Ah, where are my manners?" The king paused. He smiled at the men before him, changing his expressions and demeanor on cue. "Gentlemen, come in, come in. We can sit down at the table." He then turned toward the young guard standing quietly off to the side. "Have some tea and pastries brought up."

"Yes, your majesty," the guard said. "Excuse me, gentlemen." He made his way out of the group.

"If you will all follow me," King George said. He led them into one of the largest rooms in the estate, which was home to one of the best observatories in all of England. He passed by an enormous globe that measured over four feet in diameter. The gold globe shone brightly, reflecting candlelight from overhead. He placed a hand and spun the globe slightly, breaking the silence in the room.

The king's study had a pleasant odor, a mix of old leather books and Oriental carpets Book shelves stretched all around the room. Lustrous paintings hung on nearly every vertical surface where there was no bookshelf, while metal suits of armor and coats of arms lined the far wall, weapons glistening proudly.

The king's prized possession, however, was a large telescope that had been given to him by the English astronomer, Edmond Halley—the very same telescope that had helped discover Halley's Comet pointed out of an open window.

"Gentlemen, sit," King George said. He gestured to a large wooden table a few feet from where he stood at the telescope.

He eyed all of the men in attendance, and hoped his mannerisms would not give away his trepidation. He then turned his back to his audience. He leaned down toward the telescopic eyepiece, closed his left eye, and placed his right against the scope. The heavens danced a celestial tango beyond.

"So Captain Highmore, these men you captured—Were they rascals or common thieves?" King George pried, speaking as casually as he could manage.

Highmore smiled, choosing his words carefully. "Of sorts, you could say. They were former privateers—*your* former privateers."

The king was trapped. To admit that they were indeed his men would set himself up for an interrogation, and kings had been executed for far less traitorous acts. He smiled, realizing his best plan of attack was to just go along—rather than fighting the current, he would allow it take him on fate's adventure. The king stepped away from the telescope and then locked eyes with each man in attendance, his gaze moving from one to the next to reinforce his power as king. He knew they would listen to each and every word he said.

"Ah, yes. I imagine you are referring to Captain Arthur F. Nelson, a longtime friend of mine until just a few days ago. You see, we had a falling out recently. Distasteful words were used. He said things. I said things. It was messy to say the least. I stripped him of his medals and banned him from setting foot aboard any ships or even the soil of our great nation."

His audience nodded, accepting his words eagerly. Prime Minister George Grenville took the bait. "Ah, so those men are traitors!"

"Yes, I believe Captain Nelson and his officers are traitors to the Crown. They are dangerous men, and must be punished as such. I must express my gratitude to Captain Richard Highmore again," he said, staring at the man's fiery red hair. He silently cursed the man, who stood from his seat at hearing his name. "You should be promoted for your gallant service. Meanwhile Captain Arthur F. Nelson and his men will be hung for their treachery! They made a mockery of us!"

The guilt of lying to cover up the conspiracy weighed heavily on his heart, but by no means could the king bear to be accused of such things. England might have another civil war if that happened. He shuddered at the thought of tyranny in his country. He had waited many years to take the reins from his grandfather, George II, watching him forge a path of greatness. The king would do anything to protect his position. Anything—even if it meant hanging a few of his beloved comrades to clean his hands of what transpired.

Highmore smiled. His inflated ego clouded his judgment. "I suppose I could adjust to a new title, perhaps general, or maybe even duke, and I could retire on a plantation in the colonies. I heard the Carolinas are beautiful this time of year. I could grow cotton, or tobacco."

Taking the opportunity and distraction, King George seized the moment. He let out a booming laugh. "And so, it will be yours! This is how I shall reward your loyalty to king and country."

The men around the table replied with the customary return, "To King and Country!"

King George cleared his throat. "Men, I believe we should all rest for what is to come. Tomorrow will be a big day—we will witness justice for what has happened! Captain Nelson and his men will hang!"

The king's voice carried through the open hallway, to the ears of his young cousin Louisa Ann, who was also in love with Benjamin Manry.

※※※

A formal trial would take time, and time, the king did not have. He had to get rid of Captain Nelson and his men as quickly as he could. The crowded courtyard bustled with spectators from all across England. Word of the grand conspiracy had spread far and wide. Messengers had ventured from town to town and garrison to garrison to tell of the upcoming legendary execution.

Waiting in the dungeons was a group of gallant and heroic men that were not so lucky on this day. They had survived many such days in their shared and interwoven fates.

The chains at their ankles clanked together during their laborious walk through the dimly lit dungeons, as they made their transit through the winding passages with guards spaced evenly along the walls, and finally through the dank, last corridor.

They emerged into a wall of noise. The jeers and cheers of the crowd outside became evermore deafening as the group of ill-fated sailors walked what would be their last walk, moving slowly as a group of drummers set the pace.

It is here where the story begins for several of the gallant crew, or rather ends if you wish to call it that. Just as one event came to a stop one certainly blossomed from the ashes like a phoenix welcoming a new life.

Dressed in common traveler's rags, Captain Arthur F. Nelson let out a deep sigh as he led his most trustworthy men. These were men who had served their country time and time again—winning countless battles and upholding the honorable values of an English Privateer. Nate Brodkin, Charles Marconi, and Benjamin Manry followed their leader toward the gallows, along with several more rag-wearing men in tow.

Why had such a large crowd assembled for the hangings?

The answer was simple—these heroic sailors who'd loyally served King George III had been caught amidst an assassination attempt on Prime Minister George Grenville. By definition, this was an act of treason.

Unfortunately, the timing of the occurrence was unfavorable for Nelson and his companions. Time, as always, separates the hero from the villain, the good from the bad, and patriots from traitors.

The situation was especially ironic, because the king had been the one to set them upon this task.

A light breeze carried the lingering scent of the ocean to the sailors atop the platform.

Benjamin Manry stood tall and proud, unsure of how to react to the recent turn of events. He breathed in the soothing air. It seemed to help calm him down. He scanned the crowd, attempting to find a certain face. After searching the sea of faces, his gaze settled on Leah. She stood beside her husband and he could not help but notice a wide grin on his face.

Their intricate plan had been spoiled—instead of setting a trap, they had walked right into one.

The recently promoted General Richard Highmore displayed a sinister smile as the light breeze fed the fire that sat atop his head. His eyes burned with hatred for the young man who had held his wife's love and affection.

Leah Highmore remained silent. She was unaware of the true reason her husband had dragged her along to witness the hangings. She was a proper young woman—well educated and respectful—and daughter to the Governor of Grand Bahama. She was certain of only one thing in her young life, and that was her love for Ben.

She scanned the crowded courtyard and saw Ben standing on the platform beside Captain Nelson and Sal. She looked at the other sailors about to be hung, but did not see Ben's brother, Harris in their midst. At that moment, something deep inside her rumbled—a terrible fear spread throughout her body. She was just moments away from losing Benjamin again. She felt for Ben's medallion around her neck. Its touch momentarily calmed her nerves, but it would not be enough.

Louisa Ann, cousin to the king, also pined for the same handsome young sailor. With his deep blue eyes, thick dark hair, and a cheerful smile that brought happiness to many hearts, how could she not?

But as she sat beside the king, she cringed at the fact that she would soon witness Ben's unfortunate demise. He was the first young lad who had caught her full attention. There was several dozen suitors: rich men, successful men, high-ranking men, but there was only one she wanted—Benjamin Manry.

She had lost all will. She had cried since hearing of the upcoming hangings, and she dabbed away now at fresh tears that streamed down her face at a pace her handkerchief could not keep up with.

A church bell rang out, signaling that the hangings would commence shortly.

The king sat quietly, thinking about his relations with the doomed men. Captain Nelson had long been a friend and loyal servant to the Crown, serving as a privateer for many years and throughout the Seven Years' War. The thought of his most successful subordinate, but also his friend, dangling from the noose plagued him tremendously. He let out a long sigh, battling the internal demons that told him possible rumors might spread of their association. After many hours of thought, he had reluctantly sent messengers far and wide, carrying a bulletin acknowledging Nelson's dishonorable discharge and medal stripping. If the plan worked, no one would think the wiser that he was behind the assassination attempt.

A steady drumming carried to his perch as Captain Nelson and his men walked to the gallows. The king whispered a silent goodbye to his loyal friends as the gaoler stood in the center of the ill-fated men.

2

MODERN DAY
BOSTON MUSEUM
BOSTON, MASSACHUSETTS

Two security guards sat behind the main desk in the lobby of the Boston Museum. They silently sipped their coffees and read their newspapers. Sam looked up at the clock above his head. He sighed. "Well, Bob, it's only seven in the morning, another hour to go."

"Yeah, Sam, it's the same routine each and every time. Do you want to take the last round?"

Sam shrugged indifferently.

Bob chuckled, sipping at his cup for one last caffeine rush before getting up to explore the nooks and crannies of the quiet museum. "Okay then, I'll take it. My legs are falling asleep anyways."

"Oh come on, way to be original." Sam paused, rubbing his hands over his eyes. "Way to make excuses! But, hey, you could also use the exercise."

"Ha...very funny." Bob smiled. "Actually the wifey has me walking a few times a week now with her and Scruffy."

"'The wifey'?" Sam laughed. "It sounds like she's walking you and Scruffy! Do you wear a collar and a leash?"

"Oh, zip your mouth!" Bob shook his head. A smile quickly formed on his lips. "If I didn't know better from working this shift together for so long, I would've made you part of the museum by now!"

"Oh? What exhibit?" Sam laughed, prodding his friend with the flashlight he held in his hand.

"Probably the Sphinx and Pharaohs. You'd look good under wraps, you know; no one would see your ugly face." He stood up and gave a friendly tap to his buddy's shoulder as he made his way down the hall.

Bob's flashlight pierced through the darkness of each exhibit. All exterior doors were locked from within and all windows were closed with the shades down. He heard the central air conditioning unit vibrate overhead. The steady hum of its fans soothed his mood. His gaze moved around casually, and he was ready to embark on what he thought would be a quiet round of the museum. After all, how could anyone get inside without setting off an alarm?

✺✺✺

A violent whirlwind of energy dashed quickly through the museum's eastern wing. A blinding orange and yellow light escaped a three-foot staff that sat quietly inside the second floor exhibit. Four bodies crashed to the ground there, their robes and dress fluttering in the wind. With one last boom of sound and energy, the blast of air receded and the blinding orange and yellow lights faded into nothingness.

They lay in a circle, then looked around in shock and panic as they rose, still expecting to hear the click of a gear and their own last guttural screams before the nooses choked the life out of them. Sal and Captain Nelson both instinctively reached for their necks, feeling for a rope that had just been there, but now was not. Harris and Leah lay sprawled on their stomachs.

The glow of three medallions they wore slowly dwindled in intensity, but the warmth on their chests felt surprisingly soothing in an eerie and hair-raising way. Nelson reached into his breast pocket, pulling out the crimson journal, a leather-bound book that contained the secrets to the curse of the famous pirate Blood Bones. It still glowed brightly.

"Where are we?" Sal asked, looking from puzzled face to puzzled face.

Nelson blinked several times in shock, finding it difficult to adjust to the change of scenery. Leah quivered in fear—her breathing was out of control, in a fit of panic. Simply put, she was hysterical.

Harris stood slowly, looking around the nearest exhibit. He took a couple of steps forward, wobbling from the pain that seared throughout his body. He read the sign that hung over the glass display.

"Pirates and Privateers," he mumbled for all to hear. Turning, he stared into the display, looking at a collection of weapons and coins from the eighteenth century. Common tools and coils of line sat inside, beside a collection of nautical books and articles. His gaze then shifted to the still-glowing magical staff. He knew this piece well—it was the same staff he and his friends had discovered so many months ago in the caverns of Roosevelt Island. It now seemed a lifetime ago, when he and his friends had spent their days roaming through the hallways of their high school. Yet again, the medallion around his neck had brought him through the line of time—though he was not sure exactly where he was, or even more important than that, *when*.

He noticed a piece of paper that was framed within the glass display. Knowing it must have significance, he began reading an article headlined JUNE 26, 1763, CONSPIRACY IN THE KING'S COURT.

"Oh my God, you guys won't believe his." Harris pressed his face to the glass display to get a closer look. He saw the group's reflection in the glass.

"What is it, Harris?" Nelson placed a hand on his shoulder.

"It's an article about what just happened. I mean, when we were back in time. It's all about our capture and execution. I'll read it out loud." Harris cleared his throat. He then let his voice carry. "As the crowd screamed out, some prayed for forgiveness for the eight men about to hang for treason to the Crown. Others yelled out for their deaths, others for their salvation. Certainly the countrymen have been upset with Prime Minister George Grenville's recent indulgences, but these convicted men tried to take the matter into their own hands. Whatever their purpose, they would not be sharing it at evening meal, for the drums began their steady beat yet again. Their warrants and death sentences were read. Suddenly a swift wind carried across the platform. Their robes were ruffled as a blinding light ripped through the crowd. I myself fell backward, stumbling in fear. Whether of magic or Devil's work I cannot say, but in that flash of energy two bodies went missing. Six remained, swinging lifeless as the crowd shrieked in disbelief at the spectacle, and the orange and yellow glow faded away slowly..."

Harris stood off to the side, allowing the others to take a better look. The archived report had been by an anonymous person, and it summarized their narrow escape from death. However, reading about the lost six meant the death of a brother, close friends, and a lover, which brought tears to their eyes.

"I do not understand!" Leah cried. She looked around at her three friends, anxiously prodding them for information. She wiped away tears with her sleeve. "What has happened to Benjamin and the others?"

Harris looked at Sal. "Listen, we've traveled back through time once. I bet we're sometime in the future now, probably not too far from the time when we actually first left, or maybe even at the same time, just in a different place, obviously. It looks like the medallions brought us to the staff for some reason. Let's try and find out exactly where and when we are."

Leah cringed at the statement. She had absolutely no idea what Harris was talking about. Another wave of tears and hysteria came.

Sal nodded. "Yeah, good idea. I think you're on to something." He quietly put an arm around Leah, hoping to calm her. "It will be all right, Leah."

Nelson remained quiet, thinking of the many passages he had read in the crimson journal, which contained the many secrets of Blood Bones. He placed a reassuring hand on Leah's shoulder. He then looked at Harris and Sal to get their attention. "Leah." He cleared his throat. "There is much for us to explain. I know that this does not make any sense at all to you. This is all new to me as well, but I know that there is something we can do for Benjamin and the others."

Leah began sniffling so loudly that Nelson thought it best to wait for her to calm down before speaking again. She finally nodded for him to continue, ready to hear what the brave privateer had to say. "Our rescue lies within this crimson journal," he paused, showing her the journal, "upon these gold medallions around your necks, and inside that magical staff." He pointed into the display, where the precious stone glittered as if in mockery.

There was only one thing left to do—he balled his hand into a fist and swung with all his might. His knuckles broke through the glass. Blood quickly welled upon the cuts but he ignored it as he removed the three-foot-long cursed staff from the display. In the distance a security alarm went off at the main security desk, its sound filling the grand halls of the museum.

※※※

Sam watched as Bob walked away from the main security desk. He resumed reading, skimming an article about the local sports teams.

"Damn, we always lose!" He threw down the newspaper in disgust, then looked at the security monitor for a few minutes, watching the figure of his partner pace down a corridor. They had a few hours before the museum would open and the Saturday visitor traffic would begin to flow through.

He opened the newspaper again, but this time rather than reading the sports section, he flipped to the puzzles and comics. After a few minutes, he let out a sigh as his eyes wandered toward the digital clock on the wall. He kept thinking of the time left in his shift, hoping it would pass more quickly.

He smiled when he saw that a Sudoku puzzle was still blank. Sam picked up a pencil and began going through the rows and columns on the page, eliminating numbers as he started to solve the puzzle. He was so completely absorbed with filling in the small boxes with numbers that he did not notice a red blinking light on the security panel.

Ten seconds after the light began blinking the general security alarm went off, startling Sam. He pushed his chair back in shock.

"What the—" he called out, not realizing what had just happened.

He looked at the panel to find where the alarm had sounded. A split second later, he heard a voice on the radio at his hip.

"Sam, what the heck was that?" Bob yelled from his end.

"We got a Code Red in Sector 14: east wing, second floor," Sam radioed, still looking at the panel. "I'll silence the alarm, but get back to me with an update. I'll hold down Home Base until you return."

"Roger dodger. It's probably just a false alarm. It rained pretty heavy the other day. I wouldn't be surprised if precipitation leaked through the roof and got into the electrical system again."

"Yeah. It's happened a few times in the last couple of days. I'll log it in at 0735. See you when you get back."

Bob double-clicked the transmit button, ending the transmission. The soles of his shoes squeaked loudly as he made his way down the empty and now-quiet corridor.

✖◇✖◇✖

All eyes were on Nelson's bloodied hands as he removed the magical staff from the glass display. The beautiful scepter had first belonged to Sir Francis Drake, a gift from Queen Elizabeth in the sixteenth century, and but then was "obtained" by Blood Bones, a fierce pirate who had been hunted by all. Nelson knew the staff was one of the important components to a curse the pirate had set on his treasure.

Sal and Harris stared into the shattered display. Sirens blared throughout the hallways of the museum while flashing lights danced on the polished floors. Both Leah and Captain Nelson looked around for the source of the noise. Everything was new to them. Leah was visibly trembling in fear and confusion, completely out of the loop with everything that had just occurred, ignorant as well of the truth behind Ben's appearance—and recent disappearance—in her life.

After a few moments of chaos the alarms stopped, giving the time-travelers a second of relief.

"Well, at least we have the staff again." Sal smiled in relief.

Nelson's knuckles were still bleeding, but he ignored them and held the staff up to the light above. Used to only candles, fire, and the warmth of the sun, his expression was puzzled by the source of the light as he used modern technology to gain a closer look at the staff.

"Aye, that we have. But can we properly use it to get back to 1763 so we can save Ben and the rest of our men?" Nelson closed his eyes, wrapping his brain around the mystery before them.

Harris moved forward, getting a closer look at the object that had originally sent them back in time. "Well, should we also address how this got here into the museum? Obviously someone found it after we disappeared in the caves on Roosevelt Island. Right, Sal?"

Sal nodded. "I bet our parents came looking for us when we didn't return after the weekend. They probably found the staff, but we were nowhere to be seen. Then I guess it was sent here?" He looked around, attempting to locate there whereabouts with a clue—any clue. "Wherever here actually is."

Nelson interrupted. "Gentlemen, we have a lot to discuss, but I would advise we read through this crimson journal again." He held up the journal. "I do not fully understand how the curse works. Perhaps with your help, we can make sense of it. Throughout all of his entries, Blood Bones tells the story of how he became who he is. It is a grand tale of the transition of Hernando Audaz into the pirate we know as Blood Bones. You gentlemen are also a big part of his story," the captain said.

He was very aware that Benjamin Manry, his young third officer, was missing from this group. Just moments before they had been whisked away to the future, Ben had dangled from a noose back in eighteenth-century London. He whispered a silent prayer for his comrade.

Harris nodded. "Yeah, well, I think it's a verbal curse." He looked at Sal for anything he may have missed. "If I remember correctly, the message had different handwriting, and we read that message." But before he could continue speaking, he was interrupted.

Leah shivered and rocked slowly back and forth, holding her elbows. "Can one of you please tell me what has happened? We were in a crowded courtyard watching our friends hang, and now we are suddenly here," she spoke quickly, as if all her words were one word. She paused to catch her breath. She then looked at Sal and Harris with a deep and penetrating gaze. "What do you mean, you were sent back in time?"

Harris looked ready to begin the long story that Leah eagerly wanted to hear, but just as he was about to speak, a loud sound filled the hallway.

"What was that?" Harris asked instead.

All four heads turned, unaware that a security guard had just barreled through a nearby stairwell door, dashing down the hallway at full gait toward them.

Bob removed his 9-mm pistol from his holster and leveled it at the group.

"Freeze!" the guard screamed. He was standing about twenty feet away from the shattered glass display and the intruders.

None of them moved, unsure of what to do.

"Get on the ground!" he pointed his weapon at each intruder. "Now!"

Harris and Sal looked at each other. They both kneeled on the ground, urging Nelson and Leah to follow suit.

"Come on! All the way on the floor!" Bob held the pistol out with his right hand as he grabbed at the walkie-talkie with his left. "Sam, we have four intruders. Section 14: east wing, second floor. There are three males and one female. They broke into that Pirate and Privateers exhibit." He was unaware that Nelson had slipped the magical staff into his coat.

"Roger that. Do you need backup? Tim and Nick came in early. They heard the alarm go off from the staff locker room. Do you want us to head your way?" Sam responded.

"Yeah, I could use some help," Bob spoke into the microphone. He then looked at the intruders. "Don't do anything stupid!"

※※※

Bob continued shifting the barrel of his 9mm between each intruder. Once content that they were not going to make a difficult time of the ordeal; he lowered the weapon a few inches.

"All right. One at a time, stand up." He made the motion between each person, signaling them to move with the barrel of his weapon.

Harris stood first. Sal followed. Next came Leah. Nelson paused, determined to rearrange the cursed staff in his robes so that the guard would not notice the bulge. Once he was satisfied that it would not be seen, Nelson stood beside his friends.

"Excellent. I'm glad you are all cooperating. Everybody goes into the break room until the police arrive."

There was no response.

"Get in a single file line," he commanded. "You're going to walk straight until you stop at the corner. There will be a restroom on your left. You'll make a right and it'll be the first door you see in that new hallway."

Restroom? Leah mouthed. She shook the confusion out of her head and they started to walk as one.

Like sheep, the group was herded toward the break room. They walked for a few minutes, passing by several displays. There were different uniforms in the glass windows: British Red Coats and the uniforms of the Continental Army. Sal and Harris briefly eyed the placards below each. There were paintings also displayed, depicting numerous sea and land battles in the conflict that had given birth to the United States of America. A painting of the Boston Massacre dated March 5, 1770 came into view. The next exhibit featured an original copy of Thomas Paine's *Common Sense*. The final glass display in the corridor was of Emanuel Leutze's painting of Washington crossing the Delaware River, hidden behind a thick slav of protective glass.

They walked slowly, absorbing the exhibits. They continued on down another hallway, advancing through the years as America's wars were sequenced, with each step toward their destination. They passed by displays of the First and Second World Wars, Korea, and Vietnam.

No one spoke. Leah and Captain Nelson were perplexed at seeing various time periods unfold before their eyes. The only sound echoing through the hallways was that of their shoes upon the waxed floors, and the occasional sniffle of tears as Leah wiped her eyes with a sleeve.

Bob noticed everyone's hesitance at moving quickly. "Come on all, don't delay. This isn't a freaking tour!"

They came to the intersection and Harris paused. He looked left at the restroom door, then to the right, and saw something. A plan began to formulate quickly in his mind.

"Okay now, make another right. Don't do anything stupid!" Bob directed.

Harris shook his head, witnessing the man's bravery at escorting unarmed people through the hallways of a museum. He let out a chuckle.

"Did you say something?" Bob responded quickly.

Harris went quiet. He turned where he was told to and saw the break room door. Beside the open door, a recycling bin stood, full to the brink with bottles and cans.

Sal was just a pace behind. He also turned the corner before the other three followed in his wake. He caught sight of Harris reaching for the large green bin. Sal slowed his pace, catching on to what Harris was thinking. Just as Nelson and the security guard rounded the corner, Harris grabbed at the bin in one swift motion and hit the guard square in the chest, knocking him backward. Bob tripped over his own feet and the contents exploded out of the bin, littering the floor with recyclables.

"Run!" Harris called, leading the group past the break room. They raced down the hallway as Bob struggled to get up.

They gained about a ten-second lead on the security guard. Harris pushed open an emergency door, which set off another alarm, and found himself on a platform between staircases. There was an arrow pointing up, with the word "ROOF" in red below it. He shrugged off that idea, and moved toward the stairs heading to the first floor.

"Come on, we don't have time!" Sal yelled from behind. "Move!"

Harris took the stairs two at a time. He heard a screech as a door from below opened, and paused, pressed up against the staircase wall to hide.

He heard the click of a microphone. "Sam, this is Tim. I'm at the first floor staircase in Sector 10. I just entered it. There's some commotion above me; I'm going to check it out."

"Roger that; we just got an alarm off the emergency door above your position. Yeah; someone is definitely over there. Check it out and report back to me."

"Shit! Turn around, guys!" Harris hissed under his breath. He turned on a heel just as he made it to the middle platform, and locked gazes with the security guard below. "Hurry!"

The group raced back up the stairs. Just as they passed by the second floor entrance, the door burst open and Bob emerged. The four hurtled themselves forward as Bob and Tim followed several feet behind.

Harris pushed open the door to the roof. He rushed through and he felt the crisp, refreshing morning air against his face. Sal came out of the doorway next, followed by Captain Nelson and Leah. Harris moved to the side of the roof.

"What are we going to do?" Sal yelled as he stood beside Harris. The two looked at each other, then to the ten-foot gap between the buildings' rooftops. Harris inched toward the edge, and stared down. The adjacent rooftop was a few feet lower, and he did a quick mental calculation.

Just then, the door burst open again and the two security guards emerged into view.

"Jump!" Harris stepped a few paces back. He accelerated and reached the edge of the building, propelling his feet off the edge. His body soared through space and he landed safely on the other rooftop.

"Come on! It wasn't too bad." Harris looked up across the gap.

It was Sal's turn now. He propelled himself forward. He pushed off the edge and hurtled the gap. Nelson and Leah remained on the other side.

"Leah, you can do it! Come on!" they encouraged from the other side.

Nelson looked back at the pursuing guards. If he jumped first, he was confident that Leah would not be able to jump the gap without assistance.

"Excuse me for this." He stared into Leah's eyes, grabbed her around the waist, and took a few powerful steps toward the edge of the building. She was hurled across the gap into the waiting arms of Sal and Harris.

Just as Leah stood, she looked back. Behind Captain Nelson, one of the guards had taken a nightstick out. Reaching back in a wide swing, he brought the weapon sideways and hit Nelson in the side. He doubled over and fell to his knees.

Nelson found it difficult to breathe, but he fought on. It took him a second to regain his footing before he pushed the guard back, placing his full weight into the barrage. The first guard stumbled into the one behind him, and for a moment, Nelson weighed his options. He was in no state to jump the gap, not with the pain pulsating through his body and his attackers easily within reach. It would be a suicide attempt.

He reached into his robes and pulled out the cursed staff. Its headpiece glittered with the morning light shining off it. He made eye contact with Harris, and as if he were in a relay race, passed the baton to the next runner. Captain Nelson took a few steps toward the edge of the building and hurled the magical staff. All eyes followed it into Harris's hands.

Moments later, the guards surrounded Nelson. They closed on his position and wrestled him to the ground. One managed to get a handcuff on his wrist as he tossed and turned, fighting the other off. He knocked one man down. Nelson rolled over and stood up quickly, but a guard managed to jump onto Nelson's back just as he stood erect, bringing both men down to the tarred roof at their feet. Nelson's free wrist was placed into the other cuff.

After the skirmish, all parties were physically and mentally exhausted, panting for air. No one moved. Moments later, as Captain Nelson was pulled up to his knees, he caught a glimpse at the adjacent rooftop—it was empty. He sighed with relief that his friends had escaped. He smiled, knowing that the cursed staff was safe in their possession, and that meant possible escape for him, as well as the future rescue of Benjamin Manry and his loyal crew.

Professor Michael D. Yocklem pulled his car into his parking spot. He removed the keys from the ignition and he stared at the morning sunlight that filtered in through his windshield. He was running a little late that Saturday morning, but it didn't really matter. It was a few minutes before eight, and he smiled as he looked into the mirror. "Who goes to the museum this early anyway?" He let out a chuckle.

He reached across to the center console and grabbed his coffee mug. He let out a sigh and exited the car, moving along the silver Jaguar Sedan. Yocklem popped the hatch and grabbed a leather briefcase before leisurely making his way to a side entrance of the museum.

Placing his Museum Identification card against the magnetic reader, he opened the locked door. The hallways were empty and he moved slowly to his office. After a few minutes, he arrived in front of a closed door that had a plaque with his name and title on it: CURATOR OF NAUTICAL FINDS.

His answering machine was blinking, but he ignored it for the time being. He opened the briefcase, removed his laptop, and inserted the power cord and Internet cable. He took a sip from the coffee mug and then turned on the laptop. A few moments later the screensaver, a background of his family sitting around a Christmas tree, came into view. He double-clicked on EMAIL and then stood up from his desk.

No new emails.

Michael let out a sigh and then moved to the answering machine. He clicked PLAY.

"Professor Yocklem, this is Sam at the main security desk. There was a disturbance in Section 14: second floor, east wing, at 0735. Three males and one female somehow got into the museum without setting off any alarms and then shattered the glass display in the Pirates and Privateers exhibit. I'm not sure if anything is missing, though." There was a pause. "Unfortunately three got away. Only one male was apprehended."

Michael Yocklem frowned. Several months ago his college roommate, Tom, had called him concerning a mysterious object found in a complex cave system in St. Augustine, Florida. He was not too sure of the story behind how the staff came into his former roommate's possession. He did not ask and he honestly did not care. All he knew about it was that it seemed to have caused the deaths of three teenagers. He remembered the correspondence with their parents. This memory came to him and the morning's details began to add up. He shivered then raced through the quiet halls of the museum, hoping to discover what he could about the mysterious break-in.

3

Modern Day
Boston, Massachusetts

Harris led the group down the staircase of the adjacent building. The sun was just inching over the surrounding buildings, causing a stream of light to shimmer off rooftops. Leah held her dress by her hips, running in his wake. Sal remained a few feet behind, still wary that they might be pursued. They stopped at the first floor landing. Harris saw a sign that pointed to the loading bay behind the building. He popped open the door slowly, moving it a few inches. He sighed with relief when no alarms went off. He continued until he could slide through without difficulties, while keeping the door open only a foot.

"Come on, let's try and find a place to hide." He held the door open for Leah to pass through, and then met Sal's gaze. "All right, let's go!" he whispered.

Slowly, he closed the door, careful to not make any noise.

There were several cars and trucks in the parking lot. A FedEx delivery truck idled while nearby a man loaded several boxes onto a handcart. They proceeded past. cautiously as a group, moving from car to car, and then stopped at the sidewalk. There was a very rusty blue post office box next to them, and Harris around it, leading the others to the curb. About a hundred feet down the road to their right was a stoplight. Two cars idled there, their exhaust spewing out a cloudy smog.

Harris looked around. Once satisfied that no one was watching them, he made his move.

"Come on guys," he said. He looked back, checking their progress. "We can do this." They kept their heads low and quickly crossed the street, moving in a single line.

With every step forward, the streets seemed to get busier and busier, almost as if the city was coming to life around them. Pedestrians filled the streets; vendors were selling coffee and various breakfast foods.

Their movement drew the attention of several passersby, but they kept their heads low and followed the maze of streets until they were deep into the historic district of Boston. Ahead, they saw a group on a tour of the fort and battery that guarded the harbor. Harris thought quickly and signaled for his friends to merge in. One by one they blended into the mass of tourists and tour guides. No one seemed to notice their sudden appearance or their strange dress here.

✴✴✴

Stuck in the break room, Captain Nelson had the crimson journal open, leafing through the pages to see if he had missed anything useful. Dates progressed in the entries as Hernando Audaz described how he'd become the infamous hunted pirate Captain Blood Bones. As much as he would have loved to delve into the man's brilliant mind again, Nelson decided to try a different approach. He paced around the room, looking at the various movie and sports posters hanging on the walls. In his mind, he was comparing what he now saw to what he was used to from his previous life: oil paintings on canvas were now printed pieces on shiny material; light that had before come from oil lanterns was now provided by a long luminescent set of overhead tubes. Everything he was used to was completely different, and the concept intrigued him.

He searched the room, puzzled by many of the items around

him. There were numerous tabletops with odd-looking boxes on them. Various cords ran behind each, and also to another smaller boxy container with sheets of very fine paper stored below. Another box, of a larger size but with a similar style of opaque glass across its face, was mounted to a corner of the wall, and it took up a good chunk of the wall space. He was perplexed.

He moved toward the largest of these to get a closer look. He traced a finger around the glass plate, and dust accumulated on his fingertip. He wiped off the dust with his thumb and continued on, moving his hand toward a different colored part of the hard material of which the box was made. Clearly it was not of wood or metal. He pushed several buttons to no avail. When his finger pushed down on a green circle, the glass lit up as it came to life. The volume of the voices he heard coming from the machine was loud, causing him to jump back, completely startled.

Nelson stared at the screen, amazed by the images of human beings in a two-dimensional representation. He tried to see around the back of the machine but it was held fast to the wall. These people were talking, walking, and living creatures, and he wondered momentarily how they could have gotten so small and into the box. After trying to for several moments to communicate with them and receiving no response, he somehow sensed that this strange invention created the impression of their presence, just an illusion. He shook his head at the oddity of the thought.

✳✳✳

Three figures sat atop the fortress that overlooked Boston harbor. Sal and Harris stared off into the distance while Leah smoothed out ruffles in her dress. After a few minutes of silence, Harris cleared his throat to get everyone's attention.

"Leah, there's so much that we have to tell you. Ben really wanted to but he just couldn't. He always told me that he wasn't sure how to bring it up. I guess he was afraid or something." He paused. He then looked right into her eyes. "All I know is he loves you, and that from what he's said, and what I've observed from your interactions, you love him." He glanced over at Sal. "You see, the three of us are from the future. We stumbled upon the cursed treasure of Captain Blood Bones, and it sent us back to 1763. We're not really sure how the curse works, but that's how we crossed paths with you the first time." He looked at Leah's confused face, understanding that the concept would be completely foreign and far-fetched to her. "I know it's hard to believe, and I know that Ben wanted to be the one to have told you all of this, but Leah, I know my brother inside-and-out. You are the love of his life. I am totally sure of it. I've never heard him talk about another person as much as he talked about you." He cleared his throat. "But we need to focus on what's the most important right now; rescuing Captain Nelson. He still has the crimson journal, and I think it's a very important piece of the puzzle to get us back to 1763. For every hour that passes, it will be more difficult to find him. They might have already moved him from the museum, so we need to come up with something quick."

Sal nodded. "Yeah, I agree. We can't just leave him here."

Leah stared on, still wrapping her brain around what Harris had just said. Sal and Harris looked at each other, not sure of what else to tell Leah.

"Benjamin always seemed different. I could tell he was always thinking of something, while saying something else," Leah said.

Harris smiled. "Well, he is definitely *different*, I think he was *adopted*."

Sal laughed. "Good one!"

"All right. Enough smoking and joking, buddy. We need to figure out a plan," Harris replied. He then pointed to his medallions, as if giving Leah a brief lesson on the proper way to conduct time travel. The expression on her face suggested she was still a little confused. "I know it sounds crazy, but these medallions, the crimson journal Captain Nelson still has, along with the staff he threw us, somehow have given us the ability to travel through time. Where we are now is very far in the future from what you're used to." He waited until Leah showed a little bit of understanding. "We just traveled over two hundred years into the future. We're all going to have to trust each other to get through this—and we'll explain more to you when we have a little more time to talk about it after we rescue Captain Nelson."

He let his words sink in.

Sal smiled. "I wonder if we can just walk in and be like, 'Hey, we left our friend behind. Can we have him?'"

Harris chuckled at his friend's joke. "Come on, dude. Really? We have to look at all our options." Each of them then pondered ways to save their leader and then, hopefully, the rest of their shipmates. "I guess we could attempt something similar." Harris shrugged. "I'm open to suggestions."

Sal tilted his head, putting more thought into what he suggested. "Well, here's what we know: there is a loading bay behind both buildings. I'm sure there's a ramp where they load exhibits and packages into the museum, which could be our in. Perhaps we can steal a delivery truck and fake a delivery. We could then sneak into the museum from the rear entrance and rescue Captain Nelson."

Harris shrugged. "Well, I like the general idea of going straight back to the museum, but there are way too many variables. Too many things can go wrong. We don't even actually know if he's still there. And I imagine they would be suspicious of a delivery for an order they didn't make, especially right after the incident."

"I guess you're right, now that you put it that way," Sal said.

Leah closed her eyes for a moment. Thinking about something other than their predicament seemed to help her mood. "I think we should listen to Sal. It would seem that this is our best option, but there are still things that we would need to address."

Like the harbor below, the group was quiet again, mulling the last comment over. They reflected in the silence while watching ships, boats, and pleasure crafts resting gently at anchor or tied at the docks. The mooring lines moved lightly to and fro, creating a barely audible symphony. The sun's rays shimmered off the crests of waves in the distance.

Harris smiled. "I think I got it. Leah, I am going to tell you a few things to say, and you're going to repeat them back to me. I want you to be as serious as you can. Will you do that for me now?"

"Of course," she said. "Anything that will help save Ben and the others."

"All right, here we go. Repeat after me." Harris chuckled slightly. "Hello, my name is Doctor Aileen Smith. That's with an A and two Es. I am a specialist on nautical relics from the eighteenth century. The museum curator called me and I hopped on the first flight available from London. These are my team members. Now, if you will show me the way to the break-in."

Leah smiled, eager to assist at all costs. She went along with his request, repeating each word back. Her accent was subtle, but you could hear a distinct English tone behind each word. The little speech sounded perfect.

Sal smiled, instantly realizing what Harris meant to do.

"That was great!" Sal slapped a hand against the stone below him. "So we'll walk right into the museum, following Leah's lead?"

"That's my plan for now," Harris said. "Emphasize the spelling of your name. Also, I guess you and I would need false names just in case," he said, looking at Sal. "You can be Simon Travis, and I will be Harold Smith."

Sal chuckled. "Oh! That's good. Are you guys going to be related?"

Harris looked from Sal, then to Leah. He noticed a serious tone in Sal's question. The thought of being related to Leah was hysterical in his mind for some reason. "Bah! No! We could even play off on it. She could be like, 'Oh, we have the same last name, but we are totally not related'. Or something like that!"

Sal laughed. Meanwhile Leah nodded, listening attentively to the plan develop.

After a few seconds Leah joined in, laughing politely. "I think this may actually work."

Harris stared off into the distance, watching a seagull glide on the breeze. "We obviously need to get out of these clothes," he said. "And as for money, I don't have any modern day cash on me. Whatever I had when we were first sent back is gone. We've been through a lot in the last year. In fact, I don't even really know how long it's been since we left this time period."

"Yeah man, you're right. We've done a lot together, seriously." Sal watched the seagull as well. A few moments later, the bird came up from a dive with a fish in its mouth. "All right; well, I might still have my money pouch on me." He rifled through his robes and found a small leather bag. "Yes! I thought it fell out during the battle in Sherwood Forest!"

Leah smiled at the fortunate turn. "So it seems we have the beginnings of a plan." She was slowly adjusting to everything that had been thrown at her. "Any time I have been in need of new clothing, my mother visited the linen store and would cut the fabric and sew me a dress. She is a very skilled seamstress. Actually, that is how I met Benjamin so many months ago."

Both Harris and Sal had heard this tale many times, but as a courtesy to Leah, they let her continue.

"He saved me from two horrible men. They pushed my mother and I into a dark alleyway, and Benjamin came to our rescue."

Harris looked away from the sea and toward the hustle and bustle in the streets of Boston below. "Ben's a good kid. Now it's our turn to save him."

Sal nodded. "Yeah, you're right. We should get started as soon as we can."

"I'm sure we could find a pawn shop or an antique dealer and sell some of the coins," Harris replied. "I bet we could actually make some money off them too."

Sal smiled. "Yeah man, that's over two hundred years of inflation! We might be able to retire and live life like the kings we are destined to be!"

Harris chuckled. "You're such a dork. Anyways," he said, looking at Leah, "you are the critical part of our success here. Will you do anything and everything in your power to save Ben?"

"Yes, yes of course," Leah responded quickly. "Anything. I love him with all my heart."

"Good." Harris nodded. "Like I said, if we are to rescue Captain Nelson from the museum, our plan has to work perfectly, like a well-oiled machine, down to every last detail."

Leah smiled. His advice seemed to warm her heart, and the effect it had was a fantastic feeling. She was determined to do everything in her power to save the love of her life.

Within just a few short months, she had transformed from the well-to-do daughter of a rich governor to the wife of the stoic Captain Richard Highmore, and most recently into a brave and fearless young woman, willing to do everything in her power to save the love of her life.

✸✸✸

Captain Arthur F. Nelson shook his head, clearing his mind of the cobwebs that seemed to clutter it. He rubbed his temples for a minute and then proceeded to massage his lower back and sides with a closed fist, grinding out the many knots with his knuckles. He had taken quite a barrage of hits from the two security guards in the rooftop battle, but the pain was well worth it for by doing so he had allowed his friends to escape. It was better than the alternative—having them all captured. Closing his eyes, he slowed his breathing, trying to focus on the important tasks at hand—finding a way out of the locked and guarded room and reuniting with Sal, Harris, and Leah.

He sat down in a chair and took a few moments to reflect on the items around him. Next to him was a large bin full of refuse. He turned to it and rummaged through the contents, dumping out several water bottles, a soft, damp paper full of stale coffee grinds, and a large news daily. He had read several dailies from time to time whenever he was in port in one place or another, although he always felt overwhelmed because the news was always weeks old. That was one of the issues with being a sailor, missing out on what normal people were doing and experiencing. By the time one caught up with what had recently happened, new things were already passing by.

He smiled as he brought the newspaper out of the filth and spread it upon the tabletop. He wiped off several of the coffee grinds. He then scanned the front page, looking for a date—anything that would show him when and even where they had been cursed to. Finally he found what he was looking for. Discovering this information, he closed his eyes, computing dates and events. He was now over two hundred years in the future. This thought brought a slight smile to the lips of the brave adventurer. He had always dreamt of time travel, and living it firsthand was quite exciting for him.

Suddenly the door to the break room was pushed open, causing it to slam into the wall behind it. Papers that were tacked to a nearby bulletin board were ruffled from the rush of moving air, and a train of figures quickly entered the room. Captain Nelson casually looked up from the newspaper.

A uniformed officer, tall and massive, stopped several feet from him. He easily took up the entire doorway as he stood in the threshold. His expression was cold as stone. He was well over six feet tall and very intimidating. His skin was as black as the night, and his lips curled in an unfriendly smile full of sparkling pearly whites. Several other uniformed men stood behind the towering officer.

"My name is Colonel Dean Jackson with the Boston police." He paused, pointing to a small man behind the officers. "This gentleman is Professor Michael D. Yocklem, the curator of this museum you've broken into. I'm going to ask you two simple questions—and you're going to give me two concise answers. Straight and to the point. Who are you and where did you come from?"

He weighed his choices—the door was closing slowly, revealing a gap of just a few inches. He had to make up his mind quickly. It would have to be there and then if he was going to make a stand and fight his way out of the room, but there were too many opponents, with too many variables to consider.

He was a fighter, always aware of opportunities and quick to calculate risk versus possible outcome. This instinct had won him countless battles and earned him his reputation as one of the king's most daring and favored servants. He had moved up the ranks more quickly than all of his colleagues and he was revered for his accomplishments.

Captain Nelson was not a large man, but he certainly was a tough one. His scars carried the stories of daring feats in brawls around the world. Knowing his odds were slim to none here in a brawl against roughly half a dozen fit men, he cleared his throat as the door closed. The locking pins inside the tumbler reassured him. As much as he had wanted to fight his way out, he knew that most altercations could be easily thwarted by simply keeping a cool head, which would be his plan for now.

"Greetings. My name is Captain Arthur F. Nelson. I am an English privateer on a mission from King George the Third. God save the King!" He smiled, letting his words sink in. He suppressed a chuckle. "We were tasked to assassinate Prime Minister George Grenville. Someone who held a grudge against one of my loyal officers spoiled our plans at the last minute. We were then brought back to London, and were unfortunately found guilty for the traitorous act. As we were about to be hung, I and three others were sent into the future. We understand it to be due to the curse of Blood Bones, a pirate I captured on a mission earlier in the year."

Both the police officers and the museum curator stared in disbelief. Confusion set in, but it was mainly disbelief. "Time travel? Ha!" Professor Yocklem said. He looked at Colonel Jackson, shaking his head in disbelief. "Why did you steal that beautifully adorned staff from the display? Where did it go? Two of my guards saw you throw it to your friends. Was that your intention—to steal it?"

Captain Nelson smiled. "Ah, the magic staff of Captain Blood Bones. There is a long story of its origins, dating back to Sir Francis Drake and his circumnavigation around the globe. You see—it was a gift from the Queen of England, and it is rumored to contain many secrets, which would have proved very beneficial for Drake. Navigating itself is an art, just as it is a science. To have information not known to others would be quite helpful." He was content with his response, leading these men on a roundabout quest for learning the truth.

The police officer was tired of the man's non-concise answers. "You are speaking lies!" Colonel Jackson looked the intruder up and down. He noticed his wardrobe and eyed him warily. He then yelled. "Tell me who you are and where you come from!"

The police officers all stared at Nelson, their eyes locked on the man claiming to be from the eighteenth century.

Nelson chuckled. "Believe me if you will, or do not—it really does not matter to me. I stole the cursed staff to harness its powers to return back to the year 1763. Alongside my friends, we will then save the rest of our crew, including one of my loyal officers, Benjamin Manry. I am not quite sure what we have stumbled upon, to be honest, but there are few things I am certain of in life—and one of them is that I am a man of my word, and my word is the truth. I am no liar!"

The police officer exchanged a glance with the curator of the museum. "I guess we'll see about that." Colonel Dean Jackson smiled. "We'll be back soon enough to learn the truth." He turned, and then led the others out of the room, leaving Nelson alone again.

At the mention of the name Benjamin Manry, Professor Yocklem felt a spark of recognition and suddenly remembered a conversation he had had several months earlier with four concerned parents from St. Augustine, Florida.

4

Modern Day
Boston, Massachusetts

The antique dealer stared intently at a book of poetry spread out in his lap. He was wearing a smock with fresh paint still on it. He heard the multiple footfalls of the three visitors, but did not bother to look up as the bizarre-looking figures walked into his store. Only after finishing the stanza did he look up with a smile.

"Greetings and salutations! My name is Alfred, but I don't know anyone who calls me Alfred anymore. Well, that is a lie—I guess my mother still does." He coughed into a tissue, clearing his throat of yellow phlegm. "Ah, well, that is beside the point. So, you don't want to call me that because I probably won't respond—everyone calls me Al." He took a bow, crossing his legs and spreading his hands wide, as if he was a knight from medieval Europe. "How may I be of service to you all?"

He was apparently oblivious to their unique wardrobes.

"Hi, Al. My name is Harris. We'd like to get an estimate on some antique coins."

"Sure, of course. Let me take a look at them," Al said. He used a pencil to mark his spot in the book and then laid it on the glass countertop. Harris extended his hand, allowing Al to take the leather bag out of his hand.

Al coughed into the tissue again, then wiped at the excess saliva with his right hand. After a minute, he used both hands to hold and open the drawstring. He poured out the contents of the leather bag onto the glass countertop. Out came coins from mid-eighteenth-century England.

"Sorry about my coughing. I'm just getting over a cold." He explained, then his eyes went wide with astonishment. "Whoa! You weren't kidding. This is an amazing collection."

"How much do you think it's worth?" Harris leaned forward, trying to remain casual.

"Well, book value would definitely be over a thousand dollars—but it's hard to sell this kind of stuff because it's really special. You know, it's unique, and there aren't too many people into coins like these."

Harris looked at Sal. His friend shrugged. Harris then stared back at the storeowner. He smiled confidently. "All right, no worries. We'll take our business elsewhere—perhaps the museum will be able to assist us more." He gathered up the coins and turned around as if he was about to leave. "Thanks for your time."

Money was money, and bargaining was required in his business. "Wait a minute. Well, I could perhaps write a check for something close to that amount. Would that work?"

Harris shook his head. "Sorry, we're sort of in a bind. We need cash, and we need it quick."

Al coughed again. "Ha! I know what you mean, and I like you guys. I really do. Here, hold on." He unbuttoned the top of the smock to reveal a filthy button-down shirt beneath. There was a little bulge in the breast pocket. His fingers quickly reached in and removed a large wad of twenty-dollar bills. A rubber band held it together. He smiled. "Here's what I'm thinking—I can do $700 cash, but no more than that."

Harris smiled at the fortunate turn in events. "You've got yourself a deal then."

Harris led the group out of the pawn shop. Once on the sidewalk, he looked left and right. He went with his gut, and turned to the right. He maneuvered around a crowd with Sal and Leah quick on his heels.

"All right, we need to find two things before we can rescue Captain Nelson," Harris said.

"What are you thinking?" Sal asked.

"Some sort of identification, and obviously new clothes."

"Gotcha," Sal said. Something caught his eye—it was a sign hanging above a storefront across the street. "Well, that was pretty easy. Look over there."

The trio stared across the street, watching as several cars and trucks passed by. After the stop light changed to red, there was the gap in the traffic, which allowed a full view of the store. Sal stepped off the curb to cross the street.

The sign above the door said MA AND PA'S PRINTING PRESS. It would suit their needs perfectly.

"I think we should get some new clothes first before we get our pictures taken," Harris said.

Leah's eyes were wandering, taking it all in. Everything was so new to her, and she was beginning to love every minute of the adventure and the change of scenery from her other-century life. Her life had taken many twists and turns since her father had promised her to Captain Richard Highmore, but this was by far the most interesting thing she had ever experienced.

"Yeah, you're right." Sal gazed down the street. "I'm sure there's something close by. Let's just keep going on this side for a little bit longer. If we don't find anything in the next block or so, we can just ask for help, I guess."

Harris shook his head. He looked at Sal. "Would you help me out if I asked you a question dressed like this? I'm surprised we haven't been arrested yet. The museum knows we managed to escape. We should probably avoid the main roads until we get new clothes."

Sal laughed. "Yeah, imagine getting arrested for our wardrobe.

Crazy. If I met you for the first time and you asked for help dressed like this, I'd say you are shit-outta-luck!"

Harris was filling in as the group's leader decently enough. No one could compare to how Ben had led them since they had been cursed to the eighteenth century, even though Harris was the oldest in the group. Ben just sort of had that knack for it; when he was put into that leadership role he eagerly reached for the reins. "Yeah, totally. All right; let's keep going."

They continued walking for another fifty feet and came to an intersection. They waited at the cross walk for the signal to change. A police car was stopped at the stoplight only a few paces away, its rear license plate almost within reach.

"Whoa! Okay, stop. Turn around, guys." Harris slowly backed away. "I don't think he saw us."

The three figures turned around and scanned a storefront as if window-shopping. It was a computer repair store, and Harris led the way in. Once all three were inside, the stoplight turned green, and he was glad to see the police car accelerate out of view.

"Hello! What can I help you with?" A voice called from behind the counter. The guy was in his early twenties, with pimple scars across his forehead and reading glasses draped from his collar.

Sal thought fast and smiled. "Well, my friend's computer crashed last night. We think it's the hard drive, though. It sort of hummed for a few minutes after he powered the unit on. We were just seeing if you were free sometime this week to take a peek at it."

The guy looked at his customers and chuckled. "Are you guys re-enactors or part of one of those fort tours?"

Harris nodded and went along with Sal's inventive story. "Yeah. We're from out of town, and here for a few days, but his laptop died. We wanted to upload the photos from our trip so far." He shook his head. "Technology is so frustrating. Anyways, do you think you could help us out?"

The young man smiled. "As you can see, I'm completely free, so just bring it over whenever you get a chance," he said. He then looked at a calendar hanging behind him. "I close the store evenings all week, so you'd be more than welcome to bring it in any day this week late afternoon or early evening."

"Great. Thanks again," Sal said. Harris waved, and Leah smiled.

"My name is Ryan. I'll see you then!"

"Great. Thanks Ryan," Sal said.

Harris ran a hand through his hair, massaging his scalp, simulating stress. "Oh wait, I almost forgot. Quick question for you. We just came over from Europe and they lost our luggage. I'm really worried. I was lucky enough to bring my laptop in my carryon! I was wondering if you knew of any stores nearby for us to get new clothes, though."

"Ah, that stinks, man! I totally hate airlines—they've lost mine a few times," Ryan said. He scratched at a pimple on his neck. "Yeah, there's a Macy's just around the corner. It's about a block or so down, on Reynolds Street. Make a right when you go out. It's not too hard to find. Just look for the window signs, there are about a million advertisements."

"Cheers!" Harris said.

"See you when I see you," Ryan replied.

※※※

Harris led the group out of the computer store, making a right as instructed. About a minute later, they passed by advertisements glued to every vertical surface.

"Looks like we're almost there," Sal smiled.

Before anyone could respond, Harris paused in front of a display. Mannequins showing off the season's hottest items filled the windows.

"Sweet. I haven't been shopping in a while!" Sal laughed. "I wonder if we can get anything on sale."

"Yeah, man, it's been a while since we had the choice of what clothing to wear. It'll be nice to, like, pick out something fancy!" Harris smiled. He laughed at Sal—he always knew what to say to lighten the mood. Harris stared into the display, seeing a nice fisherman's vest. Off to the side were some fleeces and lightweight coats. "All right, let's go inside!"

Leah stared at a mannequin dressed in a flower-patterned miniskirt. "Oh my Lord! Do people actually wear these garments?" She shook her head, as if warding off demons. She would rather die than be seen in this garb. *I would be the laughing stock of the town!* She thought.

Harris laughed. "Yeah, unfortunately. I guess the trends have certainly changed! We'll find something for you; don't worry." He smiled, holding the door open for them. Sal bowed in over-exaggerated thanks.

"Why, thank you, kind sir." Sal chuckled.

A greeter stood a few feet in from the door with his hands folded across his chest. As they entered, the teenager smiled.

"Welcome to Macy's. All vests are fifty percent off, and out of season are also fifty percent off. If there's anything I can help you with, feel free to ask. Oh, and my name is Tony!"

"Sure, thanks Tony. Could you point us to the Men's section?" Harris asked.

"Just over there, follow those signs." Tony pointed left.

"Excellent, thanks. Oh, and where is the Women's section?" Harris asked.

The young man pointed to the right. "Just over there. Good luck shopping! Please let me know if there is anything I can help you with."

"Thanks." Harris led the group past several displays. Signs overhead advertised special sales. The store was packed with eager shoppers and no one appeared to notice their eighteenth-century garb.

"All right. So we'll be playing the roles of assistants to Doctor Aileen Smith. What do we wear?" Sal asked.

Leah smiled. "That's with an A and two Es."

Harris and Sal chuckled, glad to see her coping well, adjusting to the many twists and turns in their adventure together. "I imagine we'd wear either slacks and a button-down, or maybe a blazer?

I'm not really sure. I mean, we can't just walk in dressed like James Bond or anything. Right?"

Sal laughed. "Dude, I don't think I've worn a tuxedo since Uncle Johnny's wedding. I like the way you think. The three of us should all get, like, matching tuxedos."

Harris nodded. "Brilliant—you have me sold!" He looked around and saw a large rack with pants and matching jackets.

The clothes were arranged by colors. It looked as if a rainbow was being displayed for them. "What color should we pick?" Sal asked.

"Does it matter?" Harris replied.

Leah looked around until something caught her eye. "That one! It is quite beautiful."

They stared at a rack of discounted suits. There was a group of black suits, each with a white vest. An accessory rack beside it held black ties and socks. Another rack held white long-sleeved shirts.

"My name is Draben, Salvador Draben. I'll have a vodka martini, shaken not stirred." Sal laughed as he held his hands together, using his pointer and middle fingers to mock a gun's barrel. Harris made the same hand gesture, but held his finger gun to Sal's head.

"The gig is up, Draben. I've got you where I want you," Harris said in his best English accent. "Prepare to die!"

Leah laughed at the show they put on. Harris and Sal began to look for their pant sizes in the rack.

"I was a 32-inch waist before our little adventure. I think I slimmed down a little. I think not having a refrigerator in the next room made me lose a little weight," Sal said. He picked up a pair sized 30 by 30 and then looked into a mirror. He placed the pants against his stomach, gauging the size. "I think this will do." He then looked at Harris with a smile. "You're looking in the wrong section, buddy. This isn't for big and tall folks like you."

Harris shook his head. "Sal, why are you so silly?"

"I don't know! Why are you dressed so silly?" Sal laughed in return.

"All right," he said. He shook his head, mocking his friend. "Let's try these on." Harris grabbed at a pair of pants, ignoring the last comment.

"Should we try a few different colors?" Sal asked.

"Sure, let's grab a few different sets." Harris began rifling through the rack.

"What about me?" Leah smiled. "I could not possibly wear one of these suits!"

Harris and Sal both picked out their desired outfits and tossed the items over their shoulders. Harris then turned to Leah. "All right, how about we take a trip to the females' section so we can pick something for you?"

Leah nodded. "That would be nice. But please, can we choose something to my liking?"

Harris winked, then sighed. "I suppose."

Leah laughed at her friends, and then led the boys as they walked through the store toward the women's section.

※※※

The dressing rooms were filled with the hustle and bustle of people trying clothes on. Men and women moved to and fro, hanging their discards on empty racks. A young employee was placing discarded articles back on hangars, and arranging them on a portable rack so the pieces could be restocked. The wheels creaked as she pushed the rack forward.

In the corner, three figures stood laughing. Sal was kneeling, holding his hands outward. His hands formed two Ls, which he connected together at the fingertips. Every so often, his middle finger would twitch, coinciding with a clicking sound he made with his mouth. Click. Click.

Harris and Leah modeled their suits, dancing around in front of the mirrors while Sal laughed. In between fits of laughter, he said "Work it baby, work it!"

Harris paused in his tracks. Like a temperamental fashion diva, he turned on a heel, dropping his face and changing his expression completely. "I'm totally not digging this color. Next!"

He did an about-face and went back into the changing room. Leah followed the cue and went into her cubicle. A few moments later, they donned different colored suits. Sal continued his barrage of fake camera clicks.

✘✘✘

"All right, I think these are the winners!" Sal said.

Leah smiled into the mirror. She was wearing a jet-black suit—the pants were stylish and tight fitting, revealing all of her curves and features, without making her too uncomfortable with the change in trends. The jacket was long-sleeved with a two-button front. She enjoyed the feel of the fabric against her skin.

"This is so different from what I would wear back home," Leah said.

Harris and Sal tried hard not to look too closely.

"What do you think we should do?" Harris said, looking away, avoiding her eyes.

"We do need to accessorize. We're supposed to be scientists, right?" Sal replied.

Harris smiled. "Yeah, good idea. I'm thinking new shoes, sunglasses, a few pens for show, and briefcases?"

"That's exactly what I was thinking."

"I do not like the feeling of these high heels, though," Leah said with a sad face.

"Let's try some flats. You never know if we'll need to run," Harris said. "I think we all look pretty awesome though."

"Yeah, man, definitely."

✘✘✘

Harris led after they exited store. They walked down the street single file—Sal whistled a tune while Leah followed, slowly but surely getting used to her new outfit.

They were one step closer to rescuing Captain Nelson, and ultimately, Benjamin Manry and the remaining ill-fated sailors.

They passed by the computer repair store again. From the inside, Ryan recognized the group and waved. A few minutes later they were standing before Ma and Pa's Printing Press.

Harris pushed the door open and heard beads brush against the back of the glass. They entered, dressed to impress.

Mr. and Mrs. Thompson, the storeowners, looked up from a plate of cookies and milk. They were enjoying a slow work-morning, and were actually in the middle of a Cribbage game. Robert Thompson stood from the table, leaving his wife, the wooden board, and half a deck of unused playing cards behind. He greeted the newcomers.

"Hello there, my name is Robert. Is there anything I can help you with this fine morning?"

Harris nodded. "Yes sir, we've got a business meeting this afternoon, and unfortunately the airline lost all of our luggage except our carry-ons. We just had to buy new suits and we realized our ID badges were inside our bags, too."

Robert shook his head. "That's horrible. Where are you all from?"

Sal looked at his friend and then at Leah. "We just came over from London for an important meeting. If all goes according to plan, we'll be heading back across the pond later this evening."

"Ha! I've got some friends from over there; it's a small world," Robert said. His eyes clouded over, as if reliving moments from long ago. "I fought in the Second World War, and one of my best friends met a nurse while we were deployed and ended up moving there shortly after the conflict ended. It's been a while since I've heard from him," he said. He turned his head to his wife. "Lauren, can you remind me to call Caleb?"

She called from across the store, "Okay, honey!"

Robert smiled at his guests. "So you need some badges made?"

Leah nodded. "Yes. My name is Doctor Aileen Smith. I am a specialist on nautical relics from the eighteenth century. These are my two assistants. We are running a little late and would greatly appreciate any help you can give."

Robert nodded. He looked her up and down and smiled. "Well then, you came to the right place! If one of you will fill out some paperwork as to what you want printed on the cards, I can start taking the photographs of you. All three will only take about five minutes each."

"Whoa! That's great. We've still got to check into the hotel and catch lunch before the afternoon meeting. You're a real life saver!" Sal chipped in. Robert's smile grew ever larger.

The elderly couple took all the photographs and created the initial designs. Robert then typed in their names and the information Harris and Sal had written down. Just a few minutes later, three badges were laminated and ready for use.

Robert held them in his hand. "Would you like clips or lanyards for the cards?"

Harris smiled. "Clips would be perfect. Thanks. That would be wonderful. You're the man!"

Robert chuckled at his customer's comments, and moved to the cash register. He rang up the total. "That'll be $60 even. I hope your meeting goes well!"

Harris removed three twenty-dollar bills from his bundle and placed them in the man's hands. "Have a good day!"

The group waved to the couple as they exited the store.

There was only one thing left to do.

5

Modern Day
Boston Museum
Boston, Massachusetts

The trio now stood at the bottom of the staircase leading into the Boston Museum. It was just after two in the afternoon as Leah stood beside a handrail. She was holding a leather briefcase in her left hand and a small badge in her right.

"Do you both have yours?" Leah made sure Sal and Harris had affixed their badges to their breast pockets. She placed the briefcase down between her feet and then clipped hers. Content with the progression of the plan, the group nodded to each other.

"It's now or never. Let's go!" Harris smiled. "Take the lead, Doctor Aileen Smith."

Leah laughed. "That's Aileen, with an A and two E's!" She then charged up the staircase; she was determined to save Ben.

The automatic door opened and one by one, the group entered the main lobby of the museum. The panic of the morning's events had dwindled down to near normalcy, and there was little going on besides the ordinary: several guards were chatting in the corner, while a few tourists were wandering among the exhibits.

To the trio, it seemed everything having to do with their entry and the theft of the cursed staff had been swept under the carpet before the museum had opened for the day.

Harris pointed to the central guard desk, and Leah led the way. A guard looked up from a newspaper. "Good after—," he started talking before his eyes fully came to take her in. He blinked a few times, completely stunned by her beauty. "—noon. What can I do you for?" He continued to blink rapidly. "Sorry, I mean, um, what can I do for you? Excuse me!"

Leah smiled brilliantly. She closed her eyes for a moment, recalling the instructions one last time. She leaned over the counter with a teasing smile and looked at the man's identification badge. She then looked up, right into the man's eyes. "Hello, Nick." She seemed to stare right through him. "My name is Doctor Aileen Smith. That's with an A and two Es," she said, flashing her badge quickly in front of the guard. "I am a specialist on nautical relics from the eighteenth century. The museum curator called me and I hopped on the first flight from London. These are my team members. Now, if you will show me the way to the break-in."

Nick blinked a few times, overwhelmed by her sure-fire lingo. He looked from the gorgeous blonde to her team members. They all looked the part—well-dressed, calm and confident.

They had just walked into the very same museum from which they had escaped only a few hours earlier. The rush they felt was exhilarating.

A bead of sweat trickled down Sal's forehead, but he continued to stare forward at the guard, maintaining his composure.

Harris smiled, giving off a casual aura.

The guard bought it. He soaked it all up—their every word, and every action.

"Sure! Let me show you the exhibit. We had to close the floor off because of what happened this morning. We aren't positive what the heck happened. I'm sure you were filled in about the bizarre events, right? It was so weird. These people just plopped out of thin air! Crazy!"

"Of course, I am the most respected specialist in my field! Anything concerning nautical relics is forwarded to my team immediately, from every corner of the globe. I've dealt with dozens of cases over the years. Let me introduce you to Simon Travis," she said, turning her head to Sal. She then moved her gaze to Harris. "This is Harold Smith. Of no relation to me! Thank God!"

"Ha! Oh, that's too bad!" Nick replied with a teasing glance.

Leah was playing the role perfectly—she was quick on her toes, and eager to save Ben at any cost.

Nick grabbed a set of keys, and then stood up from the chair. "All right, let's go. Please follow me."

✲✲✲

Nick led the group leisurely to the main lobby elevator. He pressed the up arrow and whistled for a minute until the doors opened. He snuck a few glances at the woman who had introduced herself as Doctor Aileen Smith.

"After you." He allowed for Leah to move forward into the elevator, and he continued to eye her as she moved by.

Harris looked on. He cringed at how the guard was treating her like eye candy, but he knew that it could only better their odds of success.

Harris and Sal both entered the elevator, taking their places on either side of Leah. Nick then entered and pressed the second floor button. He continued his whistle as the doors closed.

"So, that was pretty quick for you guys to get here. It's only been about a few hours," the security guard said as he looked at each person. He closed his eyes, as if attempting to do the calculation. "I've never really traveled, so I don't really know how long it takes."

Harris smiled at the man's incompetence and responded quickly. "Yes, we have a private jet for urgent matters such as these. Usually we take a commercial flight due to the high cost involved, but this seemed like a unique opportunity. We are actually searching for a similar eighteenth-century relic as well, and we hope that it is the one we are looking for."

Nick nodded. "That's awesome! I wish I had a jet to commute to work!"

Sal smiled. "Sometimes it is impractical. Our company only lets us use it for emergencies. Luckily our boss was on vacation when we got the phone call, so we just used our gut feeling," he added with a forced chuckle. "So yeah, that's why we're here. Anyways, where do you live?"

Nick laughed. "Well, only about five miles away, so I don't know how effective a jet would be!"

Harris shook his head. "Probably not too much—you'd be in the air for all of about three seconds."

The beep of the elevator's doors interrupted their conversation. Nick stepped forward and led the group through the second floor lobby to the Pirates and Privateers exhibit. The area was roped off with yellow caution tape, but otherwise all was quiet. The group looked around, and then Nick held up the tape for the three visitors to pass beneath.

"Ah, very interesting," Sal said as he stopped before the broken glass of the exhibit. "So, in your own words, can you tell me exactly what happened?" He reached into his briefcase and pulled out a notepad and a pen. "Please do start at the beginning."

Nick cleared his throat. "Well, to be honest I wasn't actually here for it, so I didn't see anything. I was in the break room with my partner Tim when we got a call that there was a break-in. I was still changing, so Tim met with Bob to chase the intruders. Apparently four people somehow got into the museum without tripping off any of the alarms. I guess they broke through the glass display and stole that staff you mentioned earlier. We pursued them up to the roof, and we managed to capture one of them. The other three escaped by jumping across the gap. After that, I'm not really sure where they went. Boston PD sent out a few squad cars looking for them, but I haven't heard any updates. I was told they were dressed in robes and whatnot. One was wearing a dress. It was like they weren't from here, like from centuries ago or something. It's really odd, you know?"

Leah smiled. "Well, yes—that is extremely odd. We believe the missing item is a magical staff that has a curse on it," she said. It was ironic that she was the one to be explaining this. "We were told that it then went missing after the break-in?"

With dotted i's and crossed t's, their plan was unfolding perfectly. Nick nodded. "Yes, they set off the alarm when the glass display was shattered." He paused, and pointed at the remains. There was a jagged edge, where Captain Nelson's fist had gone through several hours earlier. "The guy we captured is still in the break room. We are still going over surveillance tapes. We've already had a few looks at it but we are perplexed. Four people just popped into view beside the exhibit. They stood there for a minute, and then *whamo*! The guy punched through the glass. We aren't sure if the tapes have been tampered with because it's just so weird. Boston PD interrogated him but learned nothing. He wasn't willing to cooperate."

Leah nodded. "Ah, that is most unfortunate. Well, perhaps we can speak with him? I am sure we could learn something about him, his friends, and the missing item with just a few quick and easy questions."

Nick shrugged. "Sure, that sounds good. But, I mean, I don't have the authority to let you in."

Leah bit her lip. Scrunching her face, she pouted her lips. "Oh, boo! We came all the way here from London on a hunch! Are you sure there is nothing you can do for us?"

Nick smiled. "Well, I suppose I could let you guys talk to him for a few minutes without my boss knowing. I mean, what could possibly go wrong?"

Harris snuck a glance at Sal. He then locked eyes with Leah; he was proud of her. There was a growing twinkle in her eye. "Exactly."

The door closed behind the trio. Captain Nelson was sitting alone, listening to the hum of the television. He was completely entranced by the images of people moving to and fro on the glass screen in front of him. He looked up to see Leah leading Harris and Sal. He jumped up from the chair, excited to see his friends again.

"It is so good to see you all!" He smiled.

Leah ran across the gap and wrapped her arms around Nelson's shoulders, giving him an earth-shattering hug.

"It was a close one," Harris said. "I'm glad they never moved you from the museum, otherwise we would've had to break into a jail or police station."

"And that would've been no fun," Sal said.

The group laughed, relishing in the fact that they were again in the same room.

Leah smiled. "I am glad we are all together again."

"As am I," Captain Nelson said. "How did you manage to get in?"

"Leah was brilliant. She was able to convince the guard to let us come in and talk to you," Sal said.

She blushed at the compliment. "Well, the congratulations should go to Harris. He devised much of the plan and came up with all of the phrases I might need to say in case the guard changed the topic or asked a question."

Harris laughed. "Thanks. I'm glad I came up with those extra ones, but you nailed it perfectly."

"As much as I'd like to continue this discussion, I believe we have more pressing issues to address," Captain Nelson said.

"Like getting out of here and back to the eighteenth century," Harris said.

Sal nodded. "Yeah, we don't have much time anyways. There's a bunch of guards standing around outside. I don't want them to think we're up to no good. I hope Nick is as stupid as he looks."

"Well, he looks pretty stupid," Harris said. "So that's reassuring at least." He laughed for a moment, and then looked around at each face. "So, let's make a list of what we actually know about the curse and all its components." He looked at Nelson. "You've read the journal several times through, so you have a better idea of the technical aspects. We discovered the curse, so we're good on that part, I guess." He looked at Sal for input.

"Yeah, definitely. Okay, so to start," Sal began. "We found the staff. We managed to open it. Inside there was that rolled message. We read it, but it was in Spanish," he paused. Emotions brought about by recollections of their earlier mishaps flooded his eyes. There were so many memories—both good and bad—since they had been sent back in time. "So I translated the phrase for us. It said 'you are cursed to 1763'."

Nelson nodded throughout. "So was it the English or the Spanish phrase that set off the curse?" Nelson asked. In his mind, he made a list, attempting to make sense of everything.

Both Harris and Sal shrugged, shaking their heads. "I think it was the Spanish words that did it," Sal said. "But it may be both––I'm not really sure. I guess we'll just have to find out."

"It's better to be safe than sorry. We could just say both phrases," Harris added.

Nelson smiled. "Well then, it seems that all we have to do is just say that particular phrase in the presence of the staff and the medallions. It seems to be the common element."

"Yeah, I think you're right, Captain." Harris nodded. He then looked at Sal with a mischievous smile. "Do you want the honor of setting off the curse for the third time?"

"Well, I did it the first time!" He laughed. "How about this?" He paused, locking eyes with Harris. "How about I trade you this unique opportunity for a warm meal once we get back to 1763?"

"Mr. Bargainer, that sounds like a sweet deal." Harris smiled. "I would love the opportunity to send us back to the life we have grown used to, a life filled with adventures on the high seas, of travel, and of beautiful women!"

Leah smiled. "You boys are silly." She had matured exponentially since being sent into the future. The past few hours seemed to have gone by like a blink of an eye. "I hope we can save Ben right away and end all of this nonsense."

"Well, let's get to it, then," Sal said. He turned to Captain Nelson. "Sir, could you please bring out the crimson journal?"

Nelson removed the diary of Blood Bones from inside his coat pocket. "Leah, please join us." Nelson placed a reassuring hand on Leah's arm. "It will be all right. You must have faith that we will soon be able to save Ben."

Harris cleared his throat, getting everyone's attention. "Okay, guys, and gal, make sure your medallions are intact," he paused, looking at Nelson. "And the journal?"

"Yes, it's right here." Nelson held up the crimson journal. All eyes turned to the item.

"Okay, here we go again!" Harris nodded. "I wonder where we'll end up this time!" Holding the magic staff high above his head, he said the now-too-familiar phrase: "*Le ahora maldicen a 1763.*"

And with that, the third revolution of the curse of Blood Bones was activated.

As soon as the phrase left Harris's mouth, a yellow beam of light flashed out from the magic staff. It pointed straight up, touching the ceiling of the second floor break room. Four objects in the room grew bright orange: the three medallions and the crimson journal. These orange beams angled up to meet at the yellow peak, forming a light show around the pyramid. The colored lights began to crisscross, filling in the gaps between the four legs. From the apex to the ground, the entire pyramid was full of clashing yellow and orange lights.

The room swirled around the staff and the group; a powerful gust of wind howled, originating at the top of the radiant cone and spiraling down like a corkscrew. Calendars and posters fluttered. The windows rattled. There was a loud imploding sound as the cone of light and energy collapsed. The wind stopped. Everything located within the light vanished into the reversal of time, leaving the second floor break room in shambles—papers were strewn about, a briefcase lay open, and three identification badges remained scattered on the floor where the cone of light had disappeared.

6

January 14, 1763
Boston, Massachusetts

The flames danced in each cut of the scarlet stone. As the cloaked figure pushed a coin over the tabletop, the barkeep placed a bottle of red wine easily within reach. Bringing his hand over the neck, the mysterious man retrieved the bottle between sea-weathered fingers. He sighed deeply under the protection of a large draped cloak. In deep concentration, he stroked at a well-trimmed goatee. Between swigs he took in the atmosphere, enjoying the loud music and boisterous laughter around him. He removed the ring, with its unique stone from his pinky finger and placed it in the palm of his hand, rotating it slowly. He smiled as the scarlet stone sparkled with life. The memories of its origins filled his eyes with emotion, but he fought off the urge to reminisce with a quick shake of his head. Minutes turned to hours as he sat there atop the barstool, listening intently.

A local man approached the bar through a crowd of drunks, pushing until he was face-to-face with the barkeep. "William, get me the usual. I can't take this taxation anymore. All I've saved from my last year's wages are nearly gone, between debt and these new linen tariffs. My wife can't even purchase the materials to clothe our family!"

"Aye, Jonathan. It's just not right."

"Every three months I hear that sound." The angered man pounded the table, spilling the freshly poured mead. "It utterly disgusts me!"

"Those armed carriages are beginning to sound familiar. They come from all corners of the colonies, from Albany and Philadelphia to Charleston and even Williamsburg!"

Jonathan let off another angry assault on the wooden countertop. "The king's taken all my—er—all *our* money." He paused to catch his breath. "As I came up the way, I saw the vessels taking on stores."

The barkeep nodded, wiping wet hands on a cloth tied around his waist. "Aye, I wonder how much gold's in the holds."

"Ha! Don't get me dreaming. Pour me another mead, my friend." The conversation carried to the mysterious sailor.

Hearing all that he had needed, Hernando Audaz, better known on the high seas as Captain Blood Bones, stood from the stool. Through the crowd of drunken sailors and locals, he made his way for the door, hiding his face beneath the gray cloak.

He looked over his shoulder as the tavern faded into the distance. The sun was quickly approaching its zenith as he passed by several local merchants. They approached him with the day's catches, but he ignored the crates of cod and continued on through the snow-covered streets to *La Monzón*, the sloop that had brought him his fame and fortune.

✖✖✖

A violent whirlwind of energy dashed quickly through the richly decorated cabin. *La Monzón* rested quietly beside the Boston docks. A blinding orange and yellow light filled the captain's quarters. Four bodies crashed to the wooden flooring, their clothing fluttering in the wind. With one last boom of sound and energy, the wind receded and the lights faded.

Captain Arthur F. Nelson lay sprawled on the wooden deck close beside Sal, Harris, and Leah. Each of them experienced unique emotions, and slowly the realization dawned on them—they were no longer trapped in the future, but back in the eighteenth century, one step closer to saving Ben and their shipmates The slow and steady rocking of the vessel below him immediately caused Nelson to smile. He felt at home aboard ships, having spent the majority of his life aboard a vessel of some kind or another. He stood up quickly, moving to help Leah gain her footing. She reached for his extended hand and stood up slowly.

Within a few moments, the group stood in a circle. They looked around, taking in the furnishings of the cabin they were in. They knew they were on a ship, but what ship, and whose cabin, remained a mystery.

Nelson moved across the deck, passing over an Oriental rug as he took sight of a chart atop a large oak desk. He sat and then stared at the intricate design in the wood. He then eyed the lines and neat handwriting coinciding with the position fixes. It seemed the vessel's previous voyage had been between the numerous islands that littered the Caribbean, primarily in the vicinity of Jamaica.

"Hm, this could very well be an island trader," Nelson said softly.

Beside the chart lay a position logbook. Eager to discover when and where they were, Nelson opened the cover. The vessel's name was *La Monzón* and Nelson quickly flipped through the pages. He nodded his head a few times while gathering information. The positions on the chart matched the neat penmanship that filled the pages inside. The last entry was dated January 13, 1763, with an arrival noted at Boston, Massachusetts on the morning flood tide.

"It appears we are aboard *La Monzón*, the very same vessel that Blood Bones had used in his attack on the harbor," he said to the others in the room. "We are now in Boston, just a few days before Blood Bones commandeered HMS *Courtesy* out of the harbor."

While Nelson had been occupied with the logbook and the paper chart, Sal and Harris were busy looking through the countless bookshelves that surrounded them. They were befuddled by the amount of leather-bound books Blood Bones had collected. They both were quiet, completely absorbed.

"*La Monzón*," Harris mumbled. He then looked at Sal. "We

should probably get out of here soon." He moved across the room to stand beside Nelson.

Nelson looked up from the logbook. "They made arrival on January 13, 1763, but of today's date I am not sure. I have heard it said many times that Blood Bones is a very prudent mariner, and we can all attest to that after our encounter with him months ago. He is a strategist who thinks of every outcome possible, whether it be positive or negative. I can only assume that it is some time before noon on the fourteenth now since he has yet to log in his daily entry."

Although Leah had quickly adjusted to surviving being sent into the future, finding herself back in the eighteenth century blew her mind entirely. It was as if her brain was backlogged, catching up on everything that had just happened. She remained quiet, standing to the side alone.

She then grew the confidence to speak up. She moved across the carpet to join the others. "What are we to do now? If the date that you said is correct, we are still many months away from saving Benjamin from the gallows in London. We are also an entire ocean away!" She swiped at newly forming tears.

They were in the right era, more or less, but they still had much to accomplish if they were to save Ben and the remaining sailors.

Captain Nelson nodded. "Leah, I must ask you to be strong. You proved yourself in the museum, leading Sal and Harris to my rescue. Once we figure out a plan to get out of our current predicament we can then address how to save Ben and the rest of my crew," he said. He closed his eyes for a moment, battling an inner demon. "Leah, please calm down. We have other more important things to focus on. If we are now in Boston, and it is close to the date the logbook has, I can only assume that Blood Bones will shortly commandeer the *Courtesy*." He paused, letting his words sink in. He knew that Harris and Sal were competent beyond their years. "That was my original duty, to recover the vessel, save the crew, and capture Blood Bones. The question we must ask ourselves now, is where we will be when this event occurs—will it be aboard

La Monzón, or will we be amongst Blood Bones' crew when they seize the HMS *Courtesy*?"

Sal looked around the group. "Well, why can't we just capture Blood Bones now? Think about it; we could just wait for him in here, spring a trap, and bring him back to Boston where he'll hang? That would give us plenty of time to get to London to save Ben and the others."

Harris shrugged. "Well, that would be well and dandy. Let's say we do that—the four of us could possibly take him on right here. But how would we get him off the ship without being detected by his crew? Wouldn't it look suspicious carrying a body out of his cabin, through the vessel, out on deck, and then down the gangway!" He looked at Sal, Leah, and Captain Nelson. "Plus, wouldn't that change everything that we had just lived through? If we succeed in capturing Blood Bones now in January, rather than in May, would Ben and the rest of the guys even need saving since everything would be shifted those four or five months earlier? We might not be caught by Highmore's guys in Sherwood Forest; we may not even have to *be* in Sherwood Forest."

Leah looked away at the mention of her husband's name. She loathed him, for everything he was and everything he had done. Because of this man, that she was forced to be with, she had watched the love of her life hang at the gallows.

Sal shrugged. "Yeah, I guess you're right. Who knows what we would change? We don't want to mess up the space-time continuum." Sal paused, deep in thought. He laughed to himself, thinking of a movie he had seen a dozen times as a child. "If only my name was Marty McFly and I had my trusty DeLorean!"

Harris smiled, while Captain Nelson and Leah looked puzzled. "Well, so either we mess up the space-time continuum or play the role of pirate." Harris weighed his thoughts carefully. "I guess the other option is that we could always just jump ship, manage to get across the Atlantic and wait until just before the hangings happen in London."

Sal was deep in thought. "Yeah, that could definitely work. We could hire some troops and surround Richard Highmore's goons before they capture us, or maybe, like, stop the soldiers even before they spring their trap on us."

Harris shook his head. "The issue with introducing all those new people is that there would be an even bigger battle in Sherwood Forest. There was already enough bloodshed without introducing more people."

Captain Nelson nodded. "I agree. It might even make matters worse. Fate has a way of playing tricks on you. We must be careful with what we choose to do." He paused, letting what he'd just said sink in.

Harris agreed. "Come on, Sal. We know when and where we have to save Ben, so that isn't really the problem. It's just the obvious point of getting there at the right point in time to stop the hangings from happening."

Sal looked hurt by their comments, but he shrugged it off, realizing that if they were to save Ben, they all would be contributing something, whether it was creating the plan, or acting on it.

Captain Nelson nodded. "Yes, gentlemen, you are both correct on all accounts, but time is something we most definitely have. Let me put it to you all like this—we have many months to get to London and save Ben and the others. What we have here is a unique experience that we could learn much from. I find our situation unparalleled to anything I have ever witnessed. I am intrigued and quite interested in what we could learn from this. What we have here is a once in a lifetime opportunity." He pulled out the book that contained the firsthand experiences and in-depth thoughts of Blood Bones. "I have read this crimson journal several times over. It would be even more exciting to see his doings with our own eyes, learning the ins and outs of this complex man that we were once paid handsomely to capture."

Sal chuckled. "Going under pirate cover: now this would be a great movie!" he said as he slapped Harris on the shoulder, then looked at their clothing. It dawned on him that they were once again dressed for the wrong era. "It's a shame we have to get out of these cool suits. I sort of liked being a James Bond knockoff."

Harris smirked and shook his head. "Yeah, I kind of liked the suits too."

Leah had always enjoyed Ben and his friends' company. She smiled as her friends goofed around before her. They could lighten the mood on request if needed, and for that attribute, she was grateful, because her heart was still in pain. She gasped, playing along with the tirade. "Well, I cannot wear this outfit if I am to become a pirate!"

Captain Nelson nodded toward a trunk he'd spotted in one corner. If he were right, it looked like the sort of container that might hold just what they needed to blend in again. "Aye, we will all need new clothing. We must do all that we can to not bring attention to ourselves. When the time comes, we shall all volunteer to be among the men who will seize the HMS *Courtesy*, joining Blood Bones in the attack."

Harris closed his eyes, remembering the article he had read so many months ago about the attack on the three English vessels in Boston harbor. "If memory serves me correctly, *La Monzón* catches fire and sinks. I definitely do not want to be aboard her if that happens!"

Nelson smiled, content with how his loyal friends and crew were warming up to their newly formed mission. He stepped over and opened the trunk, delighted to discover it was full of various articles of clothing. Clearly Blood Bones was a collector of more than one kind of treasure. "Lady and gentlemen, I just want to express my gratitude for how you saved my life earlier. We are all in this together, through thick and thin. First things first. Let us change out of these clothes. If we are caught now, we will be hung from the yardarms!"

The group chuckled at the many twists and turns of fate that they had experienced together, and joined Nelson at the bountiful wooden chest.

※※※

Blood Bones paced through the streets, whistling a tune as he thought of the potential prize that loomed ahead, easily within reach. He arrived at the wharf, where his vessel *La Monzón* rested easily at its berth. She was flying the colors of England and also displayed a new name plate, as his vessel was well-known. If if were recognized his mission would result in failure. He smiled at its new name, *Royal Captain*. The ship had just brought on common cargo. He was certain no one who might be watching would think twice as casks of fresh water, food, and other typical wares were slung aboard with large nets. His men hauled on blocks and tackles, singing shanties as they worked. They were all dressed in tarred linen, the common clothing of men of the sea.

He moved quickly up the gangway, nodding his head to the seaman who stood watch. "Gather the men for a meeting in the galley in twenty minutes."

"Aye, captain."

Before moving to the companionway ladder, he paced the deck to make sure all was in good order. He scanned the rigging, making sure his men aloft were safely doing their jobs. He saw several men hanging over the side on a bosun's chair painting the anchors. Content, Blood Bones then moved to his personal cabin below.

※※※

Captain Nelson rummaged through the personal garments of Blood Bones. It seemed that the pirate captain had several sets of uniforms, ranging from the officer wardrobes of the French, English, the Netherlands, and Portugal. Nelson smiled, realizing these were all just costumes—important disguises for his numerous raids throughout the Atlantic. He finally found what seemed to be common merchants' garb, and passed around a set of clothing to each of his companions, and they began changing into the new linens. Leah moved to a corner of the room and changed behind a French cloisonnette, which offered her a little privacy. Within a few minutes, each wore the new garb.

Captain Nelson placed a hand on Leah's shoulder as she stared into a mirror. Although he did not know what she was thinking, her expression indicated something deeply wrong. "I think we have to do something with your hair."

Harris and Sal nodded, while Leah shrugged and sighed heavily.

"I suppose it will grow back eventually," she said reluctantly.

"That's the spirit, Leah." Nelson pulled out a short knife, testing its sharpness on his fingernail. Content with the blade, he began slicing off the gorgeous blond locks. Harris and Sal watched as she transformed before their eyes.

Within a few minutes, Leah had short, shaggy hair, which closely resembled the men's. Nelson finished the transformation by pulling a watch cap over her head.

"There you are, Leah. You are entirely a new person now!" Nelson smiled.

She glanced into the mirror and noticed Ben's medallion peep out from under the fresh cotton shirt that she now wore. She was not sure if he was alive or dead; after all, she was still new to the concept of time travel. But there was not even the slightest doubt in her mind that she was determined to save him. After her husband's treachery, and the pain it had caused her, she knew that she would never go back to a life with Captain Richard Highmore.

"Yargh! It's a pirate's life for me," she chuckled bravely now. "If this is necessary, then let it be."

"Good!" Captain Nelson said. "I am proud of you, Leah."

"Same here, Leah," Sal and Harris chipped in.

She smiled, knowing that there was much for her to learn and adapt to if she was to ever see Ben's face again.

The group quickly worked together to clear the room of any evidence of their presence aboard.

Blood Bones sat at the desk inside his stateroom aboard *La Monzón*. He glanced down at the open logbook that remained atop his desk. He could have sworn that he'd closed it upon his last entry, but then something else caught his eye, distracting him from the logbook—the scarlet stone glowed brightly. A smile quickly formed on his face. He remembered a long discussion he'd once had with Sesostris, his personal confidant. The man was also a wizard, and he'd owned a magic crystal ball. The pirate captain had been informed of what the intense glows in the scarlet stone represented—what he saw now meant that another phase of his curse for immortality had commenced. He pulled the logbook toward him and with eloquent penmanship wrote a detailed entry about how the day was going, as well as the fortunate turn of events.

The galley of *La Monzón* was full of experienced sailors and close comrades of Captain Blood Bones. Among the horde of pirates, four new faces took refuge in the shadows, being careful to blend in without being noticed. They kept to themselves in the corner of the crowded room.

"Men, I have learned of some excellent news," Blood Bones happily announced for all to hear. "We share berthing in the same harbor as three very important vessels. These British-flagged ships are transporting a quarter year's worth of colonial taxes to London. There are two sloops of war, acting as the convoy for a thirty-two-gun frigate. The facts are simple; we cannot win in manpower or firepower."

After a slight pause, his cousin and first mate raised a hand. "Hernando, what if we engage them internally?"

"Álvaro, I was thinking the very same thing. I know that they will be heavily armed and crewed. We must focus solely on the frigate; it'll hold only a third of the enemy. We'll be outnumbered, but if we can act quickly, I am positive of a successful mission." He paused for a moment, allowing his words to sink in. "Men, what do you think? Shall we loot and plunder the English?"

Nelson and his friends bellowed and cheered for a successful mission alongside the pirates that they had previously been paid handsomely to capture. A while later he sat with Sal, Harris, and Leah, eating a meal of venison, hard tack, and boiled potatoes, while listening to the pirate shanties and booming laughter that filled the room. The food was filling and definitely above average for a shipboard meal. It had been several days since their last real meal, prior even to their capture in Sherwood Forest, and all relished the fresh food. Their moods quickly improved.

"Aye, it will be an easy haul!" a man said.

"The English are always an easy haul!" another laughed.

"Like stealing candy from a baby!" Sal cried out for all to hear. He let out a series of bashing fists against the tables, causing all eyes in the room to turn on him. Silence spread quickly through the crowd at the outlandish statement.

Harris then howled like a wolf. He acted quickly, throwing metaphorical gasoline onto Sal's inspirational, but badly termed, fire.

The mess hall let out a booming cheer. Shortly after, a man with a small fiddle began playing a tune and the pirates became enthralled with song and dance. A barrel of grog was hauled out from storage and passed around.

Captain Nelson smiled. He gazed around the galley, noticing the high morale in the room. *They must love and worship Blood Bones*, he thought. There was not one sullen face in the crowd. He was sitting among the Bloods, a group of pirates feared by all. Blood Bones was their leader, and his cousin, Álvaro, was second in command. He closed his eyes, remembering a detailed report on the men around him: Blood Spot. That was the name Álvaro also went by.

He then eyed his friends and glanced toward the ladder, signaling he wished for a meeting in private.

7

January 14, 1763
Boston, Massachusetts

The group of four moved quickly to main deck, standing beside the forward mast. Captain Arthur F. Nelson looked around, noticing a skeleton crew standing watch. There were a few men at the top of the gangway and only a few more roaming the decks. Satisfied that no one was within earshot, he began.

"Excellent! It seems that our disguises have worked. I believe no one has noticed us as stowaways. There were a few curious glances, of course, probably because we are new faces onboard, but that's common in port, to take on new crew members." He paused for a moment, gazed into the waters, listened contentedly to the lapping sound of the tide against the ship's hull. After his previous adventure through the countryside of England, he was pleased to be aboard a ship again. "If we expose ourselves around the vessel here and there, above and below, they will grow used to seeing us aboard *La Monzón*. We must blend in if we are to succeed. Our next plan of action is to volunteer to be among the men who go ashore with Blood Bones to sneak aboard HMS *Courtesy*. I imagine he will choose those members tonight or sometime early tomorrow."

"Agreed." Sal smiled. "Now all we've got to do is find out what pirates do for fun!"

Harris laughed, and slapped his friend on the shoulder. "You're a dork, man. Just saying!"

Leah had calmed down considerably since their return to the eighteenth century. And she was quickly growing used to the idea of living amongst pirates. *At least I am in the same time period as Benjamin,* she thought. It was quite the adrenaline rush. Her previous lifestyle had been a bore. She smiled eagerly.

※※※

Blood Bones sat deep in thought, eyes closed, thinking of what was to come. Planning a well-detailed takeover was always a tedious thing, helped best by a quiet room and a bottle of red wine. The bottle was half empty when a knock on his door brought him out of his reverie. Sesostris stood before him, holding a large package in his hands. He was eager to commence their session.

Sesostris was the chef aboard *La Monzón*, but he had a more important duty on the ship, primarily as the personal confidant to Blood Bones. His nickname aboard was The Egyptian. He would never tell anyone the truth of his origins, but the crew knew he had special powers. He was a wizard, and for that sole reason no one would ever cross him. It would be stupid to. He kept to himself, with the exception of his daily meetings with Captain Blood Bones.

The duo had been good friends for over ten years. They had first met in 1751, and over time the two had counseled prior to every battle or important event. The results of their discussions were astonishing. Blood Bones was feared around the globe for his successes and he was hunted by every nation he plundered, which was pretty much all of them.

Sesostris entered the stateroom upon the captain's signal. He pulled the door closed. Their counsels were always made in private, so that the secret behind Blood Bones's successes was not known.

He moved forward, taking a seat opposite Blood Bones. "Captain, good day to you." Sesostris smiled, noticing the bottle of wine he had given the captain earlier in the day. "I see that you have begun to lay out the details of the upcoming mission?"

Blood Bones nodded. "Greetings. Yes, there is something about this wine that I particularly enjoy." He laughed. "But regardless of my tastes in wine, let us begin if you are ready to do so."

"First, tell me: I have noticed several new faces aboard. Did you hire any crew since we arrived in Boston?" Sesostris asked.

Blood Bones shook his head. He paused, thinking of his secret hideout. He was the leader of the remote island where pirate ships could lay in without being seen, and refit with fresh provisions. Sailors would often switch between ships, joining a new ship to get experience on each vessel that took refuge in the island's protective harbor. "No, we have not taken on any new crew since Jamaica."

He looked down at the scarlet stone upon his smallest left finger. It radiated a glow that made his smile ever larger.

Sesostris noticed this glow as well, and he ran a hand over his ragged beard. "I would like to discuss your prophecies, for I believe them to be coming true."

Blood Bones nodded. "Yes, as do I."

The man sitting before him was in his later years in life. Rumor aboard was that Sesostris was a few years past sixty. His wrinkles nearly covered the many scars on his face. He was by far the most experienced sailor with whom Blood Bones had ever shipped, and he revered him for that. Sesostris was mediocre in the galley, which was fine, but what he lacked in food preparation skills, he made up for in battle. He was a master of the elements of a nautical battle—he knew where to place any extra yard of sail to squeeze out an extra half knot, which had saved them countless times. He knew when and from which direction weather was approaching just by a quick glance at the sky or at the waves. He was a Godsend. Working in the galley was more of a way for him to keep a low profile on board.

"Ah, yes. My prophecy for revenge against those who had betrayed me all those long years ago, and of course for eternal life," Blood Bones said with a growing smile. He paused, allowing the faces of those duplicitous men to flash before his eyes: Padre Saladino, Carlos the guard, and lastly, Captain Bernardo Bermudez. The last face lingered in his mind the longest, as Bermudez had been the one who had sentenced him to the confines of a dungeon. "I believe the curse to have been set several times now. I have noticed the brilliant colors the scarlet stone displays from time to time. Although it has a steady hue, there are often times it spikes, which catches my attention. I believe that the new members aboard of which you speak are the very same men who have discovered my cursed treasure."

"Yes, captain. I completely agree with you." The wizard paused for a moment, letting the room go quiet. "Let the rivers of destiny flow freely through your mind. Your hand alone has written your story—you have changed your destiny entirely, and for this, I am quite excited for what is to come. When Death comes to your door, you will gladly open it, only to laugh in His face. You are a brave man, my friend. Tempting fate as you have done is quite the feat. It is something to be proud of."

Blood Bones looked at Sesostris with a smile. "Thank you for your kind words. I also long for this. As much as I would enjoy dwelling on what could be, we have other matters to discuss, issues that will soon be at hand."

Sesostris nodded with closed eyes. "Yes, the upcoming events that loom ahead will need great consideration. We will prevail as always, but I believe some will perish. More than that of any other conflict we have yet to pursue," the wizard said in a mystic voice, as if he was only physically there. Where his mind was, no one could say. The crystal ball was as mystic as the man standing before Blood Bones. "You will lose many of your close comrades. Among them will be Álvaro, and this will weigh heavily on your soul."

Blood Bones had grown used to his friend's meditative state. The turn in events caused him to fret, however. He shifted his weight in the chair to stretch out a kink in his back. "My dear friend, I know not what to think on the matters to come."

The pirate captain considered several alternate plans of attack, but kept coming to dead ends with each. Frustrated, he stood from the chair. "I need a moment to collect my thoughts."

Blood Bones moved to the balcony at the aft end of his cabin. He turned the handle, opened the door, and stepped out onto the small balcony terrace.

"Do you wish me to join you?" Sesostris asked.

"No, my dear friend. I would like a moment alone." Blood Bones paused. "I need some fresh air. That always helps. I would then like to look into your crystal ball for guidance."

Sesostris placed both hands on the package before him. He began peeling off the protective layers of cloth. "It will be ready upon your return. "He raised his voice so that it would carry to Blood Bones outside. "Let me know when you are ready."

Several minutes passed before Blood Bones returned. He left the balcony door open, allowing air in to freshen the stuffy cabin. His momentary escape seemed to have calmed his nerves.

"I am ready now." Blood Bones finally sat back down in the chair.

Sesostris opened his eyes. He pushed the wrapping across the desk, being careful not to disturb the crystal ball. Blood Bones stared down at the glowing orb and began the ritual procedure. He closed his eyes. He cleared his head of all that clouded it. He touched his fingertips to the crystal ball, and within a second a fog formed within the magic crystal. A supernatural energy radiated outward, giving Blood Bones a surge of power. His body shook violently as images came and went in his head. His visions passed quickly, and then he opened his eyes.

"I know what has to be done, but I am not happy with what is required."

Sesostris looked at him with crooked eyes. "What do you mean? What troubles you, my friend?"

"As you said before, we will lose many, Álvaro among them. The men who will be aboard *La Monzón* will be captured and sent to a dungeon deep below a castle's walls. I was not able to discover the location, but truthfully, that does not matter just yet."

"Hernando, you must ask yourself just one question: Is this plan of action necessary for the mission to succeed?"

"I believe it is," Blood Bones shrugged. He thought of everything he had been told, and of everything he had just seen. He stared at the clear crystal ball again, noticing its emptiness. He then put more thought into the posed question. Silence lingered in the air while he wrapped his thoughts around the issue. "Yes, yes it is."

"Well then," Sesostris smiled. "If you know what you must do, let us begin our work and preparations."

※※※

Harris looked off into the distance, seeing the water shimmer under the afternoon sunlight. Then he looked at the others. "Leah, this is going to sound odd. Just to let you know, Ben was going to tell you the truth, but he never had a chance. He would always tell us how much he wanted to, but he just wasn't ready. He was afraid of losing you, that you might think he was a liar. I just hope you will understand that."

Leah nodded, wiping several tears with her sleeve. "Yes, thank you. I always knew there was something he was hiding. I saw it in his eyes. I knew he wanted to tell me something, but please, go on with your story."

"Okay." He paused. "Sal, if you want to add something, please feel free. I don't really know where to begin. This is all going to sound so weird." Harris paused, trying to make sense of their story. "Well, we are from the future. Our adventure begins over two hundred years from now. We are from St. Augustine, Florida and we discovered a map in a wine bottle while cleaning out our cellar. This map led us to an intricate cave system on an island that we discovered was home to the cursed treasure of Blood Bones. After discovering the treasure, we accidentally were sent through the perils of time to 1763. We climbed aboard the English vessel *Frendrich*, which is where we met Captain Nelson. At first we were thought to be stowaways, but then sort of gained our freedom by fighting alongside Nelson and his men. I believe you know the rest, with the shipwreck on the uncharted island, and the successful capture of Blood Bones when we raided his secret lair."

Leah nodded. "Yes, you all told me those exciting stories." She paused. "But what does it mean, that you are from the future? How is that possible?"

Sal decided to put in his five-cents' worth. "Well, we don't really know how exactly we ended up here. The curse is written, but we all believe it is a verbal curse as well. I can only assume there is one last phase to the curse. You know what I mean?" His eyes probed Harris's for confirmation.

Harris nodded. "Yeah, you have a point, Sal. Back in time, forward in time, and most recently back in time. It makes sense to have another cycle, I guess. The only thing we don't know is if the curse is finalized once the fourth revolution occurs. I guess we shouldn't be worried about that just yet. We still need to survive here without being caught, and then we have to go and save Ben and the others."

Nelson remained quiet. He knew it was important for Leah to hear the truth, and who better to tell the story than the young men who had lived it? He waited, then thought it wise to say, "I concur. We are aboard their vessel, among a crew of deadly pirates. They are wanted men, feared in nearly every seafaring country. Let us make the best of it to blend in. It seems our destinies have been chosen. God has written our fates. We are to become pirates! To succeed, we will need to learn the ins and outs of the vessel. Please pay attention and follow me."

Nelson waited a moment for the others, and then began the lesson. He walked the length of the deck, from bow to stern before he spoke. The trio followed in his wake. He then stopped at the anchor windlass. "I believe her to be a modified Bermuda sloop. *La Monzón* is a fast and very maneuverable vessel, with a low freeboard. Her design is unique to the vessels of Bermuda making trade with the colonies."

Leah listened, but some of Nelson's terms were completely foreign to her. "Captain Nelson, what is a low freeboard?"

Nelson smiled in return. He was always eager to teach a willing soul. "Leah, please do not call me 'captain'. I appreciate the etiquette and the gesture, but while we are aboard *La Monzón*, I cannot be addressed as your captain." His comment was directed not just to Leah, but to Harris and Sal as well.

"Of course. I do apologize," Leah said. She knew she must follow his orders, and she was slowly getting used to this new life.

He nodded his head in response, then continued. "If you take note of the numerous vessels here in port, some are larger than others, and likewise, some are very small and low in the water. What makes *La Monzón* unique is its capability to sail in shallow waters. One of the reasons pirates love sloops are for that reason; with their particular hull design they can escape from warships into the shallows without fear of being followed. Most larger vessels run aground in their pursuits, and then the pirates can turn back and capture these vessels with very little damage to themselves. It is a very commonly used strategy. Another reason that this vessel is fast and maneuverable is that it has two masts with fore-and-aft rigging. It makes it easier to sail upwind," he said, looking up into the shrouds above.

Sal, Harris, and Leah looked up. They followed the tarred ratlines from the rails beside them, arcing through the sky to the bare masts above. Dark clouds billowed overhead, suggesting a storm was coming their way.

"How fast do you think *La Monzón* can go?" Sal asked Nelson.

Nelson smiled, and then closed his eyes, reliving a moment long ago.

He paused, allowing for their anticipation to build. Once content, he began. "Well, the speed of a vessel depends on a few things of course: the vertical movement of the water, which is called tide, the horizontal movement, the current, as well as the winds. Lastly the design of the ship itself." He was enjoying taking his time, causing all three of his new students to lean in for the story. "I have stood at the helm of a ship that could exceed fifteen knots, but I will save that story for another day."

"That's not fair!" Sal said, causing Harris and Leah to laugh.

"But I do have an equally exciting tale." He paused, all were eager for the tale. "The date was the second of May, 1747. I was aboard the sloop HMS *Falcon*. She was more or less the same design as this ship, give or take some of the added guns that I've noticed Blood Bones has installed for increased firepower. The *Falcon* had ten guns, and she was fast, extremely fast. We were tasked to block off communications between the French and their colonies in North America. This was my first ship serving in the British Royal Navy. I served under Captain Gwyn, and our vessel acted as a scout and messenger for the fleet led by Admiral George Anson."

Captain Nelson had a way of blending a history lesson into his personal accounts. They all stared at him as he continued on with the story.

"I was in the crow's nest when I first saw the enemy. My eyes strained through the spyglass, scanning in all directions. Once I took sight of the first sail I quickly lost count. I bore witness to nearly thirty sails on the horizon. After what seemed an eternity of seeing sail after sail come into view, the ship's bells below tolled the time, and it brought me out of my reverie. I had been on watch for about fifteen minutes, and it would soon become a watch that strongly influenced me. It made me the man I am today—" He nearly lost track of the story here, locked in his memory, but then caught himself—"but back to the tale. It was an exhilarating chase. After Admiral Anson gave us the word, the British vessels bore down on the French. While serving Captain Gwyn, I was taught almost everything there is to know about ship handling techniques, the effects of wind, the seas, and weather upon a battle. He taught me how to properly handle a ship. It is almost as if I could make the vessel below me move as I wished it. It was almost as if I could make the ship dance upon the waves below the keel. I could easily spend hours discussing the intricacies of a sea battle, but I would not want to bore you," Nelson said. He smiled, reminiscing in the great memory.

Harris slapped Sal on the back. "Well, we've seen some of those intricacies so far." He paused, and then looked at Captain Nelson. "And I look forward to the ones to come, sailing under you."

Captain Nelson laughed. "Again, you must remember that for our plan to work, we must pay very close detail to what we say, and to whom we say it. You also forget that I am no longer in charge. I am not the master of this vessel!" The statement seemed to give him pause, as if he was reflecting on his words as well. The fact that he was no longer in charge seemed to weigh him down a bit. "But you are right. I, also, look forward to the events to come serving under Blood Bones. Our spies had no knowledge of his whereabouts after he had commandeered HMS *Courtesy* out of Boston Harbor. Rumor was that he laid low at his secret lair until things settled down. The man is a complete mystery to me. He is as complex as his crimson journal reveals him to be."

Sal stared off into the distance. "Sir, if you don't mind me asking, why are we walking around the vessel if we know that *La Monzón* sinks and that a bunch of the pirates are captured? It seems pointless to waste our time acquainting ourselves with it when disaster will hit hard."

Nelson bellowed with laughter. "You are young, and foolish! If you follow this piece of advice, you will succeed in all that you do—always become acquainted with the ship that you stand upon. Her planks, her sails—they are all things you must know inside-and-out, like the limbs and curves of a lover. Whether a week-long tussle or a lifelong embrace, everything relies on that intimate relationship between man and ship. She is a living and breathing thing. A vessel requires proper care and continual maintenance. That is why we call ships *she*."

Sal stood there, silently bowing his head in shame. Harris smiled, appreciating the advice and wisdom that Captain Nelson always bestowed. Leah blushed at the words *lover* and *intimate*. She instantly thought of Benjamin Manry and of the long road they still had to travel to save him. He was her beacon of light. Thinking of him always put a smile on her face.

"Before we go our separate ways, I think we should all have new names. From this point forward, my name will be Miguel." Captain Nelson paused, and then looked at Sal. "Yours will be Salvador." He then looked at Harris. "Yours will be Hector." Then he looked Leah up and down, pleased with the transformation of the beautiful young woman into pirate scum. "And yours will be Luis."

They mouthed their new names silently, knowing that the importance of their upcoming mission weighed heavily on quickly adapting to new identities.

Footsteps from behind warned of an approaching figure.

They turned in time to see the oncoming watch move about the vessel, relieving those currently standing duty. Moments later, the ship's bell tolled the time.

"Well, it is now 1600, let us part ways for now," Nelson told the group. "I would recommend going your own ways, observe, work with a group, see what being a pirate is all about. I will see you all at dinner!"

※※※

Later that evening, Blood Bones called for another meeting in the galley. Sitting among his loyal crew, he cut into an apple with a small blade that he removed from a sheath on his calf. He sliced off a piece and ate it. His smile brought a cheer to his men.

"Nothing better than fresh provisions!"

A well-fed crew meant a happy crew, and a happy crew meant successful missions. At least that was the philosophy of Blood Bones.

His crew laughed. "Aye, aye, captain!"

"Well, I have pondered all afternoon and have come to a decision!" He announced to his shipmates.

His crew howled as if they were wolves. For the next few minutes, each pirate made guttural noises that echoed throughout the chamber. When the noise subsided, Blood Bones continued.

"I shall split you into two groups. One will come with me to board the frigate, and the remaining crew will stay aboard *La Monzón* under the leadership of Álvaro." He paused and looked at his cousin, Blood Spot, knowing that something bad would soon happen to him. He fought off the urge to preserve his cousin, knowing that in their line of work, you died one of three ways: in battle, naturally, or at the end of the noose. Dying in battle was the preferred way, if you had any control over your destiny, which he, of course did.

"Those of you remaining on board here will get underway tomorrow on the ebb tide, sail for a few hours to give the impression that we have departed these waters. At nightfall, you will return to a position several miles off shore." He exchanged a glance with his cousin. "Remain out of sight of other vessels as well as the large cannons of the fortress."

"Consider it done, Captain."

He gave them a wicked smile. "Excellent. I have bribed several longshoremen to buy us some extra time. Every minute we have under sail will give us the advantage. The plan is simple: we sneak aboard the *Courtesy* and commandeer the vessel out of the harbor. We will get underway before the other vessels realize what has happened. The point of having *La Monzón* a few miles off shore is to give us protection if any other ship gives pursuit." He paused, silently whispering a prayer for the friends he knew he would soon lose. "We will do this under the cover of darkness and will escape under their very eyes!"

"Aye, aye!" The pirates cheered.

Blood Bones began pointing to various members, assigning them their duty stations. When just Nelson, Sal, Harris, and Leah remained, Blood Bones paused, debating where he could use the extra sailors. As he wiped at his face with his sleeve, he noticed that the glow in the scarlet stone upon his finger had intensified.

"And you four will come with me." Blood Bones smiled.

Sal nodded, giving a hoot of excitement. "To an easy victory!"

The remaining men, along with Nelson, Harris, and Leah, all cheered for the upcoming adventure, eager to fill their coffers with gold.

Blood Bones led the chosen members out of the galley. Harris, Sal, Leah, and Captain Nelson followed the other pirates. For several minutes, they traversed through the innards of the sloop, led by the light of a large lantern. The pirate leader finally arrived at a locked door in the bowels of the ship. He removed a key from deep inside his pocket and unlocked the door. It creaked as he pushed it open.

"Stay here." He looked at the line of crewmen.

Blood Bones entered the room and placed the lantern on a hook above his head.

He moved from chest to chest, staring at the name plate on each. After several minutes of searching, he found one with what looked to be an English flag painted on it. He opened the lid and pulled out leggings, stockings, and the famous red coat of the British Royal Marines.

"One at a time, please," Blood Bones said as the first man entered the small space to retrieve the new clothing.

"Hello, my friend," Sesostris said with a smile.

"Good day. It seems as if everything is falling into place." Blood Bones looked into the chest below and rummaged through the contents. After a moment, he pulled out the new clothing. "This should fit. I would like another counsel tonight if you have the time to spare, my dear friend."

"Aye. Until then, farewell."

The pirates entered, retrieved their wares, and left to go back to their quarters. Blood Bones continued this process until there were only four men standing in the darkness.

"Next," Blood Bones called. There was a moment of hesitation as Leah, Sal, Harris, and Captain Nelson stared at each other, waiting to see who would go next. "I do not have all day!" Blood Bones bellowed out. He smiled as the glow from the scarlet stone increased in intensity. In just one more phase of his curse, he would soon have all the time in the world.

Leah went first. She grunted, and mumbled an incoherent greeting. She let off a crooked smiled at Blood Bones. He passed her the new clothing.

She left the room, and then Harris went in. As before, Blood Bones gave him the clothing, and he left. Sal then entered, and received his clothing.

Captain Nelson nodded as Sal passed by. He was the only remaining man left to get the new outfitting. He looked at the backs of his friends as they walked away, following the crowd of pirates who snaked their way throughout the vessel. He then made eye contact with Blood Bones before entering the small space.

Blood Bones felt a surge in intensity in the scarlet stone upon his finger. He stared deep into Nelson's eyes. "What is your name, my friend?"

Nelson smiled. He had practiced this line several times in his head. "Those close to me call me Miguel."

Blood Bones nodded. "Excellent, I believe we will become quite close in the months to come, Miguel."

"I hope we do." He returned the smile. He wondered if Blood Bones had remembered their last interaction with each other in the alternate reality. He shrugged at the mystery. "Have a pleasant day, Captain."

Nelson's words were genuine, but the statement would echo in his head for the remainder of the day. He bowed his head slightly, and then left the space, leaving Blood Bones alone.

The pirate captain held the opened lock in his right hand. His booming laughter echoed through the ship as he placed the lock back on the metal loop, securing the storeroom. The scarlet stone glowed brilliantly with renewed vigor.

༺༻

A knock on the door caused Blood Bones to open his eyes. He was sitting at his desk, looking through records of their past voyages. He had sorted through a pile of paperwork, then placed the documents facedown. He was a very meticulous captain, paying complete attention to all details. "Come in," he said.

Sesostris entered the room quietly, carrying a large bundle in his hands. "Hello, Hernando."

"Take a seat, my dear friend," Blood Bones said. Once Sesostris was seated, he continued. "I would like you to pack a few things to take with us when we commandeer HMS *Courtesy*. The crystal ball must be with us."

Sesostris nodded. "Yes, that is not a problem. I have a satchel that I can sling to my back when we board the vessel."

"Good, its safety is of the utmost importance."

"Yes. Is there anything else you would like to discuss?" Sesostris asked.

"No, I think I will turn in soon. I am exhausted, and we have quite a mission tomorrow night. Good night, my dear friend," Blood Bones said.

"Farewell, until tomorrow."

8

January 15, 1763
Boston, Massachusetts

Leah's eyes were closed when she was suddenly shaken awake. It was roughly two hours into the four-to-eight watch when Captain Nelson walked through the berthing to wake his crew.

"Good morning," Leah said. Her eyelids struggled to open. The light in the berthing quarters was poor, but Nelson carried a lantern in his hand. Behind him, she could see the outlines of Harris and Sal.

"Good morning to you as well. I just wanted to wake you all so we could break our fasts together. I imagine Blood Bones will have a busy day planned for us ahead."

"If we were going to be so busy, we should've slept in!" Sal laughed.

Harris chuckled at his friend's humor, but Captain Nelson just shook his head. "Salvador, one day I will get used to your jokes, but it will not be this day!"

The group shared a laugh, keeping their voices soft. There were countless hammocks slung about the berthing. A ship runs twenty-four hours a day, and they knew better than to be loud belowdecks.

"All right, up with you now. Let's get a bite to eat before we find out what Blood Bones has in store for us."

※※※

Blood Bones had barely slept that night. He tossed and turned all night long, and woke up at least a dozen times. He decided it best to put his thoughts down on paper. Doing so was his remedy for concern, a thing he had done since he had escaped from the dungeons of *El Morro* so many years ago. For hours he wrote, recounting tales of the past. Each entry flowed into the next, and before he knew it, the sun was rising. Light shimmered off the water beside the vessel, casting a rainbow-like illumination into his cabin. He put his quill down and moved toward the balcony. He opened the doors and stepped out onto the small platform. The fresh air seemed to calm his nerves.

There was a knock on the door to his cabin, but from the balcony outside, Blood Bones could not hear it. A face emerged in the narrow opening, and Sesostris then moved forward into the space. He carried the crystal ball. He moved quietly so as not to disturb Blood Bones, and placed his relic on the tabletop off to the side of the room.

"Good morning, Captain." Sesostris remained hidden from view but now his voice was close enough to be heard outside the small chamber.

Blood Bones smiled at his friend's arrival. He took one last deep breath before turning around and entering the cabin. He left the doors open, and the two took a seat at their customary spots.

"Greetings, my friend," Blood Bones said. "Today is the big day. I would like to gaze into your crystal ball once last time before we set the plan in motion."

"Of course. I am ready when you are."

※※※

There were about a dozen pirates inside the galley talking quietly amongst themselves. Off to the corner sat Captain Nelson with his three friends. Harris looked down at the plate of porridge, fruit scone, and salted beef. The scone was freshly made, and was still warm in the center as he bit into it. He nodded, content with the flavor.

Leah cut into the salted beef and placed the food in her mouth. She held the fork as if she were at a banquet.

"Luis, please drop your polite mannerisms. You do not want to betray yourself as an elite member of society," Captain Nelson said under his breath. "Remember, you are the scum of the earth. Eat like they would!"

She smiled at the phrase. She felt as though the trio sitting with her were her personal saviors. Without them, she would be totally alone and completely lost on her quest to save Benjamin. She thought of that possibility, and it scared her. "This will certain take some time to get used to!"

"As with all things, change is a known factor. For everything we encounter in our lives, we will eventually change and modify our thoughts and beliefs. But for now, let us eat."

The group nodded, paying close attention to their plates and cups of grog. Leah had yet to drink the grog, and as she put the tin cup to her lips she nearly fainted at the smell. Her eyes twitched, but she continued on with the task. She let the warm liquid flow into her mouth, and she forced it down with a reluctant swallow. The burning sensation coursed through her at the speed of light, and she leaned back in her seat. It hit her then and there, and she belched loudly as a result.

The trio looked at her, as did half of the room.

"Excuse you!" Blood Bones said as he entered the room. The crowd became silent, paying respect to their leader.

※※※

The galley was now jam-packed with all of the complement aboard. Blood Bones liked to have his crew fully informed before each mission. It was common for him to lay out the details that would be attended to by each individual person. Like clockwork, he would orchestrate each aspect to a plan, with every component greased and practiced.

"Gentlemen, it is time for action. At noon, I would like to have Álvaro and the assigned crew take the ship out of the harbor. As I have said, you will set sail for the evening, but return at nightfall to a point just outside view of the fortress. Under cover of darkness, I will lead the remaining men to commandeer the HMS *Courtesy*. I have hired a few longshoreman to distract the British while on the pier. I imagine when they realize the ploy, they will start their pursuit. The longshoremen's actions should buy us the time we need to get the vessel out of the harbor."

The pirates nodded throughout the discussion, listening as the plan unfolded.

Álvaro looked at his cousin with a large grin. "And I will just be out of sight. Once you are underway and I see your sails, I will then bear down on you and offer the service of our guns as protection."

"That is the plan!" Blood Bones laughed. He stared at Álvaro, knowing this might very well be the last time he would look at his cousin. He shook out the cobwebs of doubt, and then returned his focus back to the task at hand. "As for the men coming with me, please change into the garments I provided you with last night. I would like for us to be off the vessel by noon, and assist with the mooring lines to get *La Monzón* underway. Once off the ship, we will walk about the town, blending in with the locals. By sunset, I would like to be back on the pier, just within sight of the *Courtesy*."

"Aye!" His crew cheered for the prospect of wealth. Three months' worth of colonial taxes could easily set each man up for a luxurious life.

"With that being said, are there any questions?" Blood Bones asked. He looked around, scanning the room, searching the crowd of faces. His gaze then settled on Captain Nelson and the trio that always kept to themselves. He smiled, eager for what loomed just within reach.

There was very little privacy in the common berthing area. Several pirates slept on their hammocks, their snoring drowning out other hushed discussions. Some men were changing into the uniforms Blood Bones had given them. All in all, there would be a total of twenty-four pirates joining their leader in the seizure of the British vessel.

Captain Nelson changed out of his tarred linens and into the uniform of the British Royal Marines. He closed his eyes, having a *Déjà vu*. He stood tall and proud in the cloth, maybe ten or fifteen years earlier. Memories rushed in a similar pattern: his first day aboard a ship, his first time killing a man in battle, his award ceremony, where an admiral in the fleet had pinned a ribbon to his uniform. He shook his head, ridding himself of thoughts of his prior life. He then opened his eyes and looked down at his chest. There was a distinct lack of medals and ribbons on the uniform he now wore. He was now a pirate, serving Blood Bones, and he had to get used to that fact. He was no longer in charge of men, he was just a commoner. He tucked the cursed staff into his undergarments, and straightened out the wool coat to hide it further.

"All right, gentlemen." His gaze stopped on Leah. So far, he had been careful to not call Leah by her name, or imply that she was a female. A woman aboard a ship was bad luck. Sailors were well-known for their superstitious natures. "Please, follow my lead. The sooner we are dressed, the sooner we can start our mission."

Harris and Sal were already pulling on their leggings and buttoning their waistcoats. In just a few moments, they were completely dressed. Leah stood there motionless. She had never undressed before a group of people. She glanced around, noticing that at least no one was staring at her. Her short hair and demeanor had masked her true identity so far, but she was still uncertain of undressing in front of everyone.

Harris watched Leah's wandering eyes. He began to formulate and idea. He moved over to Sal and whispered something into his ear.

The duo moved to their hammocks, which were just across from where Leah was standing. They unhooked each end off the metal circles that held the material, and began shaking the hammocks out. Dust and random items fell to the deck, but after that, they took their time replacing the hooks back on the circles. With the newly offered protection on two sides of her, Leah was essentially shielded from all eyes.

She smiled, knowing what Harris had just done for her. Quickly, she removed her clothing and began to don the undergarments of the uniform. Once she was comfortable with what she had on, she cleared her throat. Sal and Harris placed the hooks back on the metal circles, and both lay in their hammocks. No one was the wiser, and frankly, anyone who was belowdecks with them had kept to themselves.

※※※

The twenty-five pirates stood on the pier. They were scattered the length of the vessel in small groups tending the mooring lines on the bollards. Captain Nelson looked up at the clouds, noticing a fresh breeze blowing toward the water. The unique smell of civilization carried to his nose. He sniffed it in, and smiled at the blend of smoke, food, and people in general. A sailor always appreciates the smell of something other than tar, paint, and the salt of the ocean.

Blood Bones hailed to Álvaro at the railing above. "Are you ready?"

Álvaro glanced at all the remaining hands busy about the deck. Several were at the anchor windlass, ready heave the heavy anchor up aboard the vessel. Men were scattered in the yards above, ready to put out canvas. Others were standing forward and aft along the rail, ready to pull in the mooring lines. Satisfied, Álvaro nodded. "Aye!" He called down to his cousin.

"Godspeed!" Blood Bones yelled. He then turned, nodding to each group spread along the pier.

In sequence, the sailors on the pier removed the eye of the mooring lines off the bollards, as men at the rails pulled the lines aboard.

Leah put her body weight into pulling the eye off the bollard. It weighed much more than she realized, and she struggled with it. Harris and Sal shifted their positions to help her out, and the trio pulled it over the rounded top. For a moment, the eye of the mooring line sat on the ground by their feet. After the briefest of seconds, the line started to be pulled in, and they looked between the gap of the vessel and the pier as the line kerplunked into the water below. They followed the eye as it skimmed the top of the water. They watched the sailors above on deck pulling the line hand over hand, and finally the eye was on deck. The men below coiled the lines in a tight circle, readying the line for stowing.

High above, men were unfurling sail. Captain Nelson strained his eyes against the bright sunlight, only partially hidden behind a sky full of clouds. He sniffed the air, and smelled the coming of snow. The skies matched his prediction, and he estimated a snow shower before the end of the day.

Álvaro orchestrated the task perfectly. The sails caught the wind and the vessel began to float away from the pier on the ebbing tide. Captain Nelson reached down to his hip and looked at a pocket watch that he unclasped with his hand. He closed his eyes and did a quick calculation, recalling the times of high tide and low tide. It was just a few minutes after twelve. Blood Bones had obviously taken this into consideration, as *La Monzón* sailed easily out of the harbor.

9

January 15, 1763
Boston, Massachusetts

They sat inside a small tavern just a few blocks away from the docks. A fire crackled off to the side, as the twenty-five impostors ate their lunches of wild game stew, a mix of venison and rabbit and various vegetables. Steam rose off their bowls as they ate ravenously. Leah looked around the table, watching as the pirates slurped at their bowls rather than using utensils. They sopped the remaining liquid out with pieces of fresh baked bread. Simply put, they ate like animals.

Captain Nelson watched Leah's indecision with her utensil. After the briefest of moments, she looked down and grabbed the bowl on each side. The bowl was hot, and it hurt her hands, but she forced thoughts of the pain away. She had to. She had cut her hair, she had dressed like a man, and now she was eating like a commoner. The concept thrilled her, and she let off a twisted smile. She wiped her face with her sleeve, mimicking the eating practices of those around her.

Blood Bones finished his meal and stood. He was content that his men were enjoying themselves before what was to come. He moved around several tables, jam-packed with his crew, and then took a seat beside Captain Nelson. "Miguel, how are you faring this day?"

Nelson greeted the man with a smile. "Good, good. The meal was excellent, and I look forward to the upcoming mission." He was speaking the truth. Captain Nelson revered Blood Bones for his instinct and unwavering success. He then thought back to his skirmish against the man many months ago. It seemed like a different time, a different era.

"Excellent." He then turned to the other members of the group. "I do not believe we have formally met."

Harris quickly glanced at Captain Nelson, looking for any hint or suggestions. He received a nod. "I am Hector."

Blood Bones extended a hand in greeting. "Welcome." He shook hands with Harris and then turned to face Sal. "And you?"

"Salvador. Pleasure," Sal said, grabbing hands with the pirate.

"And last?" Blood Bones prodded Leah. "What is your name?"

Leah swallowed excess saliva, making her mouth as dry as possible. She then let out a weak grunt. "Luis!"

Blood Bones scanned her face. He looked down at Leah's uniform, and noticed the slightest of bulges where her bosom was. "Pleased to have you all here." He shook her hand. "I like to be acquainted with the *men* I sail with."

He emphasized the word, as if teasing Leah right to her face. Her expression dropped, but before she could respond, a violinist in the background began a song. All eyes shifted toward the noise, and the music filled the boisterous tavern, ending further conversation.

※※※

Captain Nelson studied his new friend and chuckled. He glanced down as the falling snow twirled around him. "Hernando, you look good. If I didn't know you, I'd say you could pass for a British officer!"

Blood Bones sensed the man's sarcasm and smiled. He liked the man before him. There was something about him that he couldn't quite figure out, but there would be plenty of time for that in the coming months. "Miguel, well, that is the plan after all, is it not?"

The two enjoyed a nice laugh as they led the remaining men down the wharf. Minutes later they arrived in front of HMS *Courtesy*. Sal, Harris, and Leah followed in the wake of the British Royal Marine impostors. As the officer on deck hailed down to them, Blood Bones switched to his best English accent. His Spanish skin took refuge under the blanket of darkness and sheets of light falling snow.

"Good evening. It is I, Lieutenant Clifford Johnson of your neighboring HMS *Georgia Rose*. As per our captain, we're to switch out my twenty-five best gunners between the *Courtesy* and the *Georgia Rose*. Rumor has it that Blood Bones is preying these waters, and the captain wants to be extra careful. Is that all right with you, or shall I be required to discuss orders with your captain?"

The young man appeared nervous at the mention of Blood Bones, the most feared pirate along the Atlantic Coast and in the Caribbean. "Aye, I'll pick out the men. If we do confront this bastard you speak of, we'll be well prepared. I appreciate the warning and will tell our captain. Just wait here. I'll return momentarily," he said in what seemed one nervous breath.

Captain Nelson watched the man turn and head at a quick gait for the companionway ladder that led below. "Do you think all will fall into place?"

Blood Bones rubbed his well-trimmed goatee and then ran a hand through his hair until the movement shifted the hat atop his head. "Of course, Miguel. The plan was well thought out."

Nelson nodded, still adjusting to the new name he'd assigned himself.

The officer on deck returned to his post with twenty-five marines. He cupped his hands around his mouth, hoping his voice would carry over the wind.

"Sir, I've informed my captain of the plans. I'm sending my men to the *Georgia Rose*. Again, I thank you for the warning and would be delighted to have you aboard."

Blood Bones watched as the line of men walked by, heading less than a quarter mile down the wharf. Judging the distance, he calculated the alarm would be raised in under five minutes. Time was not in their favor.

As he filed up the gangway, he lowered his head, touching the brim of his hat to the officer in salute, which also allowed him to cover his face. The young man returned the gesture as the men came aboard. Blood Bones led his men to the bow of the vessel to meet one last time before they put their plan into action.

※※※

Captain Nelson followed Blood Bones closely as the two walked toward the officer on deck at the gangway. The remainder of their group slowly spread around the main deck.

"Lieutenant, I have some requests of you," Blood Bones said.

The young man saluted. "Sir, of course. What can I do?"

"How many men do you have on deck right now?" the pirate asked.

"Sir, we've ten marines and fifteen seamen. At the end of the watch, another dozen or so will come on deck, and we'll lift anchor and sail out of the harbor in convoy with the *Georgia Rose* and the *Savannah*."

"Good. Well, I'm thinking ahead. Just in case, we can mount several swivel guns on deck. Order your marines to retrieve ten guns from below. I think if we mount four on both sides, evenly spaced, and two fore and aft, that would be enough for the defense against this bloody pirate if he indeed decides to attack."

"Aye, sir, but wouldn't it make more sense to send the ordinary seamen for the task?"

"We need them on deck to ready for sea," Blood Bones replied with a convincing air of authority. The young officer took the bait.

"Aye, sir, I'll do that right now."

※※※

As the twenty-five marines from the *Courtesy* reached the gangway of the *Georgia Rose*, the voice of the officer on deck carried down from the gangway watch station. "Hark, who goes there?"

The lead man replied. "Just reporting, sir. We've orders to join your crew. Can we be led to your commanding officer so we can go over the plans that were just assigned to us?"

The officer on deck called down in a hesitant tone. "Remain there while I retrieve the captain."

The men on the wharf stood still, chatting among themselves until two figures called down to them. "Permission granted."

Once all were aboard, the man at the front of the assembled line sounded off. "Sir, Lieutenant Alec Greenbough of the *Courtesy*, reporting as ordered."

The captain was simply puzzled. "Reporting for what?"

"Sir, Lieutenant Clifford Johnson of the *Georgia Rose* came with about twenty or so men to our vessel just before. He had a message that Blood Bones is preying the waters nearby the harbor and that you gave him permission to switch out marines between ships. He said they were the finest gunners from the *Rose*."

"Something's not right. You said Lieutenant Clifford Johnson?"

"Sir, that is correct."

The captain closed his eyes, knowing something serious was to occur. "This is not good. We need to warn the *Courtesy* that the men you speak of are impostors. I don't have anyone by the name of Clifford Johnson on board, nor did I grant those orders."

✼✼✼

Within just a few moments the deck was clear. Captain Nelson moved to the railing beside the officer on deck, glancing off into the wintry harbor. Blood Bones signaled his man with a nod of the head, and he unsheathed the knife on his hip.

"Do as I say or you will die," Captain Nelson whispered as he pressed the blade into the man's neck. The statement echoed in his head for a moment, but he fought the uncertainty. He had to, otherwise their efforts would be for naught.

The officer nodded slowly, enough to let his attacker know his decision, but not enough for the blade to inflict any damage. Only then did he notice the darker complexion of the man who had introduced himself as Lieutenant Clifford Johnson standing in front of him.

"Lock your men below deck, and batten the hatches. Get your ordinaries to cut the lines and lift anchor. Raise sails and steer out of the harbor."

The British officer's complexion reddened quickly. "And may I ask who you are?"

Blood Bones placed a hand on the brim of his tricorn, removing it with a sweeping motion across the front of his body. "My friends call me Hernando, to my crew I am Captain, but you know me as Blood Bones."

"And what if I refuse?" replied the officer.

"You'll meet Davy Jones himself, for he was the first to have refused an order of mine. Miguel, we are wasting time."

With a flick of the wrist, the young officer fell to the deck. Captain Nelson stared down at the deck in front of him. The man lay twisted where he had fallen, blood trickling out from where the cut.

A sailor standing by the gunwale nearby ran over to interrogate. "Sir, may I ask what happened?"

"An impostor. We're lucky I saw him come aboard!" Blood Bones said. "Send a man below to inform the captain of what happened. I think it's best that we ready the sails now; trouble looks to be brewing on the pier. I want the ship ready for sea immediately!"

"Yes, sir."

The seaman quickly passed the message. Blood Bones hid a smile as he watched the sailors move about the deck with haste. They were coordinated and the effort was not in vain.

"Sir, if we place a couple of swords between the handles, the hatches won't open."

"Good work, Miguel. The hatches cannot be opened from below; they'll have no way to escape. Now, hurry!"

"Yes, captain." Captain Nelson ran off to attend to that task.

With the spyglass to his eye, Blood Bones scanned the decks of HMS *Savannah*, pleased to see that there was no commotion on board the other ship. His gaze shifted toward the *Georgia Rose*. As he blinked away several snowflakes from his eyelashes, he noticed that ship was bustling with activity.

※※※

Once Captain Nelson finished blocking the hatches, he led Harris, Sal, and Leah forward to the anchor windlass. Nelson bellowed out orders to several ordinary seamen to begin the difficult task of raising anchor. A group of about six began pushing against the spokes of the windlass, slowly bringing up the anchor. It was a laborious process that took nearly half an hour.

Nelson then paced the deck to find Blood Bones and report their status.

Leah smiled, content with the physical work. This was really the first time in her life that she had performed physical labor. Everything before had been done for her. Her face dripped with sweat. She wiped her brow with her sleeve and then let out a long and content sigh.

"Good job, Leah," Harris said quietly. He was careful for his voice to not carry to the other sailors around. "We read about this attack. It was in a newspaper article back when we were home in modern day. Blood Bones was deemed brilliant for his constant and unwavering success. I guess until we captured him, that is."

"Thank you. He seems it," Leah responded.

Sal nodded. "Yeah, man. I wonder how we were so lucky catching him."

Harris shrugged. "Who knows, man. Everything happens for a reason. We're here now, which is awesome! I mean, dude, we're seeing history unfold."

Sal laughed. "Yeah, you're right."

The trio talked quietly amongst themselves, standing beside the other ordinary seamen, awaiting further orders.

※※※

The captain of the *Georgia Rose* led a squad of marines down the gangway, forming his men into columns of three. They marched quickly and with urgency, knowing that something was awry. Twenty-five unaccounted-for men had slipped past their guard. They did not know who these men were.

"It's an awfully good night, tonight," said a man emerging from the shadows.

The longshoreman led a group of ten out into the middle of the lane, obstructing the path for the marines.

The captain called out, "Get out of the way or we'll have you arrested!"

With a hand in his pocket, the longshoreman gripped the pouch of gold coins that a mysterious cloaked sailor had given him earlier. The sailor had not given him his name, but judging by the gold he now had, it was for an important reason. "But these are our docks—you must pay the toll if you would like to pass."

"You fool! We do not have time for this. Move or we will be forced to take drastic measures!"

The longshoremen fell back several feet, allowing the marines to advance further. The man replied. "Aye, that'll cost you, too. We let you have a yard," he chuckled in his half-drunk state.

"Charge them!"

The marines lowered their rifles, using them as clubs in their forward charge. One man was clubbed to the ground as the rest fled backward, allowing the marines to regain their ranks and continue down toward the HMS *Courtesy*.

The distraction had given Blood Bones the time he needed.

※※※

"All lines are cut and the anchor has just been raised," Nelson called to Blood Bones over the noise as the chain slid down the spill pipe to be stored below.

Blood Bones nodded at the news. Nelson stood beside his sworn enemy, with a newfound appreciation for the man's brilliance and leadership in the heat of battle. Blood Bones had a calm demeanor about him, as if he knew how everything would pan out. It was a great characteristic to have aboard a ship.

Under different circumstances, I would, without hesitation, consider this man a shipmate, and if time allowed it, perhaps even a good friend, Nelson thought.

Blood Bones gazed through the telescopic glass at the *Georgia Rose*. Men littered the weather decks, preparing the vessel for sea. He then adjusted his view toward the wharf, noticing his hired longshoremen had succeeded in delaying the pursuing marines. After wiping another layer of fresh snowflakes off the lens, he continued to scan the bare decks of the *Savannah*.

Blood Bones snapped to attention when he heard a volley of gunfire come from the pier. The vessel was less than half a pistol's shot away when he heard the thuds of the lead bullets hitting the decks and bulwarks of the *Courtesy*.

"Get down! Find cover!"

His men kissed the deck as the volley filled the air, and the sounds carried in the cool wintry night. The sails were let out and began filling with a strong offshore wind, propelling the vessel away from the British gunfire.

As the ship left the berthing area and passed by several anchored ships, Blood Bones looked astern to find sailors climbing the rigging of the *Georgia Rose*. She had just began to hoist the anchor and take in the lines. He closed his eyes, doing a quick mental calculation. They would have at least a quarter mile advantage on their pursuers.

※※※

"Keep your head down, Leah!" Harris put an arm around her shoulders. He placed his body between hers and the attack. "Sal, we should find some weapons to defend ourselves if something does happen."

Sal knelt beside the group, lowering his body to the deck as much as he could. His nose grazed the wood below, and he slowly inched over, covering Leah on the other flank. "Yeah, but the HMS *Courtesy* wasn't even fired upon by the fortress and it also wasn't engaged by the other vessels. They just sort of chased her until *La Monzón* tacked in to its rescue. Obviously Blood Bones navigated the ship out of harm's way, but we can't say that about his previous command." He let his words sink in. "We should be fine, as long as what we read in the article stays true."

"Yeah, I guess you're right," Harris said. He glanced astern, realizing they had increased the distance off the wharf significantly. "I wonder if we changed the past by being sent back in time? You know? What if we like, messed up everything?"

"Maybe. Who knows. I guess we'll find out soon enough. Only time will tell, as it always does." Sal stared off at the pursuing ship.

"Whoa, that was deep stuff man; since when did you become a philosopher?" Harris laughed.

Sal smiled. "Come on, dude! All my jokes over the years have subtly suggested that there were deep thoughts behind each one!"

"Right. Maybe an ounce of thought!" Harris teased.

※※※

La Monzón cruised slowly back and forth several miles off the entrance to the harbor, flying the British flag. Álvaro Audaz stood beside the several rows of gun carriages. His men waited anxiously with primed cannons, ready to fire the chain shot into the enemy's rigging when needed. With a reduced crew, maneuverability would be slow if they had to engage the enemy, so they had to make their efforts count. Only a few were on deck, a few were in the shrouds, and the remaining men were below manning the cannons.

It was a long and anxious wait for Álvaro as he continually scanned the waters around him with his spyglass. He could see the battery that protected the harbor—it looked sound asleep, hidden beneath a blanket of white. His eyes moved from the fort to the entrance of the harbor, trying to pick out the first set of white sails. He let off a large smile upon seeing the flying canvas of HMS *Courtesy*. Scanning carefully, he could see several British Royal Marines standing on deck.

✖✖✖

"Sir, they have a decent lead on us. I figure that by the time we exit the harbor and are in good winds, we'll be able to overtake them," Lieutenant Greenbough said to the captain of the HMS *Georgia Rose*.

"I cannot believe the audacity of these men. They just bloody walked on board! Someone will surely hang for this!"

"Let's hope so. This wind needs to pick up. It died down again. Look, they're almost out of the harbor!" He pointed. "The *Savannah* is lagging behind also. Hopefully it won't come down to an all-out fight against the *Georgia Rose*. They have too many guns—eight more than us!" Greenbough sighed.

"This is true, but they only had twenty-five men with them when they boarded the vessel. How will they sail the frigate out of the harbor and man the guns at the same time?"

"Well, if they all got on board ship by convincing everyone they're British naval officers, I couldn't tell you what they are capable of doing. It's like they are always one step ahead of us."

✖✖✖

Álvaro checked the angle of the guns once more before the first volley would be launched. As he stared through the gun port, a second column of canvas came into view.

"Gentlemen, man the guns. Our target is almost in sight. We need to get off an effective broadside that'll cripple their ship. We don't have much time. The fortress could come to life at any second! Let's see to it, men!"

The pirates cheered. Although Blood Bones was not on board the vessel, Álvaro was very respected and was actually a few years older than his cousin. Álvaro had recruited Hernando into his band of misfits many years prior, after he had escaped from the dungeons of *El Morro*. Blood Bones had proved himself time and time again in battle, and earned himself a reputation, as well as the command of *La Monzón*.

Inside each barrel sat a length of chain and bar shot on top of gun powder. The fuses were primed and ready. Each gun carriage leader obeyed the orders. They went down the line repeating, "Ready to fire."

✖✖✖

Lieutenant Alec Greenbough eyed the HMS *Courtesy* rounding a spit of land on its approach to the battery. He changed his view from the starboard side and looked left. The moment his eyes adjusted to the snowy darkness, he saw several bright flashes of light. Instincts took over at that moment.

"Hit the deck!" He yelled to his men. They fell as one, well practiced in the drill of battle.

The bars and chain flew through the sheets of falling snow, spinning hazardously above. The spray of projectiles nearly took off his head, slicing spars, tackles, and rigging just several feet away. A dislodged sail fell to the deck, momentarily trapping several men underneath. The central mast took the brunt of the hit, and it split in two, sending splinters flying in a massive explosion of wood in all directions.

As he lay on the wooden deck, he felt a slight pain in his calf. Once the smoke cleared above his head, he shifted his body around and analyzed the wounds. He tugged on his breeches, revealing several long gashes. He shrugged off the pain, and then stood tall and proud. He eyed the helmsman.

"Hard to port! I want to give them a broadside before they can reload their guns!"

The message was relayed to the gunners below to ready for the engagement. The helmsman fought the strain as he forced the rudder to the large angle.

As the *Georgia Rose* revealed its broadside to the attacking vessel, there was another boom of sound, and numerous flashes of light. Again, he yelled a warning as cannonballs hurtled their way.

✖✖✖

Álvaro looked on as the first volley damaged the sails and rigging, smiling at the fact that the vessel had just lost at least a knot or two in speed. The vessels ran parallel courses, just two hundred yards apart. When the debris finally settled, a full complement of the English broadside floated through the air toward Álvaro and his men. The cannonballs arced downward, crashing into the deck and through the sails. Shreds of canvas slowly descended to the men below as an explosion of splinters showered them.

The gun crews below began loading for a second volley, adjusting the angle as the vessels closed in range. Another series of chain shot flew through the air, shredding sails and spars. The English ship altered course, closing in for a boarding.

"Helmsman, hard to port—make sure we clear their bow so we can let off a broadside at minimum range. I don't want them to be able to board us just yet."

He then moved belowdecks. He shouted to get the attention of each gun captain. "Men, once clear of her bow, shower her with grapeshot."

The sailors replaced the bar and chain shot with canvas bags full of metal shards and small rods. His men were well-trained, and within moments, each cannon was ready with the new ammunition.

As he emerged back on deck, another volley from the *Georgia Rose* landed, causing more damage to the vessel. Several men were maimed with the barrage. He scanned the deck, noting the damage.

The vessels were now closing in on each other, with *La Monzón* cutting across the bow of the English ship. He felt the deck shake as the rudder continued its struggle. The instant the pirate ship was broadside to them, the cannons belched flames, sending projectiles of metal that mowed down the English marines and seamen alike. The grapeshot tore through the ranks of men.

Almost clear of the *Georgia Rose*, the English let off a volley from their after-cannons that crashed into the side of *La Monzón*. One ball entered through the gun port—the cannon exploded, killing the gun crew on the carriage. The hot metal careened across the wooden deck, spreading sparks as if it was an indoor meteor shower. Even though Blood Bones kept a clean ship, and there was very minimal gun powder unprotected or spilled on deck, a fire quickly erupted.

✺✺✺

Blood Bones peeked through his spyglass, noting the initial shots his cousin sent toward the English. He studied the curves of the ship that had brought him his fame and glory. He smiled, remembering the day Captain Blood Spot had given him command of her. It was that day where he stood before a group of pirates at their hidden lair. He spoke up, telling those in attendance a tale of deception, revenge, and sacrifice. As a result, he had become one of the youngest pirates to earn the rank of captain.

All was going according to plan—HMS *Courtesy* had passed by the battery without any detection, and the trap was set for the two pursuing English vessels. He maneuvered the ship, heading for the open Atlantic Ocean. Their rendezvous was the easternmost part of Belle Isle Inlet, out of range from the harbor's battery and out of sight of the English ships berthed in her protective refuge.

Captain Nelson stood beside Blood Bones, eager to understand how the man would orchestrate the successful attack. He took notice of the man's oddities, particularly that odd-long look of his, staring off into the distance. What the pirate was thinking, he could only guess. "Captain, is there anything that we can do to help?" He nodded toward Sal, Harris, and Leah.

Blood Bones looked down at his scarlet ring and smiled. The scarlet stone glowed vibrantly with their presence. "Yes, Miguel—please get into the rigging and see if we can put out a little more sail. Any extra yard will help get us out of the range of the big guns." He looked at the sleeping fortress again before he laughed into the wind.

Nelson led the group toward the nearest mast. They paused for a moment, taking in everything that was going on. A sea battle is a beautifully orchestrated tango of men, wood, canvas, and steel. Each battle is different in its own way, but nevertheless, the same in beauty. Captain Nelson smiled, enjoying the rush of excitement. He then looked to each, waiting for them to acknowledge his authority. "All right. I am very pleased with how we have been integrated into the crew. Blood Bones seems to trust me, which is paramount if we are to continue our escapade. We are almost out of the range of the guns and he wants us to put out as much extra canvas as we can," Nelson said. He smiled at the group. He had watched Sal and Harris grow and mature since he had found them so many months ago, floating in the warm waters of the Caribbean. "Good luck up there!"

He watched the trio move to the tarred ratlines mounted at the railing nearest to them. They stood there for a few moments, collecting the wits required for the task. The vessel was now making slightly more than six knots, and moved slightly with the ocean swells. They would not feel the movement on the main deck, but as they climbed higher and higher in the rigging, it would be more noticeable.

Harris looked at Sal, and then to Leah. "Come on guys, we can do this."

Sal reached forward, grabbing the outer edge of the tarred line. He lifted his foot and then climbed up just a few feet. He looked down at Leah and Harris, and gave them both a large smile. "It's easy! Let's go!"

The trio climbed higher and higher up into the rigging. Leah was the slowest, but she began to gain confidence with every foot gained vertically. The encouragement from the other two helped her immensely.

Captain Nelson joined Blood Bones a few moments later by the stern railing. "Sir, what do you make of this?"

"Just a hindrance, Miguel—our men are experienced. The English ship will sustain rigging damage that will take it out of the battle. Once my cousin steers the ship out of the engagement, we will rendezvous and sail southward for our lair, where we'll ransom the captured crew for more gold." Blood Bones spoke with confidence. He knew his cousin's fate already, but there was no point to dwell upon the fact. If his men knew that many of their shipmates would be captured and killed, they would not perform to their full ability.

Captain Nelson remained silent. He closed his eyes, deep in thought. He could no longer go back to the life of an English privateer. He had killed a fellow Englishman in cold blood. He had taken the man's life with a blade, and he now had blood on his hands. He had worked so hard over the years to gain command of a ship and earn the stature of one of King George III's most favored subordinates. What was he to do now with the rest of his life? Where was he to go? A man marked as a traitor had very limited choices.

The pain of that prospect weighed heavily on his heart, but then he smiled, realizing that he was alive. His heart was beating, his lungs were taking in the cool, oceanic air as the vessel below his feet moaned and groaned as it lurched forward, ever closer to its destination. He let out a resigned sigh, realizing then, at that particular moment in time, that his destiny had been written for him, and all he could do was go along for the ride, letting the fast ebb and flooding tides carry him.

"Between that and the tax money, we'll retire and buy a villa and have any woman we desire!" He played the character well. It nearly suited him.

Blood Bones let out a laugh. "Miguel, does that not happen already?"

Captain Nelson glanced off into the distance, thinking of everything that had just happened. The two snickered, leaning against the stern railing as the battle slowly waned in the distance.

✖✖✖

Álvaro heard something rumble below his feet. Without thinking, he ran for the companionway, emerging into a sailor's worst nightmare—a fire. His men were swatting the flames with their shirts, attempting to delay the fire's spread. Several buckets of water were being brought in from various parts of the ship and thrown onto the blaze. Their efforts had little effect. Trails of fine black gunpowder dust continued to catch, setting off lines of little explosions, which jumped to and fro.

"Men, we must extinguish the flames before they reach the magazine!"

Álvaro began removing anything flammable from the immediate area, and a sailor joined him in the task. It had reached the point of *in extremis*: there was really nothing left they could do to thwart the flames. He stopped what he was doing and looked around. A plan instantly came to him.

"Men, come with me!" he yelled. His voice carried over the crackling fire.

※※※

Still standing at the stern of the HMS *Courtesy*, the two figures snapped into focus when they heard the explosion and saw flames shoot out from *La Monzón*'s gun ports. Blood Bones and Captain Nelson looked on as the English vessel altered course and began to pursue his cousin's crippled command. Blood Bones gazed through his spyglass and saw HMS *Savannah* well off on the horizon. Her sails were all out, and she was closing in.

Even with the damaged rigging and several flapping sails, the *Georgia Rose* managed to close the distance between the two ships. As he continued his gaze through the spyglass, he saw grappling hooks being thrown, bringing the ships together like lovers. Marines swarmed out onto the deck of the English vessel, hooting and roaring with life. They were ready for battle.

Between the gunfire and the clinking swords, he watched his men aboard *La Monzón* back away from the fight, looking as if they were giving up. This was not like them at all. He began to think they were up to something. He smiled, knowing Álvaro had managed to make the best of what was given to him. A good mariner was able to follow a plan down to every last detail, but would have the skill set to deviate if needed.

✿✿✿

Lieutenant Greenbough and the captain of HMS *Georgia Rose* led the marines as they jumped the gap between ships. Some of his men made the leap, while others swung across the gap. They met a resistance of ten pirates, who seemed to be guarding the central companionway.

"Find out what they are hiding!" Greenbough said. Although the captain was standing beside him, he felt it was his duty to lead the charge.

A dozen marines obeyed the command, moving forward at full gait with their blades held high, ready for battle.

Greenbough's hand gripped the butt of his pistol. Taking sight of the first man he gazed at, he squeezed the trigger. The pirate fell to the deck, holding his chest. Blood seeped through his fingers. The marines continued their charge forward only to find a row of pirates who had dropped to their knees. Only one man remained standing beside the barrel of a swivel gun.

"Get out of the way!" Greenbough shouted when he saw the lit fuse.

The man pressed in the fuse—balls, nails, and shards of metal projected outward, fanning out across the deck. Numerous marines fell to the deck, clutching their throats, faces, and stomachs. The swivel gun packed quite the punch for such a small weapon. Twenty men fell with one shot from the powerful mini-cannon.

After the dust settled, the remaining marines pushed forward, cornering their enemies against the rail.

"Surrender or die!" Greenbough called out. He scanned the deck, noting the damage.

Several of the marines surrounded a pirate. A blade was pressed to the man's chest and he merely replied with a laugh. "I'm afraid it's already too late."

❈❈❈

As the flames consumed the gun deck of *La Monzón,* the powder magazine began to spit fire, sending boards and men flying upward. A hole that ran the entire breadth of the ship opened, exposing the flames of the deck below to friend and foe. Many lost their balance and slid to their fiery deaths.

The fire spread upward, engulfing the main deck of *La Monzón.* A violent explosion hurled more debris into the air, injuring men aboard the English vessel as well as wreaking havoc among the trapped sailors. Several marines began chopping at the boarding lines to free their vessel from the inferno, but to no avail. The vessels clung together in a stubborn farewell.

Within a minute, the fire had spread to the HMS *Georgia Rose,* setting it too ablaze. Men jumped from the burning ships into the surrounding waters only to have others land on their heads in the hurried escape.

"To the skiff!" a sailor yelled.

It was complete chaos, but the call saved the remaining crew of *La Monzón.* In the end Álvaro stood at the bow of the skiff. He looked at the waters ahead, and his men began rowing. Their wolf-like laughter carried over the water.

†††††

Leah watched the battle play out from the crow's nest on the other ship. From her perch atop the main mast she was high above the deck. She was standing beside Harris and Sal, who stared at the inferno with open mouths.

"I cannot believe what I have just witnessed!" Leah called out. She looked out in a three hundred and sixty degree view. The snow was still falling slightly, but she could make out the flames aboard the two vessels in the distance. The wind blew around a tassel of her short blonde hair that escaped from beneath her black watch cap. "As pirates, will we experience more of these types of adventures?"

Sal and Harris looked at each other, unsure of how to respond to Leah's question. Harris nodded. "Well, yes and no. I guess it really depends on the day." He laughed into the wind. "Do you remember all of the stories Ben told you? Of shipwrecks, battles, and time travel?"

Leah smiled. "Yes, of course. He always had a way with his words." She paused, deep in reflection. She missed Ben; there was not a bone in her body that did not. "I think I will enjoy this new life as a pirate. I have never really lived my life to the fullest! I have always had people waiting on me. I come from a home with money. I even had a servant I loved like a sister. But everything was given to me. I never had to go out and earn my keep. My hands were never dirty from doing manual labor. I look forward to all of these new and exciting experiences that I can share with you all. If I could have done it differently, I guess I would have embarked on this adventure earlier."

Both Harris and Sal listened to Leah vent. It was good for her to get these feelings out in the open. Soon, Harris broke the ice. "Well, you're here now. Let's make the best of it," he said with a reassuring smile. "I bet we'll have a ton of awesome adventures to come while sailing under Blood Bones. We have a few more months to play pirate, and then we will head across the pond and save Ben and the others."

They stared off into the distance, each thinking of their own goals and dreams. The foaming seas crashed into the bow of the vessel. The ship sliced through the water like a knife through warm butter. Sea spray carried in the wind, and its scent was just as refreshing as the breeze. They were Poseidon's brethren. They were sailors. They were pirates. The trio laughed into the wind.

Álvaro called the cadence. "Heave: one, two, three; heave: one, two, three; heave!"

The pirates pulled at the oars, propelling the vessel forward. They had disappeared into a flurry of snowflakes and were little more than thirty yards away from their burning vessels when they spotted HMS *Savannah* bearing down on them. The ship had been the last to prepare for sea, about twenty minutes behind the engagement. Álvaro watched as a man focused on them through a bronze scope. A few moments later, the ship altered its course to intercept the skiff. He knew fate had turned against them yet again.

"Men, prepare for a collision!"

The distance between the vessel and the skiff closed quickly—sail power winning the race against oar. Soon the bowsprit protruded above the man at the tiller.

"Sir, what should we do?" the man screamed to Álvaro over the crash of the waves.

Before an answer could depart his lips, the skiff dissolved under the impact, rising with the swell one last time before she sunk to the depths of the harbor. The men jumped out, bobbing amidst flotsam from the wreckage.

✹✹✹

Blood Bones looked on as the explosions of burning gunpowder filled the harbor. He could do nothing about it—there was no chance of turning HMS *Courtesy* around to rescue his fallen comrades. He was already out of the battery's range, almost rounding another spit of land that led out to the open ocean, to freedom. The scene flashed through his mind once more.

If only the British marines locked below would fire upon their own vessels, then a rescue mission would be possible, but then I would put to risk all what we have accomplished so far. We could lose this treasure that I stand upon, a frigate laden with three months' worth of colonial taxes, he thought.

Captain Blood Bones thought of his previous visions—there was no inclination toward a rescue. He heard a cheer from the men about him on deck. They were excited at their success in capturing the *Courtesy* despite the loss of their own ship. For a moment he, too, basked in the glory of their shared fortune. But there was now no possible chance of rescue for his cousin and loyal shipmates.

※※※

Blood Bones stood on deck beside Captain Nelson and Sesostris. The trio chatted lightly as the crew were busy about the ship. They had stuck sails, and drifted for a moment. An island, hidden in the darkness, was their destination. Once content with their position, Bones moved to the bow and threw a weighted line into the water. He counted the knots, which marked the depth of the water. Doing a quick calculation, he turned to the group of pirates standing ready at the anchor.

"Put out one shot of anchor." Blood Bones watched his men lower the anchor slowly by pushing the spokes of the wooden capstan. The combination of manpower, pulleys, and rope eased the anchor down.

Once the vessel settled into its course, he inspected the deck. Men were stowing gear, wrapping up the sails, and doing several other tasks. Even though he was the new master of the vessel, instincts prevailed as a good mariner. One never knows when the wind will change and the weather might take a turn for the worse.

※※※

Blood Bones paced the captain's quarters aboard HMS *Courtesy*. The chamber was beautifully outfitted, with nautical décor from around the world—Oriental rugs, mahogany furnishings, and framed charts and paintings. It slightly resembled the quarters of his previous command. He whispered a silent prayer for *La Monzón*. She now rested in the depths of the sea.

He paced to a globe that was roughly three feet in diameter. It was held with orbital bearings that were solid gold. It was truly a magnificent piece. He stood in front of it and then moved it so that he was staring at the North American continent. He let out a sigh. So much had happened to him since Captain Blood Spot had given him command of *La Monzón*. So many battles fought, all won with the mystical assistance of the crystal ball and the hard work of a loyal crew. Sesostris had given him the chance to excel, and he had done so.

A knock on the door interrupted his concentration. "Come in," Blood Bones said, his gaze transfixed on the globe before him.

Sesostris walked into the room carrying the crystal ball in its usual wrapping.

"Hello, my dear friend."

They had their routine, and as always Blood Bones welcomed him without hesitation. Regardless of where they were, what ship they were on, underway or ashore, they would meet daily. "Please sit. How was your evening?"

Sesostris sat down and then shrugged indifferently. "Well, besides the impromptu mess hours and having to do with a limited crew, not too bad. We should have brought more crewmen with us."

Blood Bones nodded. "Yes, I would agree. Unfortunately having brought more than we did would have easily alerted the British and our efforts could have been thwarted on the piers. Regardless, we've succeeded, and we now have to address what is to come."

"Yes, that we do," Sesostris said. He unwrapped the crystal ball and pushed it across the desk toward Blood Bones. "You know what to do, my dear friend."

Blood Bones closed his eyes, emptying in his mind. Once all of the day's excitement of commandeering the *Courtesy* had receded into a void of nothingness, he opened his eyes. "I am ready."

His fingertips reached out and he touched the crystal ball.

A fog within the crystal cleared, and the image of a fortress came into view. Walking through the sallyport of the fort, was a large, burly man with a white wig who paced quickly toward two horse-drawn carriages. The man turned and stood before two groups of soldiers, all standing at attention. The burly man nodded, and then his men entered the carriages. The image quickly changed to a rocky beach. There was a rowboat, with a group of men tied together. They were sitting. One man remained standing—Blood Bones thought it might be himself.

The image disappeared, and then a blinding light spiraled throughout the inside of the crystal ball.

Now the image of a wharf and a vessel came into view. A line of uniformed soldiers marched on each side of a group of men. They were wearing tarred clothing: sailors by the looks of them.

Blood Bones leaned in closer. The image sharpened, and he could see a man that looked like his cousin, Álvaro, leading a shuffling group. They were chained together, herded like common animals up the gangway and then deep into the bowels of the ship.

The image disappeared.

"What did you see?" Sesostris asked.

He closed his eyes, processing his vision. "A man from the fortress bringing men hidden in a wagon. He met me on a beach. It looked like a prisoner exchange, but I am wary of that, because then I saw my cousin and our shipmates being herded into a ship."

Sesostris nodded. "It looks like the English are trying to spring a trap on you, but we will be well-prepared."

Blood Bones laughed. "We always are, we always are. If you will excuse me, I have a message to write, and a few duties to tend to."

"I will then take my leave. Good night, my friend," Sesostris said. He wrapped the crystal ball and then left quietly, leaving Blood Bones to a sleepless night, plagued by an endless series of what ifs and what could bes.

✖✖✖

Nelson made sure his face was obscured in the shadows for fear of recognition from the English prisoners here on the *Courtesy*. He was a well-known privateer, having served King George III for the last three years as well as his predecessor and grandfather, King George II.

Leah was beside him, with Sal and Harris just behind. The group went from space to space below, shackling the prisoners together. Every so often there were a few who would fight back, but for the most part it was easy work; just demeaning to have to imprison fellow Englishmen.

When faced with three options: death, imprisonment, or joining their ranks, some of the English privateers and sailors gladly switched sides.

Once Captain Nelson and his companions had finished this task, he reported back to Blood Bones that all of the marines and sailors ha been accounted for, and that many of them had joined their ranks. The pirate seemed preoccupied, but was content to hear the report.

10

January 16, 1763
Boston, Massachusetts

A messenger rapped on the door of James Elliot, dominion governor of Boston. The stately gentleman, clad in his finest linen robe, rose and slowly made his way to the door as his legs struggled to support his weight. Before turning the knob, he donned the hairpiece that hung on a wooden peg beside the entryway.

"Yes, yes, come in."

"Sir, I was requested to bring this urgent message to you." The young lad looked up at the familiar face of the governor.

His well-manicured hands reached for the sealed delivery.

"Please take a seat."

After placing his gilded monocle over his left eye, he slid a silver letter opener under the wax seal. His heart raced as his eyes took in the mirror-imaged initials that stared him in the face. With a heavy sigh, he began reading.

Governor Elliot,

I regret to inform you that one hundred and fifty of your men are below decks, chained and ready to face my wrath if you do not fulfill my requests, which are as follows:

First, I demand that you meet me personally at the rocks of Cohasset, midnight, tomorrow night, escorted solely by the messenger that has been sent to you. You are to bring a horse-drawn carriage laden with items that will be mentioned. To put your unease to rest, I will come alone. If you have any officers following you in an attempt to ensure your safety, I can assure you—you will not be safe or alive for long.

Second, you must provide us with enough provisions to make a journey of two weeks. This entails casks of fresh water, rum, loafs of bread, and salted meat. Also, we require lumber, nails, and munitions. Limit yourself to two carriages.

Last, I wish to exchange your men for my men who survived. For this I will require an additional ten thousand gold pieces. If you want to see your men alive and well, heed my warnings and do as I say.

Blood Bones

The governor's face contorted with anger.

The messenger inquired, "Uncle, is everything okay?"

He shook his head. "Who does this man think he is?" He slammed his fist on the table with boiling rage. "We will soon end his mockery!"

Leah shivered. The group stood together in a tight circle at the stern railing. The glow of the moon was fighting the clouds and the falling blankets of snow, but its light prevailed. She stared into the crescent moon, filled with that odd sensation that only one with shipboard experience could know. The vessel lay at anchor, but they could still feel it move with the current. The rocking was calm and soothing. "I am not quite sure what to think after today. I cannot decide whether I am proud of what we did or not," she announced quietly to the others. She felt a little better after expressing her sentiments aloud.

Sal, Harris, and Captain Nelson exchanged uncertain looks.

She continued. "I mean, the day started well—I was in the rigging of this ship, underway with the wind in my hair. I felt more alive than I have ever felt." She paused, attempting to find the right words. "With, that evil, evil man, I have only looked forward to seeing Benjamin's face again." She paused, reflecting on the short-lived time she spent with Ben. "And then our paths crossed in London." She shook her head.

"Leah, please consider that what you did, or rather, what we all did today, as completely necessary for what is to come." Captain Nelson said. "I thought about this since I had first met Sal, Harris, and Ben so many months ago. We have all been brought together by the curse of Blood Bones, and to be honest, I am beginning to feel a sort of comfort with our recent actions. It is almost as if we were destined to be here, as if our combined fates had been written since the beginning of time. There is obviously a reason for all of this to have happened."

Sal and Harris stared at the man they looked up to. Captain Nelson was their mentor, and would always be, in their eyes, their captain. They would follow him into the depths of the sea.

"What do you mean?" Harris asked with curiosity.

Nelson shook his head. "To be honest, I am as confused as you all are, but ever since King George III tasked us with the assassination of the Prime Minister, and Captain Richard Highmore sprung his trap, something inside me sparked anew. I feel a sense of rebellion, a sense of pride in a new way of living and thinking. Joining up with Blood Bones has opened my eyes to the fullest capacity. I would like to say I am proud to be an honest Englishman, but after all that has occurred since I met you all, I can no longer say that. I believe there is more to this than we know, and I trust that if we work together, we will see it come to fruition. It seems that there are bigger things in store for us all."

Sal nodded. He looked between Leah and Captain Nelson. "Well, that makes a lot of sense." His eyes stopped on Leah. "We were betrayed. Your husband cannot be trusted."

Leah looked away, feeling the pressure of his gaze. "I feel I am to blame for this. I am certain that he had someone follow me. Once fate reunited Benjamin and me, my husband must have sensed that something inside me had come alive again. Benjamin brings out that warmth in me, and I must have worn it like a mask on my face." She sighed deeply. "I always felt that there was someone just behind me, lurking in the shadows. I just wish that I could have warned you all before knowledge of your mission spread to my husband."

Captain Nelson shook his head. "Leah. Do not blame yourself for this. Remember that there is something beyond our powers here at work. We are all a part of this together. There is no reason to blame yourself. If there is anyone here to blame, it should be fate. Point your finger at it, and laugh." He caught a glance of the moon coming into view again, and his eyes stared off into its glow. "We have a few months left here before we have to get back to London to save Ben and the rest of our crew. We might as well learn as much as we can from Blood Bones while we are here. I believe there is much for him to teach us."

Harris nodded. "Yeah, you're right. We don't want to overthink everything. I mean, we are all together now, and that's the important thing. We have a few months serving Blood Bones, and then we'll save Ben; just you wait."

Leah smiled at the reassurance. "You all are wondrous."

Harris placed a hand on Leah's shoulder. "Well, you are Ben's girl. We have to look out for you now. You're one of *us*."

That statement seemed to knock her back. Although Benjamin Manry had never formally asked her to be his, she did always feel a certain warmth spread through her with each thought, or even the simple sight of him. She looked down at the wedding ring on her hand, and shook her head. With eager fingers, she removed the gold band and held it up for all to see.

"Thank you and you are right—I can no longer go back to my

life with Captain Highmore. After all that has happened, it is as clear as day to me. I am destined to be with Benjamin." She thought about what Harris had just said. "You are right, I am his, and he is mine." She tossed the gold band into the water below. They watched the ring somersault to its inevitable demise. It broke the surface, and quickly disappeared to the depths of the sea.

✖✖✖

Dominion Governor James Elliot stood beside his nephew on the docks. The two oversaw the loading of the captured pirates aboard HMS *Savannah*. He smiled.

"Uncle, where are they being sent?"

"*El Morro*. To the dungeons, where they belong!"

The gang of pirates were shackled together. They shuffled down the length of the pier, to where James Elliot stood.

A young officer was leading the group and paused at the dominion governor's feet. He snapped off a quick salute. "Sir, the prisoners are ready to be loaded."

He smiled. "Excellent. Get these men out of my sight. We have much to prepare for. Blood Bones has requested a meeting on the rocks of Cohasset tonight. We will give him something to remember."

The young officer laughed. "That is good. We will get underway on the ebb tide, and make haste for *El Morro*."

"For King and Country!" James Elliot said.

The officer nodded, and led the group of pirates onward. Álvaro walked past the dominion governor and his nephew and smiled. He had overhead the entire conversation, and knew that Blood Bones would be prepared for whatever the English were planning for him. Blood Bones was always one step ahead of the game. No matter what the cost was.

11

January 17, 1763
Anchored

Time passed by slowly as the imprisoned English marines remained locked up without food and water in the bowels of the *Courtesy*. Blood Bones had tasked his men with removing all of the lanterns belowdecks. The result was a pitch-black atmosphere, and the prisoners took the brunt of it. The ship lay hidden at anchor off the Graves, an island roughly four and a half miles east of the battery protecting Boston Harbor.

Blood Bones paced the deck, waiting for day to turn to night. In his mind, he began to formulate what he believed the British dominion governor would do in response to the ransom note he had dispatched.

As midnight approached, he and a group of six handpicked men rowed from the anchored vessel to the meeting spot on the rocks of Cohasset. Between the flooding tide and the power of their oars, they soon touched bottom. The group of pirates jumped out, sending a splash as they made their way through the cool water. Once the skiff was dragged out and secured, Blood Bones loosely tied the hands of his men together with rope.

"Men, remember that you wouldn't have eaten anything in the last several days. You'd be filthy dwelling in the same disease-ridden space below deck. Act the role; we shall deceive them once again!"

Arthur F. Nelson let out a booming laugh. All eyes turned to him. "Aye! Let's fool the English another time!"

The group cheered. As loyal as Captain Nelson was to king and country, this new idea completely enthralled him.

Blood Bones looked at his crew. "Aye, Miguel. That we will."

Nelson then made eye contact with Harris, Sal, and Leah. He nodded at his friends, proud of how far they had come together. He had watched Sal and Harris grow and mature since fate brought them together aboard his vessel *Frendrich*.

They were truly going under pirate cover. There was no going back now to the life he had known and loved. But change is a constant variable in life, and in order to live life to the fullest, you have to adapt to every twist and turn fate throws your way.

※※※

James Elliot and his nephew guided the two horse-drawn carriages down the familiar streets of Boston. Inside each carriage sat a half-dozen huddled British soldiers, armed with pistol, sword, and musket. Once clear of the main streets, he navigated the caravan through side alleys and finally onto a dirt trail.

They followed the curved path for quite some time, while the dominion governor looked anxiously out the window until spying a strip of beach and the rocks of Cohasset. The carriages paused at the tree line before closing the distance to the Blood Bones and his waiting men. In just a few minutes, they were twenty paces from their fire. He glanced around, viewing the scene. Captain Blood Bones was standing alone, his gray robes fluttering in the wind. Six men, bound in rope, sat side by side before the wind-whipped flames.

The two leaders walked toward each other with their heads low, as if both were hiding something from the other.

"I have the supplies you requested," said the burly man. "Your men are safe and will be returned in the morning once the exchange is made."

Blood Bones snickered. He knew well enough that the man was

lying right to his face, but then again, he had a trick up his sleeve as well. "I have six of yours by the fire for a down payment. I shall send them to join you right now. Likewise, on the morrow I will allow your remaining men pardon, and even have them rowed out to this very beach for their safekeeping."

He turned his head slightly, still keeping the dominion governor in view. "Get out of my sight, you scum!"

The group of six stood as one, shaking sand off their breeches with tied hands as they walked over to stand behind the governor.

James Elliot watched as Captain Nelson, Sal, Harris, Leah, and two others passed him by. He took note of their wardrobe, the uniforms. *The light skin of honest Englishmen. Perhaps he did not trick us this time. Now he will be in for a surprise!*, he thought. He smiled—all was going according to plan.

✥✥✥

The moon shone through the dancing clouds, remnants of the previous night's snowstorm. A shift of the wind brought in the scent of the sea. Blood Bones could easily view the entire beach without straining his eyes. While discussing the plans for the release of the other prisoners, he scanned the area warily. His focus then shifted to the carriages. He wondered if he had been wrong in his presumptions about the man standing before him.

"Governor, I believed I asked you to be accompanied by your messenger? I have yet to see him here."

"Well, Blood Bones—may I call you Blood Bones? He had to run an errand for me and could not make it. I am sorry to disappoint you, for it is just me tonight."

The pirate smiled. He was stunned at the man's wit. "I see. Yes, call me Blood Bones." He added in a whisper, "Allow me to prove my reputation." He then continued. "Well, I lived up to the first part of my deal. I would like to see my supplies now. Tomorrow, I would like to conclude the remainder of our agreement."

"Yes, yes, of course. Let me show you the wares."

From atop a carriage, the young messenger watched his uncle manage to about-face, giving a slight nod as the man reached for the handle to the side door of the carriage. That was the signal he'd been waiting for. He took sight down the barrel of his musket, focusing on the pirate's chest, center mass.

With a cough, Blood Bones signaled his men to free themselves of the weak bonds. Governor Elliot had his back turned toward the pirate captain for just a moment, who suddenly charged and let off a yell that broke the silence.

The moonlight reflected off the messenger nephew's metallic barrel, just in time for the pirate to notice.

A loud muzzle flash erupted from atop the carriage, sending a musket ball hurtling toward Blood Bones. The ball missed its mark and nicked his left shoulder, having little effect on the man's forward progress. He barreled into Elliot just as the man's grip on the handle opened the carriage door. The hidden soldiers spilled out of the small space, joining the fight as the pirates began to split up, raising their swords to battle the six fresh soldiers.

※※※

Harris and Sal stood a few feet in front of Leah as the six soldiers exited the first carriage. Harris then looked over to the second carriage, knowing that something was amiss.

"Guys, stay here!" Harris yelled, then ran around the six soldiers to the second carriage. Sal and Leah advanced to distract them while Harris continued on.

The door inched open as soldiers from the inside were about to make their entrance into the battle. By then, Harris was running full speed across the beach, and he slammed his shoulder into the door, knocking it back into a man's face. He heard the "Ow!" associated with the barrage, and then a scuffle as the soldiers attempted to push the door open.

Harris dropped his sword and managed to hold onto each side of the carriage frame, using his body to push and hold the door shut. He struggled, and his hands began to slip. He knew that he would not be able to hold out much longer. He looked down at his fallen blade, and beside that was a piece of driftwood the size of a large walking stick. It was also several inches wide, strong enough to perhaps lock the soldiers in if he could manage to reach down and wedge it into the door handles.

The soldiers pushed back with renewed spirits, causing Harris to stumble back. One man began to shoulder his way through the opening. As the man brought out a pistol and aimed it in his face, Harris realized he was running out of time.

With a plan quickly formulating, Harris retreated, allowing the door to swing open a little more. In one fluid motion, he reached down and grabbed his sword by the handle. He sliced upwards at the man's wrist, and the pistol misfired into the carriage, shooting a comrade. He heard the man fall down with a loud thud, and the others seemed to back away.

As the smoke dissipated, Harris charged forward with the long piece of driftwood, jamming it into the handles and locking the British soldiers inside.

"Phew! That was close," he mumbled as he knelt down to catch his breath. The odds of winning the battle were slowly swinging toward their favor.

He enjoyed just a moment of temporary relief before he joined the conflict.

※※※

Governor James Elliot slashed at the air beside Blood Bones. The blade missed the pirate captain's face by an inch as it clinked into the rocks at their feet. Blood Bones had toiled with swordplay in his early years, receiving lessons from his father and honing them during his short stint in the Spanish navy, but as a pirate he had mastered the art in countless battles.

The two leaders touched blades multiple times as the surrounding area began to fill with redcoats engaged in hand-to-hand combat. Each of the deceptive pirates had a piece of rope tied around his right elbow to distinguish him as friend or foe.

Blood Bones was surprised how well the obese man managed his blade. He studied his rival's quick, strong slices, looking for weaknesses. *The governor only fights from one side, leaving his the other vulnerable. He parries well, although at times he is slightly delayed. His attack is stronger than his defense,* he carefully observed.

With a quick feint, he tricked Elliot into blocking high, revealing a small window of opportunity for his blade to slice at the man's stomach. Drawing blood, he continued on the attack, slashing high and then low, left and then right. His blade was parried away each time, but he continued on, eventually cornering the dominion governor against the carriage. Blood Bones changed his fighting style once again and now slashed in quick arcs.

※※※

This was Leah's first time holding a blade in combat. Throughout her marriage, she had occasionally been curious enough to see what weapon had been safely snug inside a sheath. Her husband had had an armory of various blades and other army paraphernalia. But actually using one of these tools was unlike anything she had ever experienced. Adrenaline pulsated through her veins. Her vision widened a little, making her more aware of her surroundings. Her ears seemed to pick up on every sound within earshot. She smiled, ready for battle. She relished in the moment.

A British soldier approached at full gait. She was not exactly sure what to do, but her husband had brought her to witness several drills in the barracks. She smiled, knowing that regardless of how much she hated Highmore, he had taught her things that could prove valuable in this new life she found herself living.

Leah quickly sidestepped, letting the man rush past her. As he around, Leah swung with all her might. The soldier was lucky enough to parry the blade.

The man charged again and his weight crashed fully into Leah, knocking her down to her back. He brought the sword even with his right ear, swinging it around for the briefest of seconds. As he brought his hands down for the final kill, Leah kicked with all her might. The man's kneecap took the brunt of the kick, and it was just enough to alter the course of the blade. The razor edge missed her face, and the tip was buried into the ground beside her.

He grunted in pain while Leah rolled to her right. In one swift movement, she picked up her fallen blade and swung with all her might at the man's left foot. From her kneeling position, she watched as the blade sliced clean through the man's ankle. Skin, muscles, and sinew parted as the man fell face first into the dirt, screaming in agony. Leah then stood to her full height.

She looked around with darting eyes. Her heart was beating a million beats a minute. She looked down at the man, still writhing in pain. *Whether to finish the fallen man before her, or bring the fight to someone else*, she thought. She scanned the battlefield and noticed Sal and Harris, who were busy fending off two British marines, while two soldiers slowly surrounded Captain Nelson. She saw them approaching on each side, about to catch him by surprise. Her decision was easy.

✺✺✺

Captain Nelson had remained by the fire. Like a composer at a symphony, he could see the skirmish unfold. From his viewpoint, he could tell where his men should hold, advance, or retreat. It was always a good tactic to have reinforcements. Sal and Harris had moved off to the right, touching blades with two marines, while Leah had her own little battle going on. It was a strategy that had won him many conflicts over the years, saving his as well as his men's lives. Then he realized it wasn't he who was in charge of the battle, but Blood Bones.

In his peripheral vision, he noticed a man on each side flanking his position. They were hiding in the shadows cast by the fire. He stood there, acting as if he had not seen them. He did not want to warn them of his early notice.

As if they had been drilled on the practice field, the men made their move simultaneously. He had mere seconds to decide his move. He weighed his options quickly. To block one man's attack would leave his entire back side vulnerable. He instinctively dropped to a knee and rolled forward, avoiding the initial assault by mere inches.

He regained his footing and slashed quickly, knocking the blade out of the closest man's hand. It crashed to the ground with a loud clang against the rocks that littered the beach. Then Nelson brought his blade back, readying for the final kill. He glanced to his right just in time to see the blade of the second marine coming his way for a strike.

Leah had crossed the battlefield just in time to thwart the attack on Captain Nelson. Her full body weight crashed into the man's exposed side, causing him to stumble sideways into the fire pit. The blade missed its mark, clanking close to Nelson's feet.

"Ahhh!" the man yelled. He quickly regained his footing, but his wool uniform caught fire. He dropped to the sand and began rolling back and forth, putting out the fire.

Leah watched the man rolling on the ground while pointing her blade at the remaining marine, who was still unarmed. It was not in her nature to kill. She did not even know if she was capable of taking a life. What she had done so far had been in self-defense, or at least, justified by saving someone's life.

"Do you gentlemen surrender?" Captain Nelson stared at the fallen man. He too, had his blade out, held high. He stepped forward, angling to where he could watch both of the redcoats.

"Yes, we surrender," the unarmed marine said on behalf of his colleague. Multiple areas of his uniform were burnt off: there was a large gap on his side missing, almost his entire right sleeve was gone, and several black rings on his left trouser leg revealed his white skin beneath. The man's eyes were closed and he clearly was in a great deal of pain.

"Remain where you are," Nelson said with authority. He had always fought with honor and dignity. When the white flag of surrender was struck, an enemy quickly became a friend, or at least, friendly. It was a code of honor that he had upheld in his training as an English privateer.

The soldiers obliged. From their vantage point, they watched Blood Bones and the dominion governor battling.

※※※

As Blood Bones continued clanking blades with the governor, his men overcame the remaining British soldiers. They watched, cheering as he parried with the skilled governor. Minutes passed as they exchanged blows that were blocked by each other.

Sweat glistened on both men's brows due to the strenuous efforts. Blood Bones now tried a different approach—instead of arcing the attacks, he now lunged with quick jabs, the first of which caught the man by surprise, slicing him low under his ribs. The blow knocked Elliot back, and he crashed hard into the carriage, revealing a clear path toward his neck. His blade instinctively met his opponent's weakness, slicing deep into the man's throat. The governor fell to his knees, a sheen of fresh blood flowing fast down his chest.

In one last death throe, the man struggled to regain his footing. He had lost too much blood, however, and the wound was deadly. He fell face first into the sand, mere feet from Blood Bones.

"A worthy adversary," Blood Bones said, bowing his head in silent respect.

He kneeled beside the fallen man and checked for a pulse. Dead.

※※※

Having no clear shots, the messenger John Elliot lay down his musket beside his hip. All he could do now was watch his uncle face his slayer's blade. The thought disturbed him. He had never seen any man kill another, whether in battle or in cold blood, and now it was his own kin being slain. In his two brief years of service to the Crown, the most serious thing he had seen were mere paper cuts from the many piles of letters strewn throughout the offices in the battery.

He watched as Blood Bones commanded his troops to throw the dead and injured bodies into the empty carriage. They locked the doors once all the British were inside. Shifting the blanket, he made sure he was shrouded from their view.

"I can't believe they forgot about me. Thank God," he whispered in relief.

"What now, captain?" said Arthur F. Nelson.

"Miguel," Blood Bones said as he turned to his men. He shook a fist into the air. "Burn it all. There's nothing of value here. This, this will show the British!"

John Elliot watched as two men grabbed a handful of boughs from a nearby bush and headed toward the bonfire.

Captain Nelson and Harris walked slowly towards the fire. Out of earshot from the others, Harris cleared his throat. "Captain, I don't feel comfortable doing this."

As they squatted beside the fire, they placed the greenery into the fire. The shrubs were wet, and refused to catch fire. "I know, neither do I." He paused, letting his thoughts form. "Listen, Harris. I pride myself on never killing a man in cold blood, but if this is what we have to do, so be it. Remember, Blood Bones is *our* captain now. Since we have all agreed to sail with him until the time is right to go save Benjamin, we must listen and obey his commands. Regardless of what he asks."

Harris nodded. He knew that everything Captain Nelson said was true. Finally, the green shrubbery caught, and they returned to the carriages holding the blazing branches high above their heads like torches.

"Come on, lads, get it done with. Someone knows of the meeting also." Blood Bones paused, laughing into the night. "When they come to investigate, they will realize that we mean business."

The two pairs of horses whinnied in fear as they spread the fire, tossing burning tree limbs onto each carriage.

"Set the horses free. They are innocent—they have done nothing wrong here except deliver these men to meet their fates," Blood Bones said.

Once done, they watched as the flames kicked up. Suddenly there was a stirring motion on top of the first carriage.

A young lad jumped down, landing hard on the ground. The boy curled in pain as he held his sides. He coughed for several minutes until he could manage to breathe regularly. Once he regained his composure, he looked up at pointed blades.

"Ah, you must be the messenger." Blood Bones smiled.

The teenager looked at the man who had slain his uncle. His body shuddered with another series of coughs.

"You are killing innocent men!" he managed to say through gritted teeth.

Blood Bones replied. "By associating themselves with these scoundrels, they can no longer claim innocence!"

"Then go along and kill me! I am loyal to the Crown, which means I am guilty as well." His chest stuck out with pride.

The pirate snickered. "You are brave, boy. Now off with you. I shall soon send a message to your uncle's replacement, but until then, be gone with you."

The boy unsheathed his sword, ready to fight any who dared cross his blade.

"Do you have to learn the hard way? Obviously it runs in your family. Now get out of here!" Blood Bones waved his hand in disgust. He dismissed the teenager quickly, but the boy still stood there.

After a long stalemate of gleaming eyes, the messenger's sword found comfort in the scabbard. He looked deep into the pirate's eyes and said, "This is not over. You will be slain."

Captain Nelson, Harris, and Sal overheard that last part. The trio sort of chuckled, thought the boy thought it was in jest, however, it was highly ironic, since in what seemed a previous life, they had captured Blood Bones and watched him swing from the noose.

With that, the young messenger hurried off into the dark of night, not looking back once for fear of being chased.

Blood Bones called the cadence as his men rowed back to their anchored vessel. HMS *Courtesy* rode easily at anchor. The wind had picked up since they were ashore, and was now out of the northeast. From their vantage point, they could see the vessel's bow pointing into the wind-curdled seas. They maneuvered the longboat into position below two block and tackles that dangled from above.

"Salvador, Hector." Blood Bones looked at Sal and Harris. "We will rig the falls fore and aft. He then looked at Leah and Captain Nelson. "Luis, Miguel, please ship all the oars."

Leah nodded, trying to comprehend the task. She paused, allowing Nelson to begin the task so she could mimic it. He pulled the oar closest to him and stowed it inside the vessel by his feet.

Leah smiled. She was a quick learner. She stepped over the nearest thwart and with skilled balance, pulled in the oar closest.

Sal and Harris moved to opposite ends of the longboat, where they noticed the eye of a spliced line secured to the forward and after ends of the vessel.

They were familiar with basic knots and tying and untying small boats, so the task was quite simple. They placed the spliced eye onto the hook below each block and tackle.

"Aye, captain," Sal said. "Forward end is connected."

Harris followed suit. "After end is connected."

Blood Bones smiled, content with his new crewmen. They could fight, and obey orders. What more could a captain want in a crewman?

"Excellent." He then looked up, seeing several sailors by the rail. "Hoist us up!"

As the longboat was raised, Nelson made eye contact with Sal, Harris, and Leah. He was very proud of how they had handled themselves.

John Elliot returned with haste to the safety of his home. When he rapped on the door, he was sweaty and breathing heavily. His mother opened the door and instantly knew something was unusual.

"What's wrong, dear?"

Between pants, he managed to explain. "Uncle took me … We went with twelve men to make a prisoner exchange … The pirates deceived us, killing everyone except me … I need to pass word to his replacement."

As John's words slowly sank in, all the color drained from her face. She had lost one of her closest childhood friends and her brother-in-law.

She closed her eyes in silent prayer. "Oh my Lord." She opened her eyes. "Your father is sleeping; I'll go wake him. You go wash up. You're a mess!" she said, attempting to lighten the mood with her normal motherly duties.

He ran to the changing chamber and dunked up to his wrists under the cool water. He swirled them around and then bent down, splashing water onto his face. He could feel the sweat and ash slide off his wet cheeks and into the bowl.

When the family reunited beside the fireplace, his mother passed him a blanket to warm up. His father was tying on his leather boots as he trembled with fear.

"I'm going to the governor's headquarters. John; you can stay here with your mother."

He shook his head. "No, I would like to come."

Mrs. Elliot watched as her husband and son stood up and walked to the door.

"It's all right. There is nothing to worry about. Go to bed, we will be back by sunup."

They hurried around the house to their backyard. There was a watering hole, several bales of hay, and three beautiful white horses.

Several minutes later, the two figures passed by the front porch at a full gallop. John craned his head as he passed, and saw his mother standing at the window in the flicker of candlelight.

They rode on through the town, heading toward the dominion governor's large estate.

※※※

Once they made their way from the cobblestone main streets onto the brick inlaid walkway, they hopped off the white stallions, and tied the horses to a wooden post beside the soldier's barracks.

They approached a group of laughing figures silhouetted in cigar smoke. His father paced up the stairs to the landing. "I'm Nicholas Elliot, the governor's brother. I need to come in right away."

The men sensed the urgency in the other's voice and waved them inside.

After being led to a group of officers finishing the night's last paperwork, Nicholas looked for Victor Smith, his brother's favorite subordinate.

"Victor, I've some rather unpleasant news. The governor and a small force of troops went to meet Captain Blood Bones to discuss the prisoner exchange."

"Yes, I am aware. He mentioned that prior to his departure." Victor Smith said.

"Well, my son was there, and he was lucky to have survived. Those bloody pirates killed every last one of our men, burning the dead and the injured, and showing no remorse. Something has to be done!" he said with an angry tone, smashing a closed fist into an open palm.

The officers closed their eyes, and each said a silent prayer for their lost comrades. Victor's face turned red with anger. "How shall we address this?"

His gaze was not focused on any one person; the question was directed to all those present. John craned his head back and forth, looking at the faces of each man in attendance.

Finally a man replied. "We should hunt him down. I believe all the captured pirates from the wreck were sent to a stronghold—the name escapes me at the moment."

Victor added on, "Yes, I was informed of that this morning. They will be brought to the fortress of *El Morro*. I suppose we could send someone to look for Blood Bones? Bloody hell, this pirate has already deceived us twice!"

Nicholas chimed in. "Yes, it's the least we could do for my brother. Do we know of anyone capable of finding this murderer Captain Blood Bones?"

The men pondered for a long while, thumping their hands against their sides. "I had a man do a few errands here and there, but I don't think he is capable of this sort of mission," a voice called out.

Victor ran a hand through his long salt-and-pepper hair. "I know of a man—his name is Captain Arthur F. Nelson. I worked with him several times, and he has an impressive record. What time is it?"

"Sir, three hours into the midnight watch," said a voice listening in.

Victor continued. "If I'm not mistaken, he will be arriving in St. Augustine within a week or so. We can send out a dispatch rider immediately. Do we have any messengers available?"

A man replied, "No, sir. My messenger was dispatched four days ago; he should arrive within a fortnight."

Victor shook his head. "No, that will not help."

Another officer replied, "I believe I might have one also, but he won't be in for another three days."

An air of disappointment filled the room. All seemed to be lost. "Is there anything we can do then?" asked the favorite of the late dominion governor.

At the age of fifteen, John Elliot showed the qualities of leadership needed for such a brave and daring mission. "Sir, I will dispatch the message to St. Augustine."

All eyes turned to the corner of the room.

His father replied instantaneously, "No, you will not. This is very serious."

"Yes, but, Father, ask any one of these men. I've carried messages for each and every one of them."

Nicholas Elliot sighed. "This is different, however. This is not just an ordinary message."

"Father, if you had been standing in my shoes and saw what happened through my eyes, it would be a different story." He paused, sticking out his chest with pride. "I am as capable of any of the others; I'm a skilled rider and could get there more quickly than anyone else."

Victor smiled slightly. "I will agree only if your father allows you."

"No, it is settled; my son will not ride."

"Father, you don't understand. I have to do this. This is what Uncle would want. Plus, I know these trails well. Better than most."

Finally, after all pondered their choices, Victor spoke again. "All in approval of sending our own John Elliot to dispatch the message, say aye. All opposed, say nay."

The responses were unanimous; John beamed. The scenes of what had happened earlier that night flashed before his eyes, and he remembered then what he had said.

Victor dismissed everyone except the father and son. The man took out a sheet of parchment and placed it before himself. Opening the ink jar, he dipped the quill in and began writing. The sounds of the pen etching into the paper made John jump in anticipation. Finally, Victor took out a block of wax and held it over the candle that lit his workspace. Melting the wax, he let several drips pour onto the fold of the letter. Before it could harden, he placed Boston's seal on it, labeling it as official business. He then began writing another letter.

He nodded for John to come near. "Whatever you do, do not let this slip into enemy hands. You must get this to St. Augustine with haste. The survival of one hundred and fifty of our marines, retrieval of the lost taxes, and justice for your uncle's death depend on this." He paused. "The first message is to be brought to the harbormaster at the port; this will end up going to Captain Arthur F. Nelson of the vessel *Frendrich*. The second must be brought to my representative at the Castillo de San Marcos. Now, off with you and rest up. You have quite a long journey ahead of you."

The young lad stood at attention, saluting his uncle's favorite.

"Aye, sir, I'll dispatch the message."

"Dismissed. Good luck and Godspeed."

As his son turned and began to walk through the doorway, Nicholas Elliot placed a hand on his shoulder and said, "Son, I'm proud of you."

✠✠✠

Sesostris hovered over Blood Bones. A lantern hung high above them, casting light on the bullet wound the captain had received in the skirmish. The injury had barely affected him in battle, but several hours had passed by the time he could have it looked at. With steady hands, the wizard, cook, and now surgeon, moved the forceps to separate the wound. Inside the small gap of flesh he saw a small metal ball.

"Ah, there it is."

Blood Bones kept a straight face as the cold metal touched his skin.

"One of your lesser wounds, if you will say," Sesostris said with a teasing smile.

"It is nothing. Just a mere flesh wound."

Sesostris pulled out the small ball with the forceps. He then moved to drop the ball into a metal pan beside the tabletop. He caught a glimpse of his friend's back, and saw the criss-cross of scars on that covered the man's entire backside, as well as several healed wounds from years of battles.

"You have been through a lot, my friend."

Blood Bones smiled. "I suppose it comes with the job of being a pirate."

They let out a booming laugh.

"Before you go, pass word to the crew. I would like a meeting at sunup."

"See you then," Sesostris said. He left Blood Bones with a nod and a wave.

12

January 18, 1763
Anchored

It was two hours into the four to eight watch when Blood Bones mustered his crew in the galley of HMS *Courtesy*. Several of his men were above deck, standing watch, while others were below guarding the one hundred and fifty marines.

His chest was still sore from the battle wound, but he hid the fact from his crew. There were only a few who'd seen him get shot, and only Sesostris handled the wound in the privacy of his cabin.

He cleared his throat. "Men, I would like to get underway at sunup." He closed his eyes, recalling a calculation he had done the night before. "It should be roughly 0710, plus or minus a few seconds."

His men laughed. The man was known for his detailed calculations—down to each component.

"Are you sure it is not 0711?" Captain Nelson laughed. He had integrated well into the crew, and men even looked up to him now as a leadership figure.

This caused an uproar of laughter and Blood Bones just smiled. There was nothing really to do but let his men have the moment. They had earned it.

"Miguel, I am quite sure." Blood Bones smiled. He then turned his gaze from Captain Nelson and his friends and made eye contact with the rest of the men in the group. "I would like to express my many and continual thanks the past few days. You all performed well." His men were silent, eager to hear what the their captain was about to say. He continued, "Our next plan of action is simple—I would like to get underway, as I said just now, at sunup. With the rising sun in our enemy's eyes, we will set sail. We will then proceed south, following the coast."

Someone interrupted him. "Captain, are we heading straight to our lair?"

He thought about this for a minute before responding. "No, I think we will stop somewhere on the way." They could also stockpile their wares and trade with other pirate ships in Jamaica. He closed his eyes, remembering a dream from just a few hours before: the crystal ball and three young boys finding a buried treasure—his buried treasure. When he opened his eyes he scanned the crowd of faces. His gaze settled on Miguel, Salvador, Hector, and Luis again. The scarlet stone on his finger glowed fierce and bright. He smiled. "But alas, there is much to do. We will discuss those matters in a day or so. We have an hour to ready the ship for sea. Let us see to it, men!"

"Aye, captain!" His crew bellowed out. Several new faces in the crowd joined in—English sailors who had willingly agreed to join with Blood Bones. His men dispersed throughout the vessel, carrying out their assigned duties. Sails were hoisted, the anchor was heaved, and soon enough, the wind filled the canvases and propelled the vessel eastward into the rising sun.

❈❈❈

Captain Nelson climbed high into the tarred ratlines with Leah, Sal, and Harris quick on his heels. Heights no longer bothered Leah, and she climbed with confidence and ease. Soon enough, the group of four stood atop the wooden platform. They scanned the deck below, seeing men moving to and fro. The addition of nearly a dozen English marines and seaman to their crew made sailing much easier. For the first few days, it had been just Blood Bones and his original crew manning the vessel; now there were almost thirty souls assisting.

"Blood Bones seems very content with us." Captain Nelson stared off into the distance.

Harris nodded. "Yeah, but it seems like he eyes us more often than he should, you know what I mean?"

"Yeah, totally." Sal chipped in. "It's like he knows who we are."

"Do you think that is even possible?" Leah asked curiously. "It is only January. I thought he was captured in May." Of the group, she had been exposed to the concept of time travel the least. Captain Nelson, on the other hand, had had numerous conversations with the young teenagers, and was well-acquainted with their stories.

"Yeah, but this could be an alternate time and place, I guess." Harris responded. "I think that's how it would work. So, if that's true, maybe he carried some knowledge of us with him as we were sent back in time?"

Sal shrugged. "Who the heck knows! It's so confusing." He laughed into the wind. He paused, looking at the sun as it continued its ascent into the sky. "Blood Bones does look at that ring often."

Captain Nelson smiled, putting the pieces together. "You are right. He does!"

"Do you think that the ring has anything to do with the curse?" Harris asked.

Captain Nelson placed a hand inside his coat pocket, and removed the crimson journal. "Absolutely! I think the ring, the cursed staff, the medallions around your neck—" he then held up the crimson journal—"and this journal are all key components to the curse of Blood Bones. You should read his words; the man is a genius."

Harris smiled. "I haven't read a book since we were sent back in time."

Sal laughed. "Really? I didn't know you knew how to read!"

Harris playfully pushed his friend, and Sal stumbled dangerously close to the edge of the crow's nest. "Holy shit!" Sal yelled.

He caught himself on the tarred rigging, and then turned his head toward his friend, looking angry. "Come on, dude!"

"That was for your bad joke," Harris said. "And for your information, I do read. Sometimes. On days that don't end in 'y'."

"Ha! I knew it!" Sal goofed around.

Leah laughed, enjoying their spectacle.

※※※

Blood Bones walked around the deck of the HMS *Courtesy*. During their escape, the ship had taken several shots from the British Royal Marines' pistols on the pier. Nothing seemed seriously damaged, but since he was in command of a new vessel, he decided to inspect it from the top down. As he moved from the exterior spaces to the interior spaces, he made a checklist of all the work he wanted to do.

The sun was now reaching its zenith, and he had his men muster up for the noon formation. Although he was just a pirate—albeit a very successful one that—he followed a very similar naval presence aboard. He had a must three times a day, to pass word to his men. Unless a sailor was physically on watch, his presence was required at these musters.

The watch rang eight bells, marking twelve noon. Men seemed to come from out of the woodwork, as the crew made their way to the main mast. Blood Bones leaned against the wooden mast while eating an apple. He bit into it and chewed, watching as roughly twenty or so men came to stand at loose attention.

"Men, we have some work to do today. I would like the vessel scrubbed top–down; the British are not known for the standard of cleanliness that is expected of a ship commanded by yours truly." His men laughed. "From you to you," he commanded, pointing at a section of the crowd, "scrub and sweep the main deck, fore and aft." He then pointed to another group. "Inventory our stores and wares. See what we have on board, and determine what we will need to purchase at our next port of call." Blood Bones then hesitated. The last four crewmen had not yet been assigned a task. "Miguel, you will come with me; I would like to have a word. Luis, Hector, and Salvador, there is some damage to our stern, where the pistol balls hit. Please sand and repaint that area."

"Aye, captain." Blood Bones watched as his men dispersed to carry on the afternoon's work, while Captain Nelson remained behind.

Nelson approached and stood before the pirate. "Yes, sir," he said.

"Miguel, Sesostris and I have been discussing things, since you and your friends came aboard while we were in Boston…" Blood Bones let his statement linger, and tension built. "As you know, I would like to stop for some goods and wares as we proceed south to our lair."

Captain Nelson sighed. He'd thought the conversation was going to be about something else. He nodded. "Yes, you mentioned that earlier this morning."

Blood Bones closed his eyes, going over the dream he had had the night before. Many years ago, when he had first met Sesostris, he'd had a vision of the coast of Florida, a cavern system, and three young teenagers discovering a treasure inside the largest cavern. He opened his eyes and smiled. "Do you know of any suitable locations en route?"

Arthur F. Nelson nodded. "Of course; I know that coast quite well." He recalled pulling into St. Augustine once before, where a message had been waiting for him at the harbormaster's office. That was where he'd received his mission from King George III to hunt down Blood Bones and bring him in for hanging. Fate has a terrible way of being ironic. He stared right at the pirate and smiled. "St. Augustine. Everything we could possibly need, we could find there."

"Excellent," Blood Bones replied. "Does it offer any concealment of goods?" he asked.

Nelson laughed. "Concealment of goods?" He let his statement linger. "What sort of goods?"

Blood Bones smiled back. "Oh, you know, of the treasure-kind."

Although Captain Nelson did not know the specific location of the cave system, he knew he could easily have them help him in the quest. "Of course. Let us set a course for St. Augustine, and I shall show you something beyond your wildest imagination."

Blood Bones let out a booming laugh. He rotated the ring upon his finger, and as always the scarlet stone twinkled with life. "Yes, I would surely hope so!"

✴✴✴

Harris placed several tools in a leather bag and tied it closed with small line. He led the bitter end of the rope over the railing, and slowly hoisted the bag and its contents down below to Leah. She sat on a bosun's chair, dangling off the edge of the vessel. Sal controlled her movements, holding a piece of line wrapped several times around the rail.

"How bad is it?" Sal called down.

Leah inspected the damage. The area starboard of the captain's balcony had been showered with pistol rounds. There were at least a dozen small holes in the vessel's wooden planks. "Just a few splinters. It looks manageable."

They were all new to the task, but it seemed self-explanatory: sand the area down, fill the holes with a putty that Sesostris had concocted, wait for it to dry, and then paint over it.

Leah was the lightest member of the group, and she had volunteered for the job. By wrapping the line around the rail, Sal could easily hold her in a position to do the work. She had a harness around her chest made from several strips of canvas. She seemed to enjoy the task.

HMS *Courtesy* continued its southward journey, and its bow sliced through the cool Atlantic waters. The wind would often carry the sea spray up, and Leah could feel it accumulate on the bosun's chair. She glanced around, noticing the sun's descent in the western sky. She looked up and saw her two friends above. She breathed in the fresh air, and it made her smile.

"This is great!" she yelled up. "It is so refreshing!" This new way of life was so exciting for her. She reached over to the leather bag that was dangling close by and pulled it to her. Slowly, she sorted through the materials and looked for a small metal file. She then went to work, digging out several of the metal balls that were stuck in the wooden planks. She filed the edges, evening the splinters out. Working with her hands was medicine for the soul. She basked in it.

※※※

Arthur F. Nelson nodded good-bye to Blood Bones and left his personal quarters. He maneuvered through the interior spaces of the vessel, and then made his way to main deck. He looked around, searching for his friends to update them on his conversation with the pirate. He moved toward the stern and saw Sal and Harris manning the lines.

"Gentlemen, good afternoon," he said.

"Howdy!" Sal smiled. "How'd it go?"

Captain Nelson stood beside them at the railing, and glanced down to see Leah filling the holes with a gooey putty. She had a natural talent for working over the side. Most men he had sailed with would draw sticks to avoid that job. Not only was it dangerous, but he knew some sailors also had a fear of heights. The thought brought a smile to his lips. He then realized Sal had asked him a question.

"Oh, the meeting with Blood Bones went well. He asked me if I knew of a location off Florida where we could bury treasure."

Sal and Harris exchanged a quick glance. Florida. Their home.

"Whoa!" Sal said. "That's awesome! What'd you say?"

Captain Nelson laughed. "Well, I told him that we knew of a location in St. Augustine. I don't know the exact location, but you both do."

The cavern system they had stumbled upon so many months ago on, what seemed then to be just another weekend camping trip, had spiraled quickly out of control once they had discovered the buried treasure of Blood Bones. And now they were being asked to guide that very pirate to the location!

"I don't believe it!" Harris whooped with excitement. "This is nuts!"

"Yeah, man!" Sal chipped in. "It's completely crazy." He faced Nelson. "So, what's the plan, then?"

Nelson shrugged. "Well, I believe we are another five days or so from St. Augustine now. I would have to check our noon position to confirm this, but I am just doing the rough calculation in my head." He let his words settle with the group, and they enjoyed a few moments of silence. "How is the work going?"

"Leah's doing a great job down there," Harris said. He leaned his head a little bit over the railing to see her progress. "It looks like she just started painting over the sanded area now."

"Good! Blood Bones will be quite pleased," Nelson said. "I must continue my walk around the deck. Good job with the work so far."

"Thanks. See you at dinner," Harris said.

13

January 24, 1763
Underway

Blood Bones stood on deck by the foremast. He held a sextant up, with his face pushed to the eyepiece. He fiddled with the micrometer drum, waiting for the sun to reach its zenith and then called mark. "Time?"

Arthur F. Nelson stood beside the pirate, and he took note of the time using a pocket watch. "Twelve-eighteen and forty-five seconds."

"Thank you, Miguel." Blood Bones said. "Gentlemen, did you see how we observed local apparent noon?" He glanced between Leah, Harris, and Sal.

Nelson smiled, enjoying the pirate's ease and attitude toward learning. Although he had already taught Harris and Sal these navigational skills several months earlier aboard his own vessel, practicing was important for a mariner. Historically, sailors would observe this position each day at local apparent noon. The group watched Blood Bones quickly work out the mathematics for the observation. His fingers navigated the nautical publications with ease. He would extract a number here and a number there, and then with simple arithmetic, achieved his answer. He circled the result, and then looked up from the notebook in his hand.

"The sight puts us at latitude thirty-two degrees, and forty-one minutes north." He closed his eyes, remembering the position of Charleston, South Carolina. "We are just a few miles south of Charleston, and just outside of visual contact from their shorelines." They had skirted the coastline of the American continent since they'd left Boston, always staying out of sight of land during the day, and occasionally closing the distance at night. "We should be off the coast of Florida tomorrow evening."

"Excellent!" Captain Nelson said.

"Yes, Miguel. I am quite excited for this next adventure. Once we are in sight of St. Augustine, I would like to put a boat ashore to explore this cavern system you all have told me about. It seems suitable for our needs."

His statement lingered for a moment, and Harris cast a sideways glance at Sal.

What exactly is 'our needs'? Harris thought.

※※※

Harris and Sal stared off into the distance through their telescopes. They paced the deck, looking off at various angles. They had rotated onto the midnight-to-four watch, and enjoyed the quiet that came with it.

"So, what are you thinking about?" Harris broke the silence.

Sal shrugged. "I'm not really thinking about anything in particular."

"That's a first." They shared a laugh. There was a splash off the starboard bow, and they both instinctively looked over into the water. They scanned the foaming seas and saw a pod of whales about a hundred feet away.

"This is the life, man! Going to school was getting so boring!" Sal said. "As much as I miss home, this is kind of cool, you know?"

Harris nodded. "I totally agree, man." They watched the marine life play in the water, splashing and cutting across the bow waves. "I wonder what happened to Ben, like, did he die?"

They mulled over the hangings back in London. "Well, I guess you could look at it like this—he's alive now." Sal said optimistically.

"Yeah, I guess you're right." Harris responded. He said a silent prayer for his brother. "It's weird not having him with us, you know? I've known him my whole life basically."

"Yeah."

"I mean, don't get me wrong, Leah is great. She's been holding her own since we've been here, but not having Ben around is just—odd." Harris said. He stowed his spyglass, sliding it back into a pouch he slung over his shoulder.

"I get that, man. Totally." Sal said. "Tomorrow is going to be equally as odd."

"Yeah, those caves—kind of weird how we are actually going to be burying treasure there—treasure that we find in the future."

They laughed, passing the remainder of the watch with idle chitchat.

***

Blood Bones had his dinner brought to his cabin. As he lifted the metal lid off the tray, steam billowed out from beneath. It was a simple meal of chicken, potatoes, and greens, but he began to eat. After he chewed a mouthful, he would cleanse his palate with a swig of red wine.

He ate every last bit of food on the plate, and then let out a loud, content sigh. He had not had a moment's rest since they had commandeered the vessel, and things were finally slowing down. He slipped off his shoes and remained at his desk, just staring off into the distance.

A knock on the door brought him out of his reverie.

"Yes, yes, come in." He looked over as Sesostris peered through the opening.

"Hello, my friend. Do you wish company?" the wizard asked.

"Always. Take a seat." Blood Bones smiled.

Sesostris carried in the crystal ball, wrapped in a heavy blanket for protection. He placed it carefully on the table and smiled. "Do you wish to gaze into the crystal ball? We have much to come in the next few days. Your visions have been coming true, and with each day reveal new and exciting events."

Blood Bones shook his head. "My friend, I am tired. I do not seek the assistance of your crystal ball today." He paused, scanning the room. His gaze settled upon the chess board. A leather bag containing the black and white pieces was nearby, and he smiled. "Would you care for a game of chess?"

Sesostris followed his gaze and stared at the board. "Yes! It has been quite some time since our last game."

"That it has." Blood Bones stood and moved across the room. He reached for the board and brought it back to the table.

"Black, or white?" He offered the wizard the choice.

Blood Bones removed the string that tied the leather bag, and poured the contents out.

Sesostris glanced down and reached for the piece closest to him. "Black."

"Black it is," Blood Bones said, and his fingers eagerly retrieved all the white pieces. The two began to set up the board, and after a few moments they were ready to play.

"Would you care to join me for a glass of wine?" he asked.

Sesostris nodded. "Yes, yes, of course. I will have what you are drinking."

The wine bottle beside him was half full, and he poured a glass for himself and stood, then moved toward a rack in the corner. He picked a glass, and then walked back to the table. The liquid easily poured out into the glass, and he slid it toward the other man's waiting hand.

"Cheers. To our previous successes, and most importantly, our future ones!"

They clinked glasses, and then began the game.

Blood Bones closed his eyes, putting thought to a strategy. He smiled, reached forward and grabbed the headpiece of one of the pawns. He moved it two spaces forward.

Sesostris reached for a pawn of his own, and moved it one space.

They went back and forth: moving pawns forward, bishops diagonally, rooks to and fro, and knights with their infamous L pattern. The game progressed smoothly, each taking several pawns.

They finished their first glass of wine together, and they both eagerly eyed the bottle. Blood Bones let out a booming laugh, and poured them each another glass, leaving an empty bottle and a half-finished game.

Sesostris took his queen with a knight; Blood Bones took the very same knight with the right-side rook.

They exchanged blows, as if they were two boxers in a ring. In turn, each eliminated one another's pieces, until finally all that remained were their kings, a rook, and a knight for each.

They set up traps, which were avoided with careful planning. They finished a second glass of wine, and Blood Bones quickly found another bottle in a cabinet.

"At least the vessel's previous master had a good taste in wine!" he jested. Sesostris laughed. They clinked their glasses together in toast again.

As they resumed their game, Blood Bones studied the board. He played out all the possible moves that he, or his friend, could play. He would lose, if he played his next move. Then it hit him. He retreated his king one spot back. The move accomplished absolutely nothing, and left his most valuable piece vulnerable.

Sesostris jumped on the bait, moving a piece into a check. Blood Bones countered, moving the king sideways. Again, just a minimal move, but he had bigger things in mind.

When it was next his turn, Blood Bones made the move he was waiting for.

"Checkmate."

Sesostris studied the board. He replayed the last five moves of each in his head, and realized his downfall. He would have won, if he had not chased the king.

14

January 25, 1763
Anchored

HMS *Courtesy* rocked gently at anchor several hundred yards off the port of St. Augustine. The crew had changed into the clothing of ordinary seaman and of the British Royal Marines. The setting sun hit *Castillo de San Marcos* and it seemed to glow as the sailors aboard stared off into the distance. Blood Bones had selected men for a small expedition party, and they all gathered at the main mast for one last meeting.

"Gentlemen, are we ready?" Blood Bones looked around. He saw the familiar faces of Miguel, Luis, Hector, and Salvador, along with Sesostris behind them.

"Yes, we have packed several tools and lanterns for the journey inland." Captain Arthur F. Nelson said.

"Excellent, Miguel." Blood Bones then shifted his focus, and stared at Sesostris. "My friend, you will stay behind. Make sure none of the captured men come above decks, and no one is to go ashore."

Sesostris nodded. This was not the first time he had been left in command while Blood Bones or his cousin, Blood Spot, went on a random mission. Sesostris was quite capable of command, even though he acted as the cook aboard ship.

"Of course, Hernando. It will be seen to." The wizard smiled. "When should I expect your return?"

Blood Bones looked inland, toward the west. The sun had just set, and the sky shone in brilliant reds and oranges. "Well, we will row inland following the river. We will make camp, and then start fresh in the morning. We will spend two days there and return back the afternoon of the twenty-seventh."

Sesostris, as well as the others, all nodded, listening to Blood Bones giving the breakdown of events. Harris and Sal had told Captain Nelson about their discovery of the cavern system back in the future, and how there were manmade contraptions and booby traps inside it. The woods surrounding the caves would be completely overgrown. It would take time to traverse the beach, the woods, and make it into the twists and turns of the underground cave system. They would have to span the cavern's raging currents in complete darkness. It seemed a suicide mission.

"My friend, good luck."

With that, they loaded their goods into a longboat, and several sailors began lowering them to the water below. The boat creaked down slowly as the men labored on the deck.

When the boat eventually touched the water, Blood Bones reached over and ran his fingers through the water. It was cold to the touch. He rubbed his hands together, drying them off a bit. Even though it was still January, the sky above was clear and the temperature was in the sixties. Florida was known for its year-round good weather.

"Man the oars," Blood Bones said. "Hector, Salvador, please disconnect the falls."

They did as they were told, while Leah and Captain Nelson put their oars into the water. They awaited further instruction as Blood Bones sat in the stern, holding the sweep oar firmly.

Harris and Sal quickly maneuvered to their respective areas, and disconnected the falls as the longboat road the crest of a wave, and the falls swung behind as the boat lurched forward.

"Forward now, once!" Blood Bones called out. Leah and Nelson put their weight into each oar, and gave one strong pull each. The bow of the boat straightened out, and Blood Bones gave the sweep oar one strong pull also, pushing the bow to the right.

Harris and Sal stepped back into their seats and picked up their oars.

"All together now, forward!" Blood Bones called again. "One, two, three, pull!"

They kept to the easy cadence as they propelled the longboat forward. Night would be their blanket as they maneuvered past several anchored ships amid the docks of St. Augustine. The fortress and her many guns loomed in the distance, as if teasing Blood Bones.

Harris exchanged a glance with Sal and then whispered, "Hey, do you remember any of the articles we read before we found the treasure?"

Sal nodded. "Yeah, for the most part. I mean, I couldn't like, quote something from them. What's up, buddy?"

Harris shrugged. "I remember it saying that Blood Bones and several of his crew had been seen ashore early in the year, some time in January 1763."

Sal smiled. "Yeah, that actually rings a bell. I never thought it would be us, though!"

They laughed softly together as they continued rowing the longboat.

✣✣✣

They rowed on, keeping Polaris on their starboard quarter. Harris looked up at the Big Dipper, and followed the two pointer stars to the North Star. It was a star that had guided an infinite number of sailors safely home, and on this night, it would guide the group of pirates farther inland.

They rowed in relative silence, with the exception of Blood Bones continued calling a gentle cadence.

"How much farther?" the pirate captain asked. He stood by the sweep oar, with his hands firmly grasping the wooden handle.

It was hard to gauge the distance they had traveled, or even the distance remaining. They had navigated through several streams and rivers since passing the harbor of St. Augustine just hours before.

Harris closed his eyes, doing a mental calculation, crunching numbers of speed, distance, and time.

"I'd say we are almost there," Harris said. He looked up again, finding Polaris as a reference. It was now bearing slightly off the starboard bow. "Maybe another thirty minutes or so. We're heading up what would be Bulow Creek."

Sal looked over in recognition of the name. "That sounds about right."

"Yeah, we rowed south from where *Castillo de San Marcos* is," Harris continued. "Then we hooked a right, following the southern tip of St. Augustine."

Blood Bones nodded. "That is good."

They continued on for another half hour, and then off in the distance the shape of an island came into view. Blood Bones peered through his spyglass and scanned the island under starlight.

"Gentlemen, it seems the island you speak of is in view." He slid the spyglass back, and placed it in his leather pouch.

Leah smiled, knowing landfall would give her a break from rowing. She was still adjusting to the life of being a pirate, and the physical labor was beginning to take its toll on her body and her mind. Meanwhile, Harris, Sal, and Captain Nelson increased the pace. She struggled to keep up, but she was tough and she matched their pull.

"Come on, guys, we're almost there!" Sal said.

They closed the distance, and soon the longboat touched bottom. The group of five jumped out and pulled the boat forward onto the sandy beach of the island. Harris pointed over to a pair of large boulders, and Sal caught his gaze. It was almost as if they had never left. The beach appeared to be the same, and the boulders marking the landing area were still there.

"All right, time to set up camp," Blood Bones said. "Luis and Salvador, please gather some wood and start a fire; put on something warm—tea or coffee, perhaps. Miguel and Hector, please set up the tents."

"Yes, captain," they responded in turn.

"I will be back shortly. I would like to walk around."

They set to work as Blood Bones disappeared into the underbrush, using the light cast from the heavens above as his torch.

***

Leah and Sal piled rocks in a circle about three feet in diameter. They then combed the beach, looking for driftwood that they could use for the fire. Off in the distance, they could see Harris and Captain Nelson nailing in wooden poles and stretching long strips of canvas across the frames they had made.

"How you holding up, Leah?" Sal asked. He reached down and picked up a small piece of driftwood.

"I am so sore!" Leah said. She looked off into the distance and saw a downed tree. She walked over to it and began breaking off branches. "My arms are all numb. I can barely feel my fingertips!"

"Ha! I know how you feel," Sal said. He followed her to the fallen tree, and also broke off dead branches.

They eventually each had a large pile in the crooks of their arms. "I think we've got enough for now. This should last the night."

"Okay, let's head back," Leah said. "Will you lead the way? I am awful with directions and I do not see well in the dark."

He scanned the beach and realized they had walked a little farther than he had thought.

"Yeah, follow me." Sal moved forward, skirting the lapping water. She waited for him to get about ten feet away before she started. Every so often, he would look back to see Leah lagging just a few paces behind, and he could see their combined footprints in the soft sand.

She caught his gaze, and smiled. "I always loved seeing footprints." By the moon's glow from above, they could make out the lapping water filling some of the prints as the tide came in.

"I know what you mean. It's kind of like a temporary reminder of where you were." Sal stared ahead. He could barely make out the outlines of Harris and Captain Nelson. "Come on, let's get back to camp."

"You are right; we've taken long enough," Leah said. She adjusted the driftwood in her arms before signaling Sal that she was ready to continue back to camp.

✺✺✺

Captain Nelson held one of the wooden poles firmly against the ground. He glanced down at the mix of rock, dirt, and sand. "Harris, could you grab a mallet from the bag and hit this in while I hold it?"

"Of course; hold on." Harris jogged over and reached into the bag. He pulled out a wooden mallet and returned back to where Nelson was squatted. "All right, you ready?"

Captain Nelson nodded. "Ready when you are!"

He smiled, and then with a measured hit, swung the head of the mallet down. It drove the pole down about an inch. Harris brought the mallet around for another hit, and then drove it about an inch and a half further. "What do you think?"

The experienced sailor glanced upward at the heavens. He saw very little cloud cover, and no visible signs of a change in the weather. "That should suffice."

Captain Nelson stood to full height and paced forward two times. "All right, Harris, this is where we will drive the next stake in." He held the wooden pole down. "Ready when you are."

Harris drove in the stake twice, just like last time, and then the two of them pulled a length of line between two stakes, wrapping the rope several times around each pole, before they anchored the line around a sapling a few feet away.

"Excellent. Now comes the tricky part!" Captain Nelson laughed. "I always had a difficult time with these sorts of things. I guess that is why I always found it more comfortable to be standing at the helm of a ship, with my bow crashing into the foaming seas."

Harris smiled. He nodded, and then said, "Absolutely! We would have to become professional tent setter-uppers if we wanted to join the army!"

Captain Nelson chuckled. "And that is why I shall stick to what I know!"

They had begun to work on getting a second tent rigged when their laughter was interrupted by the arrival of Leah and Sal.

"Hey guys, get that fire started!" Harris smiled in jest. "It's kind of dark."

"Yes, your majesty!" Sal laughed. With Leah following quickly on his heels, they dumped the driftwood beside the circle of rocks in the middle of camp. "If you want to stack the excess, I'll start making the fire."

Leah nodded. "Okay. I'll prepare a light meal and some tea."

By the time Blood Bones re-entered the camp, all three tents were rigged and the campfire was burning bright. He stood in the bushes, out of sight from the others and observed. They were very close, and he smiled as the group talked and laughed. They could fight, follow orders, and by the smell of it, could cook a meal, too.

※※※

Blood Bones took a seat opposite Leah. She had been standing over a metal pot, and a pleasant smell drifted over to him. He took in a few deep sniffs, and smiled.

"Luis, what is that you are making?" the pirate asked.

"Coffee. I found it in one of the bags we packed," Leah responded. "I'm also heating up some of the dried meat we had in storage—pork."

"Most excellent!" Blood Bones said enthusiastically. "I could use something warm right about now, and my stomach was growling on my walk." He let out a booming laugh.

The temperature had fallen by a few degrees since they had beached the longboat and set to work. The group sat in a rough circle around the campfire, warming their hands against the flames. They all wore the wool coats Blood Bones had provided several days ago, before they had commandeered HMS *Courtesy*. Leah began to pour the contents of a pot over the fire into small mugs. In turn, the four others stood from their respective logs and thanked Leah for the coffee.

"The pork should be ready in a few minutes," Leah said. She took a wooden spoon and moved the contents around in the metal pot.

They drank the hot liquid and sighed with relief as the warmth spread through their bodies. Leah gagged a little as the bitter liquid hit her tastebuds, and she forced herself to swallow it down. The others drank the coffee with satisfaction. Blood Bones smacked his lips together in contentment.

"Ah! Nothing better than a good cup of coffee!" The pirate said. "It seems that you are not used to it?" He stared at Leah.

She shook her head. "No, my father only had tea in the house. He was very English in that sense. I am almost certain he refused to have coffee one time at a dinner party because it was too American."

"Ah, I understand that. He was used to something, and did not want to adapt." Blood Bones paused, thinking of what to say next. "Where did you live?" he pressed.

"I lived in Freeport, Grand Bahama. My father was the governor there." Leah smiled.

"Ah, that may be one of the ports I have not been to!" Blood Bones laughed loudly, and then let his words fade away. The group sat there on the logs, drinking the warm coffee. All that was heard was the occasional crackling of the burning driftwood. Blood Bones stared deep into the embers. "Men, I would like to share a tale with you all tonight." The statement made each shift slightly on their logs. They inched forward, ready to listen.

"We are ready when you are, Hernando," Captain Nelson said.

Blood Bones smiled at the informality. He liked the men before him. They were friendly, loyal, and most importantly, key factors in his quest for immortality. He glanced down at his ring, and saw the scarlet stone shine with life. He stood up from the log and reached toward the pot containing the pork.

He smiled at Leah, and then stuck his face above the pot. He took in a deep breath, inhaling the aroma of the meat. He grabbed the wooden spoon and angled it, sliding a piece of pork up the side and onto the spoon. He brought the meat to his mouth, and blew on it for a moment to cool it down. Once certain he had cooled it, he placed the piece in his mouth and chewed. His gave them all a large smile as the juices splashed between several gaps in his teeth. Some of the juice dribbled out of the corner of his mouth as he chewed, and he wiped at it with his sleeve.

"Tonight is a perfect night—I have good food, a warm drink, and loyal comrades!" He placed the spoon back where he found it, and then resumed his seat. "I will start my story now. Please, if you would like to try some of the pork while I regale you with my tale, feel free."

He had their complete and utter attention. "My tale begins many years ago. I was sixteen years young and a messenger for the Spanish navy. I carried important documents between the seaports in Spain. I knew the roads better than most, and I could ride fast. On one of my missions, which as I look at it now, was my last, I reported back to my commanding officer a little earlier than expected. I had walked into an act of treason, and as a result, they sentenced me to the dungeons of *El Morro*."

They had all heard of *El Morro*, either through stories or banter aboard the various ships they sailed on. He continued on with the tale of his transformation from Hernando Audaz into the fierce pirate Blood Bones. "While in the depths of the dungeon, I befriended one of the priests there. Of course, I put my full and complete faith in the man, and he stole the one possession I had." He closed his eyes, thinking of the necklace his mother had given him. "I was beaten, over and over again. They were trying to break my spirit, but I prevailed. One night, I found a way to escape and seized my chance."

His audience was enthralled with the story. Even though Captain Nelson had read of it many times, and he even had the journal in his possession, it was special to hear it in first person.

"I jumped off the high walls and somehow survived the fall. I washed up ashore, and with only the tattered rags on my back, barely deemed clothes, I found work in a tavern. I cleaned dishes for food and a place to stay and would tell my tale of escape to those who were inclined to hear it. Of course, they paid for the tale!"

His men laughed. Captain Nelson smiled. "Hernando, will you charge us for this telling?"

Blood Bones shook his head. "No, I think not!"

Once their laughter settled Blood Bones continued. "I finally met a group of pirates that took me in as one of their own. They knew my cousin, Alvaro, and welcomed me into the Bloods with open arms. I set sail with them and after several battles, earned my name, Blood Bones. I had saved my captain, Blood Lust, in the heat of the fight. I was soaked to the bone with blood; hence my nickname."

"Wow!" Harris exclaimed. "That's insane!"

Blood Bones chuckled at the young man's interest.

He continued on. "I had told my story at the Bloods' strategic dwellings. That will be our next stop, by the way. You will see how fantastic it is. The island has an entrance that blends into the surrounding woods, and from a distance, looks uninhabitable. There is a large harbor where nearly a dozen ships can anchor unseen by searching eyes."

Captain Nelson nodded, remembering just how hard it had been to find Blood Bones and his men in their secret lair. The story kept unfolding, and it just caused him to have more affection and admiration for the pirate. The man was certainly interesting, to say the least.

"Blood Lust then gave me command of *La Monzón*. So many of the sailors around the campfire that night wished me luck on my new adventure, and even joined me on what was to come."

"That is certainly a grand tale!" Captain Nelson laughed. "You are quite an interesting man!"

Blood Bones smiled. "Thank you, Miguel. I could say the same about you all."

A rumble in Sal's stomach brought him out of his reverie. He stood up and walked to the metal pot and spooned out a piece of the pork. "Anybody want some?"

He noticed several nods around, and spooned a few pieces onto a small wooden dish. He walked to each and let them pick the piece they wanted.

"For the most part, that is my tale," Blood Bones said. He stretched out a kink in his back, and then stared up toward the heavens. "There is, of course, a bit more to the story, but I do believe it is getting late. I shall save the tale of my revenge for tomorrow. I would like to turn in for the night. We will get started at sunup."

"Excellent. Good night, Hernando." Captain Nelson stood up and then looked at his friends. "We have much to do on the morrow; let us turn in as well."

With that, Blood Bones took a tent for himself, Nelson and Sal shared a tent, and Harris and Leah went into the third and final tent.

✤✤✤

Leah wrapped a blanket around herself, warding off the cold. Harris noticed her shifting around and looked over.

"Hey, are you cold? Do you want my blanket?" Harris asked.

She nodded. "I don't do well with the cold."

Harris pulled off his blanket and passed it to her. As she reached for it, Ben's medallion fell out into view. Her hand grabbed the blanket and she looked down at the gold medal around her neck.

Harris caught her gaze, and she paused. She was frozen there, deep in thought.

"Hey, are you okay?" Harris said, concern in his voice.

She shrugged, pulling the wool blanket over her other blanket. She then reached for the medallion and held it up to her face. The campfire was still burning bright, and from this angle, the flames reflected off the medallion.

"I just wish I could be with Benjamin." Leah sniffed back newly forming tears.

"Yeah, I understand. I miss my brother too, but there isn't much we can do right now. January is coming to a quick close. We've got less than a week before it's February, and then soon after that it will be March, and then, whoa! All of sudden it's April! And then before you know is May and then we'll save Ben in June!" He hoped his words would settle Leah's spirits. When he thought she was okay, he continued on. "We'll explore the caves the next few days, then head down to that pirate lair. We'll probably stay there for a few months, I guess, and then do whatever pirates do for fun," he said. His words sounded ridiculous, and he chuckled slightly at the imagery now in his head.

A bead of tears trickled out and followed the curve of her face, and one splashed onto the medallion in her hands. She brought it to her mouth and kissed it. "You are right. We will do what needs to be done, and then we will save Benjamin and the others."

"That's the spirit, Leah." Harris was proud of her. She had transformed from a friend to almost a sister ever since their paths had crossed. "You and Ben are destined to be together. I'm sure of it."

Harris closed his eyes, reflecting on everything they had just discussed. His words were almost more inclined to that of a son comforting his mother as his father went off to war. He shook the odd thought out of his mind, and then opened his eyes. "Good night, Leah."

"Good night, Harris. Thank you for everything."

15

January 26, 1763
Roosevelt Island

A beam of sunlight came in through an opening in the tent's canvas. Light danced across the ground as the sun inched upward. Finally a beam settled onto Leah's face and it caused her to stir. Her hand instinctively reached for her eyes, and she rubbed out the night's sleep. She had slept very little throughout the night, and even now distinctly remembered several nightmares. She yawned and then pulled her wool blanket closer to her chin.

Harris heard the movement and craned his neck to face Leah. He saw her hiding beneath the gray blanket, and he let out a chuckle. "Afraid to see a new day?"

Leah slowly pushed the blankets back to reveal her face. She chuckled, and then shifted her weight to look over at her friend. "I am just really tired. I lived a life of luxury. I have never slept on the ground before. Adjusting to the hammocks aboard ship was only slightly easier than this. I think I twisted and turned all night long."

Harris nodded. "Yeah, I hear you on that. I mean, when I was growing up, my father would take Ben and me camping a lot, so I sort of just got used to it, I guess." At the mention of Ben's name, Leah closed her eyes. Harris noticed this and cursed himself under his breath. "Sorry, Leah. I'm still getting used to him not being here. It's going to slip from time to time."

Leah nodded. "You are right. I can deal with adjusting to this new lifestyle of being a pirate, of sleeping in hammocks aboard ships, or on the ground on some remote beach, but losing Benjamin has been the most difficult thing I have had to deal with." Her words settled into a silence, and then she continued. "And the funny thing is, I was never his to begin with. I was so mad at my father when I heard that he had arranged my marriage to Captain Richard Highmore."

Harris had heard the story many times over, but clearly Leah was upset. He smiled at her. "It'll all work out, Leah. You are the toughest gal I've ever met, physically and emotionally. We're going to save Ben, just you wait!"

Leah laughed. Harris always was able to put her in a better mood. "Thanks." Her stomach rumbled, and she sat up. "I guess we should start our day."

"Yeah. I wonder if anyone else is up yet," Harris said as he stretched. "I haven't heard anything outside and I've been sort of just laying around for the last half hour or so."

Harris made the first move, and in a semi-crawl, semi-haunched action, skirted underneath the tent's canvas. He stood to his full height and looked around. Blood Bones was carrying two metal pots back from the beach.

"Good morning, Hector," the pirate said. "How did you sleep?"

Harris smiled. "I slept well. I kind of like sleeping outside; it's soothing, you know?"

Blood Bones let out a hearty laugh. "Aye, that it is. I've spent many a night with the sky above as my blanket, and the earth below as my pillow. You chose the right profession, then! Our adventures give us the opportunity to see many beautiful things, and sleep in various conditions." He paused, concentrating on placing the metal pots back on the stakes by the campfire. The pirate had rekindled the flames before cleaning the pots and filling one with water. In the other pot he placed several pieces of the dried pork. "I will tell you one thing, though; from all of my experiences—I wouldn't trade my decision to become a pirate for anything. Is it morally wrong to steal and profit from the skills of my blade?" Blood Bones curtsied in mockery. He spread his hands wide, as if he was a conductor of a symphony. "Maybe—but it is not as if I steal only from the British. I also loot the French, the Dutch, the Portuguese, and anybody who has something of value! I've even taken a few Spanish prizes from time to time."

Harris smiled. It was odd how at first he, his brother, and Sal, had feared Blood Bones. They had found the skeleton of the famous pirate down in the cavern system back in the future. It had been tattered and had lain hidden for hundreds of years. They had even researched the man standing just a few feet from him now, and everything Harris had learned then was completely different from what he was experiencing now. *Blood Bones is a brave leader. His men love him. He's even making us breakfast*, Harris thought.

Blood Bones sized up Harris. "So, this cave system—Miguel told me many good things about it. I look forward to seeing it firsthand."

"Yeah, it's pretty neat. There was this river with all these poles sticking out; there were dead bodies and booby traps throughout the caves!" His imagination flared at recollecting his previous adventure. He wasn't sure how much Blood Bones knew about their knowledge, so he didn't want to give away too much information. "It's the perfect site for us to bury our treasure."

Blood Bones gave him a twisted smile. "Well, some day in the future, someone will be bound to find it…" he trailed off. His words lingered in the air just as Leah crawled out from under the canvas tent. Just as she stood, Captain Nelson and Sal also joined the ranks. "Ah, welcome all. Good morning. I'll put on a pot of coffee, some mashed grain, and a few pieces of the dried pork. Breakfast will be ready in about ten minutes."

※※※

Blood Bones stood in the bow of the longboat. He opened a storage compartment and passed two lanterns to Sal and Leah. Next, he pulled out three machetes for Harris, Captain Nelson, and himself.

"Anything else?" Nelson asked.

Blood Bones looked at his friend and nodded. "Miguel, catch." As he said the words, he tossed a heavy coil of line toward Captain Nelson.

With a split second to react, Nelson dropped the machete to the ground and its sharp blade pierced an inch into the ground, vibrating with a whir. With practiced skill, Nelson grabbed at the eye of the line as it flew through the air. Using the momentum of the line, he swung it around his midsection, and stuck his head and torso through the eye, using his body to carry the heavy rope. He winked at Blood Bones, who erupted into laughter. He then kneeled down slightly, and with his left hand balanced the coiled line and with his right picked up the machete.

"Ready when you are!" Nelson said.

Blood Bones eyed his crew. He let out a mischievous smile, and then took a long bow. His head reared forward, and then like a gunshot, he snapped to attention. He glanced down at the scarlet stone on his finger, and noticed it was glowing with life. He focused his gaze on Harris. "Hector, where is the location of the cavern system exactly?"

Harris turned his lip up as he concentrated. He thought of the zig-zag path they had taken across the island. It was definitely the longest possible route to the cavern system. There were a few sections of booby traps, and he remembered the area where tree limbs seemed to have a haunted life of their own. Goosebumps formed on his skin as he remembered the quicksand that Sal had stumbled chest deep into. "I'm almost certain it is exactly in the center of the island. Based on where we are now, we should just have to hike straight in." He paused, looking up at the sky. He noticed where the sun was, just an inch or two above the eastern horizon. "It should be half a mile or less if we hike mostly north."

Blood Bones nodded. His eyes were closed, and he was sketching out a map inside his brain. Details were hewn into the imagery—distances, speeds, and time were all calculated. As he opened his eyes, he gently swung the machete around and placed the straight, dull edge on his shoulder as if it were a walking cane. "Luis, Salvador—if you will please light the lanterns." He then let out a laugh as they set to the task. "It seems we have a destination, then. Now, let us begin."

They stared at the underbrush ahead, eager for what was to come.

✺✺✺

The jungle was thick and untamed—more than likely, the island had never been seen by man until now. There was no evidence of habitation. Their machete blades created a symphony of noise as they slowly progressed through the thick woods. The terrain was relatively flat, with only a few inclines or declines here and there.

They could barely see the sky above, as the tree limbs combined to form a dense canopy. Sal and Leah held their lanterns high above their heads, casting enough light for the other three to hack a path. They would stop every thirty minutes or so to take a quick breath and rest. Harris switched between his dominant right hand and his left, hoping to conserve as much energy as he could.

Finally, they emerged before the cavern entrance. The group stood there staring at the ten-foot-high mouth of rock in the hillside. It was almost as if the rock face smiled, welcoming them. Harris and Sal exchanged a sideways glance.

Sal placed a hand on his friend's shoulder. "I don't think there's treasure in there this time around, so you probably don't want to just run in there like last time!"

Harris smiled. "You're such a goon." He closed his eyes for a moment, recalling the aforementioned event. On that adventure-seeking trip, the Manry brothers and Sal had stood at the entrance of the cave just like they were now. Harris had plunged without thinking into the cavern, like a moth to a flame. "This is kind of wild, man. Who would've thought we would've gone through all of this not just once, but twice!"

Sal shrugged. "I hear you on that, man. This is one hell of an adventure."

Blood Bones listened to the exchange. He had been carefully observing them since they had crossed paths in the port of Boston. They were different somehow, and their mannerisms were odd. He smiled. "Luis, Salvador—please shed some light upon this dark situation!"

They moved forward, and the lanterns cast enough light so they could see a half dozen feet in front of them. Their movements would be slow at best.

The group of five stood in a small atrium. As their eyes gradually adjusted to the dimness, a narrow passageway, just wide enough to walk through side by side, seemed to materialize before them. Sal held his lantern high and gazed at the ceiling of the cavern. "Dude, check it out!"

Harris followed the lantern's light and saw a jumble of bats hiding amongst the cobwebbed stalactites above. He shuddered, feeling as if he was a delicacy in the mouth of a large whale. Sal lowered the lantern and then moved it from side to side, slowly. There were also stalagmites coming up from the rocks by their feet. As they made their way slowly forward, they came to realize they were following a noticeable slope downward. The rocky walls that encircled them were covered with ghostly cobwebs that danced with the slight draft that wound its way through the complex tunnel system.

"I do not think I have ever seen something this dark!" Leah said. Fear mixed with an edge of excitement in her voice.

"This equals what I've seen in the innards of a ship," Captain Nelson said with a smile.

"Aye, I can attest to that also," Blood Bones said. His face was illuminated by Leah's lantern. She looked at the smile on his face, and it was one of pure joy. A sailor talking of ships is like a poet speaking of love.

They continued on for another half hour through the winding path. The descent took them beneath the massive body of water on which they had just been canoeing.

Harris and Sal led the way forward, and they felt an odd sense of familiarity in the cavern. They could hear the gurgle of water coming from around the bend, and soon Sal stood at the edge of a deep ditch. He held the lantern high and could not see the opposite bank.

The five now stood, their feet mere inches from the edge of what looked like a miniature canyon. From their vantage point they could really only see down and what appeared to be the trickle of a very small, slowly moving stream.

"Weird. This used to be a raging river." Sal stared down. "I wonder what happened to it."

"I think—we happened to it." Harris knelt down, getting a closer view. "Hey, pass me the lantern, I want to see something."

He grabbed at the lantern and placed it carefully near the edge. He was now lying on his chest, as if he was about to do a pushup. He could see farther than the others, but it was still not enough. Spotting a pebble next to his hand, he gave it a little flick. It somersaulted down into the dark abyss, and just a moment later, he heard the pebble hit the ground, roll a bit, and then splash into the nearly still water.

"I think we're going to have to climb down," he said to the others from his prone position. "There's definitely water down there, but it's not much. Then we'll have to climb up the other side."

"Are there sufficient hand holds to climb?" Blood Bones kneeled down beside Harris.

He looked over at the pirate who was just a foot away from his face. At a point in a parallel universe—in a different time and place—the two had fought against each other as enemies. Now, however, they were working together as comrades. Blood Bones had shown compassion to him and his friends since they had joined him aboard *La Monzón*.

"I'm not sure," Harris said as he looked at a few of the juts and outcroppings of rock. They were spread out several feet between each. "I mean, it's probably doable."

"Nevertheless, we will take the proper precautions." Blood Bones looked at Captain Nelson. "Miguel, if you would, please uncoil a length of line."

He did as instructed, and passed the bitter end of the line to Blood Bones. He lowered the end of the rope slowly, and with practiced skill determined the depth of the descent. Leah followed the pirate's gaze as he began to scan for an anchor, and found a suitable stalagmite to tie off to. He closed his eyes and made a mental calculation of the proper length. His hands moved effortlessly as he found, and then cut the line at the desired spot.

Sure enough, once he secured the line around the stalagmite and tossed the rope down, it just reached the ground below. Although he couldn't see his handiwork, Blood Bones was quite confident with the attempt, and let off a victorious smile. "So, who shall go first?"

The group exchanged a few glances, and Harris shrugged. "I'll go first." He tucked his machete into his belt, and then picked up the rope. He maneuvered to the edge and took up the slack in the rope. He faced his friends as he placed his feet on the edge. He leaned back, and the line became taut. His body became perpendicular to the vertical shelf of rock as he rappelled down. He quickly disappeared from view.

At the bottom, his feet scuffed lightly against the cavern floor. He wiped sweat from his brow, and then called up, "Hey, I made it. Piece of cake!"

"Good job!" He heard a combination of voices calling down. "We're going to lower a lantern to you now."

The glow of the lantern seemed almost alien as it floated slowly down to his awaiting hands. He quickly untied the lantern's handle and then stepped back away from the rock face to explore the immediate vicinity.

※※※

Five explorers continued onward, leaving behind a conquered obstacle. It was difficult work in the near pitch-black cavern, but they had prevailed. Blood Bones led the group, with Sal and Leah on each side holding their lanterns high. Captain Nelson came up on the right flank, with Harris on the left. Together, they pierced through the darkness like a wedge of light. The tunnel sloped down farther into the earth. After having gone perhaps one hundred yards, they emerged into another, smaller cavern that was roughly the size of a shipboard cabin. The ceiling was no more than eight feet high and the room itself was perhaps twelve by sixteen feet.

The space was completely barren. Sal held the lantern next to Harris and whispered. "This is where the skull and cross bone mosaic was…" his words trailed off.

Harris thought for a moment. "Wait." He then laughed. "Or more accurately, will be. I am getting that weird feeling that we're the ones who design all of this."

Sal thought for a moment and his friend's idea was not that farfetched. "I think you're right. This is insane. Completely insane."

Captain Nelson watched their exchange and it caused him to smile. "Where to next?"

"There was like…a trap door, or something." Harris said. "Leah, can I see the lantern real quick?" She nodded and passed it to his eager hands. "Thanks."

He turned his body around and retraced his steps, noting where they had entered the space. He looked around and closed his eyes, transporting back into a memory that seemed so long ago, but in reality would take place hundreds of years in the future. As if he were watching a movie, the scene unraveled and he smiled. He opened his eyes and took a few measured paces forward. He skirted the group and then stopped, searching frantically for the passageway that would lead to the third mini-cavern.

"The next passageway should be right here!" Harris said with a flare of anger.

Blood Bones observed silently. He moved over to the young sailor and then stood next to him. "Hector, let me see the lantern, please."

He placed the lantern on the floor and slid the glass open to reveal the burning wick.

Five sets of eyes watched the flame dance with life. Captain Nelson smiled at the pirate's brilliance.

"There is a breeze, which means the passageway that you speak of is right here."

He knelt down and pressed his face closer to the wall. He could feel where the breeze was coming through, and the lantern's light cast enough glow to even see several slits where cobwebs and dirt had co-mingled. He pressed the tip of his machete into one of these slits, and began wiggling the blade back and forth. Sure enough, pebbles began to cascade to the ground, slowly at first and then the hole opened more quickly as sand and pebbles poured to their feet. Blood Bones paused for a moment, realizing that it would still take quite some time to make an opening large enough for one of them to fit through. He scanned the surface of the rock wall more closely, holding the lantern mere inches from it. He exposed the wick as he had done before and it flared at certain spots. As before, he inserted the tip of the machete into a crack, and opened it just an inch or so. He spent a few minutes strategically picking the locations where he could ply the machete. After a few more attempts he stood to his full height and gave the lantern back to Harris.

"Now, all we have to do is push," Blood Bones said with a smile.

Harris, Sal, and Captain Nelson moved forward. They emptied their hands of machetes and lanterns and then took up positions against the rock wall.

"On the count of three we'll push through," Blood Bones said loudly. "One, two, three!"

The combined effort worked beautifully. Blood Bones had weakened the wall by drilling the holes, and rocks crumbled to their feet. Dust flew upward as the miniature cave-in revealed yet another passageway.

When the dust settled, Blood Bones bowed theatrically. "Luis, would you lead us forward?"

Leah had remained quiet, and the fact that Blood Bones wished to let her lead made something inside her swell with pride.

They continued forward by the lanterns' soft glow. Leah led the others slowly, and after about fifty yards they ended up in an even smaller cavern than the previous two. Sal cleared his throat. "This one goes up. We're going to have to climb."

Captain Nelson stepped forward this time to volunteer. Jokingly, he touched his toes as if to warm up for the climb. He stretched his back by swinging his shoulders from side to side. The group cracked up, laughing away in the darkness. "Here goes nothing!"

They watched him move up the vertical wall. He tested the rock slowly and methodically for handholds. They held the lanterns up as high as they could to provide light for him. He climbed roughly twenty-five feet up, and then was able to swing his legs and pull his body over the edge. It was completely dark in the small perch. He leaned his head over the edge and looked down.

He could see the outlines of his friends below in the glow of the two lanterns. "I am going to lower the end of a line. Can one of you tie off a lantern so I can pull it up."

Just a few moments later, Captain Nelson was pulling the rope so that the lantern rose mid-way up the wall—there the lantern came to rest. He gauged that the climbers would have enough light the entire way up with the lantern in this position.

One at a time, the four remaining crew climbed. Their ascents were faster than his had been, and soon enough the group stood atop, eager to continue.

The group walked down the corridor and emerged into a spacious chamber. On either side there were tunnels—six in total. They stopped to explore each vein of the cave system, and discovered only more emptiness. The rooms were nearly identical in size, with high ceilings and broad entryways.

Blood Bones smiled. "This will certainly make for a suitable location. It looks like we have much to do, but for now, let us return to camp. We will spend another night here, and then row back to join our men aboard ship on the morrow."

The group enjoyed just a few moments's rest before Blood Bones made the move to return, and now they had to do the entire cavern transit in reverse. By the time they exited the caves, then trekked through the woods back to their tents, they were too exhausted to cook or chat idly by the fire. Each of them fell asleep the moment they lay their heads down.

16

January 27, 1763
Port of St. Augustine

Blood Bones once again called the cadence as the group rowed the longboat through the harbor. They had been underway for a few hours now, leaving with the rising sun. Now they could see several boats anchored to the north as they neared the harbor of St. Augustine. After another thirty minutes, they were within sight of their vessel. A sailor in the rigging spotted their approach, and a bell rang out, signaling all available hands to tend the lines for their retrieval.

Without even a command from Blood Bones, Harris and Sal gracefully moved within the boat to each end of the vessel. They balanced carefully as the boat rocked, riding the waves that crashed into them. Leah watched as Harris passed by, and he quickly connected the longboat's bow to the forward fall. He made eye contact with Blood Bones, and made the report. Sal finished the task just a moment after.

Blood Bones nodded. "Ship the oars—it's time for us to rise!" He looked up at a few sailors standing at the ready, waiting by the railing above. "Hoist us up!"

※※※

Once the group of five were back aboard HMS *Courtesy*, Blood Bones called for a meeting in the galley. The group of pirates still wore the garb of the English Royal Marines. They were careful to deceive watchful eyes, knowing that if another vessel saw something awry here it could mean detection and ultimately death by hanging. Piracy was not well-looked upon in the colonies.

Blood Bones stared at all of his crew. He had been gone for less than two days, and the crew welcomed their leader back with open arms.

"Men, we have explored the island and with great satisfaction deem it worthy of our efforts."

The crew hooted with excitement. When the noise died down, Blood Bones continued. "I checked my navigation journals, and the ebbing tide will occur two hours before sunset. That gives us a few hours to relax before we set to work and ready for sea. I would like to be underway as the tide changes, with our secret lair our next destination!"

Again, the pirates cheered. He made eye contact with Sesostris, and the wizard nodded, knowing that Blood Bones wished a meeting in private to discuss all that had happened. Blood Bones valued his friendship with the mysterious wizard, and whether they were discussing fate and destiny with the assistance of the crystal ball or just enjoying idle chitchat or a game of chess, the man was an invaluable asset aboard ship.

✣✣✣

Captain Nelson swung in his hammock. He was tired from the excursion, and it was nice to get off his feet. The ship rocked lightly at anchor and he quickly dozed off. Leah, Harris, and Sal chatted quietly in the corner of their berthing area.

"That cave system is completely barren. It's kind of cool to see what it used to be like, you know?" Sal looked at his friend.

"You mean, before we showed Blood Bones to it?" Harris laughed. "I still don't one hundred percent believe it. It's crazy!"

Leah watched their exchanges—words, facial expressions, everything. "I do not fully comprehend time travel, but what if this was all meant to happen?"

"You mean, like fate?" Harris looked at Leah.

She nodded. "Yes! Exactly!" She beamed a brilliant smile. Obviously Benjamin Manry had come into her life for a reason, and everything she was dealing with now was directly related to the handsome brunette who held a strong grip on her heart.

"You're probably right," Sal said. Captain Nelson began to snore, and the noise carried over to the trio. "I think we should squeeze in a quick nap. We've had a busy few days!"

The group laughed, and then spread their wool blankets over their hammocks. Their heavy eyes closed quickly.

✖✖✖

Sesostris sipped at a small glass of red wine. He smacked his lips, relishing the taste. "That was a lovely toast, my friend!"

Blood Bones smiled in response. "Thank you—for everything you have done over the years." Likewise, Blood Bones took a sip and let out a small chuckle. "The young men led me on quite the adventure over the past few days!"

"You are like a brother to me, Hernando! But tell me of this cave system. How did it compare to your visions?" the wizard asked.

Blood Bones closed his eyes for a moment, comparing this recent experience with a vision he had had many years prior. The images fluttered before his eyes in a crystal-clear fashion. He smiled, concluding it was the very same cave system he had once imagined. "Yes, yes, I believe it is the same. The cave system is spacious, and will be very suitable for our needs."

Sesostris sipped at the glass of wine again. He let out a very content sigh. "Well, that is good. I am glad the trip inland went well."

Blood Bones nodded. "How was it aboard ship while I was gone?"

"Quiet. I had the bosun carry about the vessel with a skeleton crew, keeping just the watch above decks. I also had several men inventory the ship further to see what we have aboard."

"Excellent. Do we have sufficient supplies to get to Port Royal?" Blood Bones asked.

"We have enough for a trip there and back, if needed. Plenty of water and fresh provisions. Our armories are full with gun powder, weapons, and various types of cannon balls. We've got spare sails aplenty, and the carpenter's shop is loaded with all sorts of wood," the wizard reported. He knew that Blood Bones liked the details. He heard the bell above ringing the time, and he shifted in his chair. "I've got to get back to the galley and prepare for the afternoon meal."

"Ah, yes, it seems it is that time. My stomach is growling, too!" Blood Bones laughed. "I will walk with you."

The duo stood from their respective seats, and exited the stateroom, ready to get their fill of food and drink.

※※※

HMS *Courtesy* hoisted anchor. Men high above deck stood in the tarred ratlines, letting out sail. The wind caught and the vessel propelled forward out of the harbor.

Castillo de San Marcos faded in the distance as the ship increased speed. The sails were now filled with wind, and Blood Bones maneuvered delicately around several other anchored ships. He pointed the bow nearly due east, and soon enough, they could feel the ocean waves more prominently as they moved out into open waters.

Captain Nelson stood beside his three friends as they helped secure the anchor on deck. They lashed it to the deck for sea travel. Harris wiped at his brow.

"That went very well," Nelson announced to the group. "I believe we will be underway for a little less than a week before we arrive at the lair."

Harris and Sal nodded. "Not bad," said Harris. "What do you think Blood Bones will have us do until then?"

Captain Nelson shrugged. "Well, there is not much to do. We already fixed the damage from the skirmish in Boston."

"Yeah, that's true," Harris responded.

"Maybe we'll do some training?" Sal said. He leaned forward, placing his chest against the railing and sniffing the fresh air.

"That could very well be," Captain Nelson said. He thought for another moment, and then continued. "Blood Bones is known for that sort of thing. When we battled him, we narrowly won. It could have gone either way, to be honest."

"The wind wasn't in our favor, that is for damn sure." Harris added. "I remember you were delayed because you had to fight the wind and current."

Sal smiled. "It was awesome, though, when we were battling on the beach, and then all of a sudden we saw the bowsprit and the sails pop into view. It gave the men a little more fight, you know?"

Harris nodded. "Absolutely. We fought with vigor! It was great."

Leah stared off into the distance, listening to her companions reminiscing about their previous battle. Slightly off the port bow, a white smudge appeared on the horizon. She noticed this, and turned to face it more directly.

"Do one of you have a telescope?" she asked politely.

"Of course," Nelson said. "Every mariner should have one!" He jested, pulling out a bronze telescope from his leather pouch. He passed the piece to her.

She pressed her face to the eyepiece and squinted. A white sail came into view, and then another. She moved the telescope slowly, scanning the horizon. "I see a ship!" she said excitedly.

Captain Nelson moved to her side. "May I see?"

She passed him the telescope. Coming into view was a very familiar ship, his former command, *Frendrich*. "I do not believe my eyes."

"What is it?" Harris asked.

The ship was angled for an approach into St. Augustine. As the vessel came closer, it grew in size until the group could see it without needing a scope.

Sal and Harris echoed Captain Nelson's exclamation. "That is crazy!"

Sal slapped his mentor on the shoulder in jest. "You are on that right now!"

"I wonder if you can see yourself!" Harris smiled at the odd thought.

Nelson looked through the spyglass and scanned the deck. He knew the lines of his ship so well—almost like knowing the freckles and birthmarks of an intimate lover. He stopped for a moment, focusing in on a figure standing beside the helmsman. His jaw dropped, recognizing that the man holding his gaze was himself.

"I need a drink!" He laughed. He shook his head for a moment and then turned to face Sal and Harris. "I do believe fate has brought us all together, and to be honest, even though this adventure has had many ups and downs, I would not have it any other way. We have become quite close since I found the three of you aboard my ship so many months ago." He was of course referring to Benjamin Manry as the third person, but he then turned his eyes toward Leah. "We will get Benjamin back, and the two of you will live a long and happy life together. I am sure of it!"

17

January 28, 1763
At Sea

The HMS *Courtesy* continued its southward passage down the coast of the colonies. The following day, Blood Bones called for a meeting. As usual, the pirates sat in the galley, eager for what their leader had to say.

"Men, if the wind holds, we will be in the comfort of our lair within five days." Blood Bones announced. He paced back and forth, and with every step he could sense their gazes following his every move. They cheered. "We have worked very hard these last few months, especially with our latest success. As always, we will stick to our normal underway routine. We will split the crew into sections—one for maintenance, one for training, and obviously one for watch."

Blood Bones began pointing to various groupings, splitting up the men into assignments. Nelson and company were all assigned to training. After Blood Bones dismissed the group the men went their various ways.

"All right, let's go up to the weather deck. Training will be held by the foremast," Captain Nelson said. He led Harris, Sal, and Leah, along with others also assigned to training. Sesostris tagged along as well.

Sesostris hauled a large bundle onto the main deck from one of the weapons lockers below. He placed the large canvas roll on the wooden deck, and then untied the straps that held it secure. He slowly unrolled the canvas, revealing dozens of various nautical weapons. Each weapon had been slipped into a pouch within the roll. It was a convenient way to store and keep the weapons dry.

Captain Nelson was essentially winging the training session. Blood Bones had appointed him as the training leader for the morning's exercise, while Sesostris would take command in the afternoon. Nelson talked quietly with the wizard off to the side, while the remaining men stood by the railing, enjoying the fresh breeze and the warmth of the sunlight on their faces. Once content, Sesostris remained to the side to observe. Captain Nelson studied the various tools and weapons. After the briefest of pauses, he closed his eyes and ran through various memories of his shipboard experiences.

"All right, men, please gather round," he called. About half a dozen sailors stood at loose attention as Captain Nelson began. "My name is Miguel, for those who do not know me." He had made it a point to tell Sal, Leah, and Harris to make themselves known throughout the vessel, and subtle exposure over time had completely worked in their favor. As for himself, he was now one of the right-hand men of Blood Bones. Their last adventure had sealed the deal in that respect. He held up a solid wooden shaft. "Men, this is called a belaying pin." In a slow arc, he moved his arm so the men could see it. "This is a device used to secure lines. It can be inserted into a hole in a wooden pinrail." He knelt down beside the bulwarks. "If a line needs to be released quickly, the belaying pin can be lifted out and removed, releasing the line."

Leah's eyes followed each movement as Captain Nelson demonstrated the use of the belaying pin. Harris and Sal had seen it used a few times before, and the other pirates in their group all looked on with what seemed to be bored looks. Blood Bones had these routine training sessions to keep everyone on board up-to-date with shipboard tools and weapons. In battle, you had to be prepared for almost anything.

"So, what else can this be used for?" He called out, hoping to spark a little interest in the crowd.

"A club?" A man grunted.

"Exactly!" Captain Nelson smiled. "Trust me, I've whacked a few in the face with one before, and it surely does the job!"

The group laughed and he continued on. He bent down, replacing the belaying pin into its pouch. "Next is the boarding axe." He hefted the three-foot-long axe and swung it in a few wide arcs. It had a sharp blade on one side and a blunt hammer on the other. "This can be used to cut the ropes of boarding hooks thrown by enemies. You can also chop at a mast or at rigging. I've personally used it to knock in a door or a hatch." He let his words sink in. "Can anyone think of another use for it?"

"I was a gun-crew member a few years back. We took a full broadside that raked our vessel from bow to stern. There were several cannon balls that got lodged into the wooden deck, so we used the boarding axes to chisel the balls out," a sailor said.

"Exactly!" Captain Nelson replaced the boarding axe back into its respective pouch, and then pulled out a grappling hook. There was a fifteen-foot coil of line that went with the metal hook. "This is rather self-explanatory, but I shall give a demonstration."

He glanced at his target: an empty barrel. He gauged the distance and began swinging the hook around his head. Once he was content with the speed behind the metal hook, he released and watched as it flew toward the wooden barrel. Two of the metal hooks caught the uppermost edge of the barrel and Captain Nelson then pulled on it with a hard tug. The barrel flipped over, causing the sailors to cheer at his display of skill.

As before, he replaced the grappling hook back into its respective pouch. Next, he pulled out what looked like a large tack. It had four sides, and at any given point, would have one dangerously facing up. "This is the caltrop, and let me tell you—stepping on one will definitely make for a shitty day!"

His audience had warmed up to his technique of splicing jokes and personal stories into the training. "I remember tossing a few of these aboard a ship before we made our attack, and it was almost as if they were dancing on hot coals. It distracted them to the point that we were able to clear the deck in under ten minutes."

He watched several heads nod and smiled. "All right, now to a few of my favorite weapons!" He decided to combine this next lecture: in his left hand he held a dirk and in his right he held a cutlass. "In hand-to-hand combat, this pair of weapons could be deadly." He stepped forward with his right foot, and began a little routine of slicing and dicing, blocking high and then low. His attack rotated between using the smaller dirk and the larger cutlass in his hands. "Both weapons can be used in battle, or even for simple shipboard tasks."

"I actually prefer the pike," a man said. "It puts a little distance between my enemy and myself."

"Ah, yes, well the pike most certainly has its advantages," Captain Nelson said with a smile. "But it surely is a clumsy weapon in the heat of battle."

There was a chuckle from the crowd, but the man seemed a little offended at his words. "If you say so. It has saved my arse a few times."

He thought quickly, not wanting to offend the man further. "And that is the point, everyone. Each of these tools and weapons I have displayed thus far can be used." He held the blades point down, letting his muscles relax for a moment. "I believe that should suffice for this morning's session. Now it is your turn to practice!"

Captain Nelson returned the two blades back into the pouch, and then invited the men around him to practice. He walked over to Sesostris and smiled. "That went over fairly well!"

"Aye, that it did," the wizard said with a smile. "My afternoon session should be a little more fun."

Captain Nelson laughed. "An explosion always lightens the mood!"

※※※

Blood Bones lay in his bed reading a book of poetry. His eyes eagerly moved across the pages, creating beautiful images in his imagination. Green fields, flowers, a setting sun. The words brought him somewhere else entirely. There was a knock on his door and he shifted on his bed. "Come in!" he called.

Sesostris opened the door slightly and poked his head in. "Hernando, just reporting the morning's training went very well."

The pirate captain placed a feather to mark his page and then closed the book. He swung his feet and placed them on the deck, standing to his full height. "Excellent! What did he talk about?"

The wizard smiled. "General shipboard weapons, and edged weapons. He covered them in detail and then let the men practice with each. He has a natural skill with conveying knowledge to others, plus he is quite skilled in his own right. Miguel will provide you with many services, I feel."

Blood Bones nodded. He had grown to like the man very much. "I do think you are right. Fate has brought us together." A rumble in his stomach distracted him. "It seems like it is time for lunch!"

Sesostris laughed. "Aye, that it is!"

※※※

After lunch, they resumed their afternoon training session. This time, however, Sesostris took over. He cleared his throat, projecting his voice loudly enough for all those around to hear. "All right, if you thought this morning's session was fun, you're in for a surprise," he said. He cocked the flintlock pistol in his right hand, aiming down the sights. He focused on a red circle that had been painted on a barrel some distance away on the deck.

"Always exhale prior to pulling the trigger," he said as he exhaled. The breath left him, and in the moment that followed, he realigned his focus and pulled the trigger. A flash of light sparked as the gun shot, projecting the ball forward right through the red circle. "Easy as that, men!"

They bellowed with laughter. "Obviously, it is more difficult in the heat of battle. So, when the time comes for you to practice, perhaps you should—oh, pretend that you are under attack!"

"I have an idea for that," Harris smiled.

"Yes, Hector?" Sesostris asked.

"We could have the target attached to a series of pulleys. We could use the block and tackles to move the target, and we'd have to adjust our sights and attempt to hit it!" Harris spoke excitedly.

"That would prove a great test of skill, combining that with the vessel's motions," Sesostris said. He then placed his hands on his hips, still holding the pistol. "Miguel, can you and Hector attend to that task?"

"Absolutely," Captain Nelson said. The two left the group, leaving Sal and Leah behind.

"So, the next weapon will be the *grenadoes*," Sesostris said with a large smile. "This may be my favorite weapon of all, simply because of the damage it inflicts." He placed the pistol back in its pouch, and then pulled out a small metal ball, roughly four inches in diameter. "Obviously due to the one-time use nature behind this weapon, I shall be the only one to demonstrate its use." He let the murmurs die down before he continued. "Timing is key with this weapon. You do not want to throw it at your enemy too early, because if they are quick enough, they can send it right back to you and you're left to deal with the result—which, as I have seen, is not pretty!"

Again, the crew laughed. He pressed the fuse into the small hole and delayed just a split second before hurling it away from the ship. It spiraled through the air, and all eyes were watching as it exploded, sending shrapnel in all directions over the water. All who were above deck stopped what they were doing and looked at the cloud of smoke dissipating.

"It sure packs quite the punch!" The wizard laughed. "Next, we'll go below decks and shoot off a few cannon balls. We'll rotate between the different jobs of a gun crew. Later on, we'll have an accuracy contest once the pulleys are rigged with the targets."

18

February 1, 1763
At Sea

Blood Bones stood beside the helmsman. Off in the distance were the Bahamas, but he had just changed course toward the eastern end of Cuba. The next leg would take them on a southwesterly course, heading for their hideout near Port Royal, Jamaica. The sun had been up for maybe ten minutes, filling the sky with a deep blood-red color. White caps filled the horizon.

He had been awakened by the watch to alert him of a change in the weather, as well as for the upcoming course change. "Red sky in morning, sailor take warning. Red sky at night, sailor's delight," Blood Bones recited aloud.

"Aye, looks like a storm is a-brewing," the helmsman said.

Blood Bones looked down at his ring and caught the lively glow of the scarlet stone. Everything was connected—in this life, and that. His curse for immortality was well underway, and he smiled at the fact that all was falling into place.

※※※

Another day passed as Blood Bones captained the ship to its destination. He steered for the hidden opening that was known only to those deemed worthy of such knowledge. Here they often joined their fellow brothers of the sea—pirates who would band together and seek refuge and shelter in the well-protected area known as Hunt Bay. For the last several years, Blood Bones and many others had met here on a regular basis to trade their plunder and escape from onlooking eyes.

They lived by a secret code, and few knew the hideout's location. If this location ever fell into their enemies' hands, it would be the end for the men who dwelled upon these hidden beaches. The hills that engulfed the bay were large enough to shield the tall masts of the numerous vessels that could be found there at any given time, and the entrance was small so that from a few miles out, it was not easily distinguishable through the surrounding landscape. The foliage blended together: it was a perfect location.

❈❈❈

As Blood Bones and his crew maneuvered the sails, the HMS *Courtesy* passed astern of several moored ships. A horde of men ran out to investigate the vessel that had dropped anchor just a cable-length away from the smooth beach lining the bay. A red pendant flew just inches below the black pirate flag, as was customary to prove their true identities.

Blood Bones found his usual spot and ordered the anchor lowered. Captain Nelson and a handful of men took in sail and secured the canvas up in the riggings. Once the flukes caught and the vessel stilled, Blood Bones went about to make sure all was in order. Once satisfied, he had his crew unload their wares. He kept minimal provisions aboard, in case a hasty departure was required. Otherwise, all their stores were moved ashore to various huts and shacks on the island.

❈❈❈

Later that night, Blood Bones met with seven other ships' captains who were present on the island. The group sat around a large table made from a rich mahogany. Various bottles of wine were spread around the table, easily within reach to all.

"My brothers, please listen closely. I have captured an English ship, and deep in the holds are one hundred and fifty British marines and a quarter-year's worth of colonial taxes. We shall disperse the profits accordingly." He continued once all had smiled. "I believe we should put these prisoners to work—have them build larger huts for the captains, along with other structures, perhaps an improved pier?"

Several nodding heads caused him to go on. "The blasted pier we have now I built using the masts of a captured Dutch merchant. Or maybe we can work them in the sugar fields!"

"That would be most profitable," said one man.

"Indeed," said another voice from across the room.

The group began fantasizing of the ever-increasing amount of gold that would fill their already laden purses. Their laughter rang throughout the encampment, reverberating against the chains that latched each pair of marines together. The captive soldiers had been forced out from the dark holds belowdecks and loaded into a vast array of dinghies that ferried them to the beach to be locked up under a careful watch once more.

※※※

Captain Nelson sat by the campfire staring idly at the dancing flames. Sal sat on a log a few feet to his right, where he was poking a stick into the fire, moving a log onto the coals. Harris drank fresh water from a leather pouch beside Leah, who remained quiet, watching the flames flicker to life with Sal's tending.

"What do you think Blood Bones will have us do next?" Leah asked, finally looking up from the fire.

"Well, he seems like he is a firm believer in constant training, so I imagine we would continue with that to pass the time." Captain Nelson looked over the flames at her. "Perhaps some maintenance aboard the various ships, or some work on the island itself."

"There were a lot of fields behind the campgrounds, if you guys remember." Sal said. He was still adjusting a log, and pulled his stick out once content with its angle. "I think it was sugar cane?"

Harris nodded. "Yeah. Maybe Blood Bones will work us in the fields!"

The group chuckled. "I doubt that," Captain Nelson said. "We do have the captured British Marines now, which means we will have to keep a guard on them so they don't rebel."

"Yeah, that's true." Sal agreed. He paused, thinking of their previous experience on the island. "I don't remember too much of the layout here. It was kind of a blur, you know? Like with the whole battle and everything."

"I agree." Harris shrugged. He remembered Captain Nelson's advice about getting to know your ship. "It wouldn't hurt to explore the island tomorrow, get familiar with the island."

"That would be wise. It's late. Shall we adjourn for now?" Captain Nelson asked the group.

"Yeah, that's probably a good idea." Harris looked over to their leader. "Did Blood Bones tell you where we were going to sleep?"

He nodded. "Yes, there are several dozen huts for each ship at anchor. He explained that there are essential common areas for those dwelling here. If we were to board ship and set sail into the sunrise, our cots would then turn over to the next sailor seeking refuge."

Sal laughed. "Sounds like Blood Bones has got himself a nice little resort. If only there was a jacuzzi or a spa!"

Harris shook his head, mocking his friend. "Holy moly, you are ridiculous!"

Leah tried hard to suppress a giggle, but it escaped her lips. "Goodnight!"

The group dispersed into the shacks farther inland. They were crudely made, but each offered a roof and small cots for a half dozen people.

19

February 12, 1763
Pirate Lair

Just over a week passed. Blood Bones gave his men a well-earned break for their efforts in Boston. The crew were free to come and go, assuming they were not standing watch at the various stations about the island. It was almost as if it were a holiday, as pirates could nap well into the afternoon. Some would go for walks, while others played various instruments around campfires, passing around bottles. Others played cards or dice. Overall, morale was very high.

Four figures sat together, enjoying a relaxing day.

Harris held a log between his feet. He sat next to the fire pit debating the fate of the piece of wood.

"To burn, or not to burn. That is the question!" He laughed. His giggle carried to the others and caught their attention.

Sal smiled, watching from across the flames as his friend mimicked Shakespeare. Captain Nelson was writing some thoughts down in a logbook, while Leah was caught in a daydream of Benjamin Manry and their future together, assuming they could save him in time.

"I think the fire is warm enough." Sal glanced into the flames that were now stretching vertically, lapping to and fro.

"Yeah, I guess you're right," Harris said. He took his machete from its sheath and began to shave the log down. He stripped off the bark and then began to whittle it.

"What are you up to?" Sal watched his friend slide the blade down, slicing off strips of the wood.

"Not sure yet; I'll let you know when I figure it out," Harris responded, absorbed in his work. He was completely focused on the task at hand.

After about thirty minutes, there was a pile of shavings between his feet. Harris had whittled the log into a crude baseball bat. He stood up from his seat and spread his stance—placing his feet shoulder-width apart. He dug his bare feet into the sand, like any ballplayer might before taking that big swing to win the game.

"It's the bottom of the ninth, two outs, three and two count. The bases are loaded. We are down by three runs. The pitcher winds up, and hurls a fastball down the middle."

He tossed a stale piece of hardtack into the air. He shouldered the bat, and waited until the hardtack began its downward fall. He gripped the handle of the bat tightly and then swung with all his might. He connected the head of the bat with the stale biscuit. For a split second, the two objects clung together like stubborn lovers, but then the hardtack flew through the air, sailing to the water's edge about fifty feet away. Pieces of the biscuit trailed like a comet's tail, crumbled off in flight. Several heads turned.

"Home run!" Sal screamed. "Ahhhhh! Grand slam! Ahhhhh!" He let out a cheer, encouraging his friend.

"The Marlins win! The Marlins win!" Harris whooped with excitement. "Oh man, that's one of the things I really miss about being home."

"You're totally right, buddy—relaxing on a nice weekend afternoon. Ice tea and some lemonade. Home cooked meals." The two looked off into the distance, both equally distraught, caught in dreams of another place and another time.

*B*lood Bones sipped at a glass of red wine from inside his hut. From his relaxed perch, he saw a group of his men by a fire. Four of them hung off to the side. He noticed they were always together, never completely mingling with the others in his crew. He stared from afar at their faces, intrigued by their differences, then down at the scarlet stone upon his finger, noticing its sparkle.

He stood and made his way across the sandy beach to where his men were. Somewhere off in the distance, he heard a fiddle playing a tune. Men sang shanties here and there while several danced barefoot in the sand, enjoying the day.

But what caught his eye were two of his younger men standing aside, one of whom had just tossed something high into the air. Then the lad swung mightily, as if he was chopping firewood but at a different angle, bringing the wooden bat from a resting position against his shoulder to swing in a wide arc.

Blood Bones smiled as the piece of wood smacked the biscuit. The sound carried and he moved closer to get a better look. He approached slowly, and once he was within view, he smiled. "What is this game called that you are playing?" the pirate leader asked.

Harris stared deep into the man's eyes. He smiled, toeing the line of danger that he and his friends had shared since joining the pirates many months prior. It seemed that at nearly every moment since they had gone undercover as pirates, Blood Bones had been questioning them, or even testing them. Nelson had cautioned them not to stand out, and to always attempt to not be noticed. But here he was again. Blood Bones, the fearless pirate that they had captured in some alternate timeline, was standing right in front of him.

Harris took a moment to breathe before responding. He placed the head of the bat into the sand and leaned against it like the famous Babe Ruth had posed on an old baseball card his grandfather had given him on his twelfth birthday. He winked at Blood Bones. "Baseball. Where I'm from, we call it baseball."

"Ah, I would very much like to see how this game, baseball, is played. Perhaps you can tell me more of it later, and maybe organize a demonstration at some point?" Blood Bones looked between Harris, the flickering flames, and his three friends.

Harris smiled, delving into his imagination in a world of endless possibilities. "Of course, Captain."

20

February 28, 1763
Pirate Lair

Several more weeks passed by and Blood Bones had put his men to work on the old pier. Using wood in their stockpiles or from the carpenter cages on the vessels, the workers replaced nearly half of the pier that had been damaged over the years. Then they extended the pier another thirty feet, and fabricated rope fenders to protect smaller boats that would be tied off there. They took their time with the work, enjoying the relaxing pace, focusing on quality.

Another group worked in the sugar fields. A group of about thirty pirates commanded various work parties of the captured British Marines. Between these groups, men focused on the stages of turning raw sugar canes into various products. One group focused on the sugar itself, which they could sell in the colonies. Another focused on making rum, which the island dwellers loved. The prisoners were worked hard but they were not abused. Blood Bones had been treated poorly as a prisoner and had a personal grudge against it. He fed the marines quite well and every so often he would even give them a rum ration.

A few vessels had come and gone since Blood Bones had pulled into this port of refuge. The newest vessel, *Changing Tide*, had entered the harbor just that morning. There were now seven vessels anchored in the protective waters of their island paradise. Blood Bones called for another meeting to introduce the captains to each other.

✖✖✖

Blood Bones stared across the table, observing the newcomer. "So, tell me your name, young lad."

The newest captain paused, looking at Blood Bones curiously. Of all the people around, he was the one who spoke first. *He must be the leader*, David thought. "David Hawley, sir. I am the navigator aboard *Changing Tide*."

Blood Bones smiled. "Ah, no need for formalities. Call me Blood Bones. I was about to say that you looked quite young to be a captain!" The crowd laughed. The newcomer was by far the youngest in the group of pirate captains. "How old are you if you don't mind my asking."

"I just turned twenty-two several weeks past." David looked around at each man. It almost seemed as if they were testing him. He held their gazes, and then returned his stare to Blood Bones. "My captain was sick the last few days of our voyage and he is not able to attend the meeting. He sent me in his stead."

"Excellent. Well then, make your report." Blood Bones sat back in his chair. As if by subtle command, the tension in the room diminished as the pirate captains casually waited for David to begin.

"Well, there is a crewman aboard my ship—actually the boatswain Oscar, if you want to be technical—who had a personal letter from a Spanish acquaintance stationed in Cadiz," David said excitedly. This was big news for the pirate captains. His statement piqued the interest of all those around the table. "Oscar was informed of a treasure fleet moving from Veracruz, containing eight transport ships, with four escorts. The transports are thirty-gun galleons, and the escorts are forty-four gun frigates. The fleet is to get underway on the third of April. They will pass through the Windward Passage en route to Cadiz."

"That is certainly great news. How reliable is the information?" Blood Bones asked.

"Oscar's contact is his brother, so it is quite good. My captain has followed his hunches several times before, and it has made us richer than sultans." David smiled, pitching the scheme well to the pirate captains. "As most of you know, Veracruz was an Aztec city that contained riches beyond our wildest imaginations—gold, emeralds, rubies, and more."

"We will need all of our ships to join forces then," said one captain.

"We would be fighting against *twelve* ships!" another said, his voice growing louder as he finished his statement.

"We've gone up against similar numbers before," a third pirate said.

"Aye! And under Blood Bones we have never failed!" another yelled for all to hear.

Blood Bones smiled, happy that his colleagues were voicing their opinions. He was eager to begin planning for the task. "Gentlemen, it is settled then. It looks like we will be severely outnumbered, but as it has been already said—we have overcome other obstacles similar in intensity." He paused, allowing all to hear his words. "If you wish to partake on this mission, we will start our preparations in the morning. However, if you do not wish to partake, I would recommend departing our lair on the morning tide. I will not judge you if you choose to embark on other ventures. There is much to lose by going up against such a large complement, but likewise, there is also much to gain."

He let his words sink in with the men around the table. Blood Bones was strict, but fair. He had set his rules and boundaries for the upcoming mission. The pirate captains stared amongst themselves, gauging who was in and who was out. After several minutes of light discussion, they came to a decision—six heads gave a nod, causing Blood Bones to smile.

"Talk with your crews this evening; let them know our intentions. I would like to have a meeting tomorrow on the beach with all of the island dwellers." He paused, watching the men nod in excitement.

※※※

Captain Nelson stared into the clay furnace. That day he and his three friends had been assigned to refining the sugarcane. They were boiling the raw sugar into what looked like molasses. After that, they would further refine it into rum. Since they had been on the island, Blood Bones had rotated his men's skills between the fields, the pier, and sugarcane manufacturing. It gave them something to look forward to the next day, something different that they could experience rather than the monotony of doing the same task over and over again.

"This is really neat!" Sal laughed. "I never thought I'd be on some secret pirate hideout refining sugarcane."

Harris smiled at his friend. "Honestly, same here."

Leah held a pan of the boiling sugarcane over the flames. She moved the pan back and forth, and then replaced it on the metal grate. "How much longer do we need to heat this?"

Captain Nelson snapped out of his daydream and glanced into the pan. "Probably just a few more minutes; it looks thick. We'll need to let it cool, and then we can send it over to the rum makers."

The group laughed. Just a few weeks ago they were part of a crew that had commandeered a British vessel out of the port of Boston. Their adventures had had many ups and downs so far, but all had brought them closer together.

※※※

Blood Bones and Sesostris sat together, passing a bottle of red wine between them. The wizard had been asked at dinner to bring the crystal ball with him to their meeting. Blood Bones poured a few inches' worth into his glass and then topped off his friend's.

"Thank you for joining me, as always." He paused, taking a sip. "There has been quite the development today—" he told the wizard of the treasure fleet leaving Veracruz. He told him how they would be greatly undermanned, and most importantly outgunned. "I would like to gaze upon your crystal ball again for guidance."

Sesostris nodded. "Yes, of course, Hernando." He reached down for the bundle of cloth by his feet. He placed the crystal ball on the table and slowly peeled off the layers. "Clear your mind, and when you are ready, you will see what fate has in store for you."

An image of the sea came into view. This then transformed into the rough outline of Cuba and Haiti. A fleet of ships, seen from an aerial view, came next. Blood Bones counted twelve in total. The image seemed to zip by, zooming in on the flags and pennants billowing in the wind. Spanish royal crests. The ships sailed nearly due east, hugging the southern coast of Cuba. Once at the gap between Cuba and Haiti, Blood Bones could see there a long spread of ships flying the jolly roger. The pirate ships slowly forced the Spanish ships close to the Haitian mainland. Cannons shot from the beaches. A trap had been set. The vision then shifted into images of the dark holds of each vessel. Treasure, and lots of it.

Blood Bones sat back in his chair, exhausted. He blinked a few times, ridding his mind of the flash of visions. It was similar to the feeling of having stared at the sun for too long, and then seeing images dance before your very eyes.

"What did you see?" Sesostris asked quietly.

"Many things, my friend. The treasure fleet will sail south of Cuba, not north. They will hug the coast and sail through the Windward Passage."

"Is that all?" the wizard interrupted.

"No, we bore down on them from the northwest, pushing them into *Canal de la Tortue*. We had cannons on the Haitian beaches that fired upon their ships."

The wizard nodded. "It seems that we will spring a trap upon them."

Blood Bones smiled, staring at Sesostris. "That it does."

21

February 28, 1763
Pirate Lair

"We do not have much time!" Blood Bones yelled to the full island's complement. The sun filled the eastern sky, casting a shadow upon well over five hundred pirates spread across the beach, representing the seven pirate ships anchored safely in the bay. Some of the men were missing—standing watch aboard the vessels, or at the lookout tower hidden in the foliage, to watch for approaching ships. "We have less than a month to prepare for our upcoming mission. Three weeks, men! Three weeks is all we have before we must spring into action." He let his words sink in at the haste they would soon need. "The treasure fleet will set sail from Veracruz and head through the Windward Passage between Cuba and Haiti. The only downfall is that the stretch of water is fifty nautical miles wide, so there is plenty of sea room for their ships to navigate around our trap—this means our plan needs to be well-thought out, perhaps more thoroughly than anything we have done in the past."

"Captain, what are you thinking?" Captain Nelson asked loudly, his voice carrying so that those all around could hear him. He had been used to giving orders in a powerful voice that would carry to anyone aboard a ship, no matter where they were. Faces in the crowd turned their heads from him back to Blood Bones.

Blood Bones stared at the man, this recent accomplice who had proven himself time and time again in the past few weeks. His men looked up to the experienced hand, and he was eager to hear what he had to say. "Miguel, my idea is simple, although implementing it will be quite difficult."

It seemed like all in attendance moved several inches forward, waiting to hear what their leader would say.

David Hawley cleared his throat, and then raised a hand. "If I may contribute." He waited for Blood Bones to nod, encouraging him to continue. "The Windward Passage, as you have said, is over fifty miles wide. We could possibly spread our vessels out every few miles, creating a sort of spiderweb. Once the treasure fleet clears Cuba, heading through, we can then bear down on them."

"Yes, that could work." The suggestion essentially mirrored his vision, causing Blood Bones to smile. "I was thinking of something similar, myself."

"What about creating the illusion of having more ships?" Captain Nelson looked between the pirate captain and the young sailor who had just spoken. David had a youthful tenacity that was beyond his years. He admired him for that; it reminded him of himself a decade or so earlier, when he had first made the rank of an officer. He smiled, caught amidst happy thoughts of himself as young man, shaking hands with King George II and earning his commission. Blood Bones turned to him, cleared his throat, and nodded for him to continue, bringing him back to his senses. "I've seen this done before: each vessel tows a raft with several lanterns, confusing the enemy about the size of our vessel, the amount of vessels, or even the direction we are going. It makes for slow maneuvering, but it has proven successful."

"Miguel, I like both ideas, but obviously that would only work during the night." Blood Bones stared at Captain Nelson and thought for a moment. A cloud of silence spread over the heads of the horde of pirates. He scanned the crowd of faces, and finally found the captain of a xebec, *El Viento*. He knew of that type of vessel and the high speed it could attain, making it very valuable to smugglers and pirates alike. "We will talk more of the details later. For now, we have other things to address—José Silva, you have the fastest vessel of us all. My task for you is to get underway and visit several seaports that are within a day or two's sail from here. Nothing farther. Recruit men and ships. The more we have, the better."

"Understood, Blood Bones," José Silva said.

"The rest of you," Blood Bones gestured with wide arms, "will begin to work tomorrow morning with the rising sun. I would like to construct several dozen rafts. I would also like to place a handful of cannons upon the Haitian beaches, so we will need to coordinate that. I want an inventory of the stores we have between all seven vessels, as well as what we have on the island. We will break into groups to attend to these details. We will need to also keep an eye on the movement of the treasure fleet. It will take them eight days to sail from Veracruz to the Windward Passage. That gives us until the eleventh of April before they fall into our trap!"

The large group of men cheered, eager to begin their quest for gold and glory. Their combined voices echoed off the hilltops protecting their lair.

⚜⚜⚜

Once the pirates had been dismissed to go about their duties, David walked over to join Captain Nelson and his friends.

The young man stood tall and proud. He had the light skin of an American or an Englishman. "Good morning, my name is David Hawley. I just wanted introduce myself." He extended a hand.

Captain Nelson smiled, extending his hand at the gesture. "Good morning to you, as well. My name—" he hesitated momentarily, almost giving Hawley his real name, "—is Miguel. I've sailed as captain for the last few years as an English privateer."

David laughed. "Ah, I see—." He wrapped his mind around the sight of the white-skinned man standing before him. Then name clearly did not match the face. He smiled. "—and then you went rogue?"

Nelson thought about the statement, but there was much more to the story than he was going to tell a new acquaintance. "I suppose you could say that. Fate has a funny way of changing a man's destination. Your vessel will be steering a course, and you will attempt to correct for set and drift, but more often than not, something outside your control will bring you elsewhere. You just need to hold fast, and enjoy the ride that is life."

David paused for a moment, digesting the man's words. "That was well said and quite true." He extended a hand to the others, introducing himself. Harris, Sal, and Leah each took turns giving him their fake names. At each exchange, a twinkle sparked in the young man's eyes. *Clearly, they are escaping from something*, he thought of his new comrades.

After the greetings were finished, David gazed back at Captain Nelson. "I was born and raised in Connecticut. My family ran into—a few hiccups—with English law. My family told me to stay home and adjust to their laws and rules, but I just couldn't have it, so I found a berth aboard a pirate ship and have grown to like it! I wanted to be free of English bonds then. With each day, my disdain for their rule grows!"

Captain Nelson noticed a twinkle in the man's eye as he said that last phrase. It inspired him, for he too had had that fire in his chest since King George III had not stuck up for him. They had been friends for years. He had served the king's grandfather before him. It hurt knowing that it had all turned out to be just a *façade* of smoke and mirrors. He had been used by the king, and carelessly thrown to the ground like scraps to the dogs. He had been pegged as a traitor by an unfavorable court decision, and sentenced to death. What if the curse of Blood Bones had not transported him from the gallows in London to the future, essentially saving his life?

He smiled at the irony, as he was now serving the very same pirate. "And tell me David, what is it that you aspire to? What would you wish to happen in the colonies?"

The young man thought for a minute. A smile creased his lips. "A revolution. Independence for the colonies. A new nation!"

What the man said would be considered treason anywhere else, and punishable by death; but then again—they were pirates, bound together by loyalty, blood, and brotherhood.

Images of what could be fluttered before his eyes. Captain Nelson instantly liked the man and what he stood for. A man's beliefs are a testament to their character, and he knew at that moment that he and David would become good friends. "Even though I am an Englishman by birth, I do look forward to the day that the thirteen colonies become independent of British rule. An ocean separates them from their tyrant, and that is too far a distance for him to play puppet-master."

"An Englishman named Miguel. I find that quite interesting." David teased. "But I am sure you have stories that you will share with me when the time is right. I could complain of British rule for days, but let us get to work. We've much to do," David said with a smile. "Do you have any specific design for the rafts?"

Captain Nelson took a kneeling position in the sand, and indicated for the group to join him. With his finger he traced a rough square, about a foot in size in the sand. "Just your standard raft. I'm picturing a design of roughly eight feet by eight feet."

"Okay," Sal said, nodding.

"Do you think we should make it bigger, though?" Harris inquired.

Captain Nelson shook his head. "No, I do not think so. We will have a central mast, which would carry the lantern, so the structure needs to be large enough to accommodate that without flipping over. I have a good understanding of stability, although I have no exact formal training with it."

David laughed.

The group looked at David with puzzled faces. "Do you find something funny?" Captain Nelson asked, not sure whether David was mocking him.

"I studied advanced mathematics at King's College on the island of Manhattan. I was there for two semesters before the little incident that was the—catalyst—for my becoming a pirate. I was in the top five percent in my class each year, and excelled with the calculations of construction and stability." He let his words sink in with the group. "Shipbuilding has intrigued me since my younger years. I have always been drawn to the sea; it is in my blood."

Captain Nelson closed his eyes, recalling various dates and names in his head. "I do recognize your surname. It rings a bell."

"Yes, shipbuilding is quite the small circle. My great-great grandfather was a well-known shipbuilder. Various members of my family followed suit, and it was passed down from father to son, uncle to nephew until I had my hands on an adze at the young age of seven. Shaping the wood that would comprise a ship, it is such a great feeling—like contributing to something bigger than myself." David stared off into the distance, reliving memories from years past. They were happy memories, causing a smile to form on his face.

Leah stared at the young man. He was handsome in his own right, obviously very smart, and clearly confident with his abilities. David was about the same height as Ben, with sandy blond hair, as opposed to Ben's dark locks.

Harris caught her staring at David, and wondered what she was thinking. He knew that she loved his brother beyond a doubt. She noticed Harris looking at her, and then smiled at him. "So, it seems that we should have an easy time constructing the rafts, since you are such an—expert with these things."

The group laughed, enjoying Leah's joke. "Absolutely! Since the rafts are solely for distraction, we can get away from having exact measurements. Between the five of us, we should easily be able to make a raft a day. If we planned on using the rafts to hold us in them, we would have to take our time to make sure they are seaworthy, but these are purely for illusion."

"Well said," Captain Nelson said. "I suppose we could take our time and make the rafts capable of holding us, just in case something happens. It's always better to be prepared for the worst."

"So, let us begin then!" David replied, eager to show off his skill. "I am a perfectionist in any case, so I will not settle for mediocrity."

❈❈❈

Blood Bones walked with Sesostris between the various groups about the island. He had assigned a group to organize their stores, counting the quantity of gun powder, balls, and cannons they had, as well as various tools and weapons that would be used in the assault. Next, he talked with each ship's captain and discussed the layout of each vessel. How many cannons? How many able fighters aboard? What speed could each vessel attain? Things of that nature.

They walked through the sugarcane fields, content with the work still in progress there. Blood Bones then led his friend back toward the beach, and caught sight of the five men huddled around a raft.

"Let's see what Miguel and the others are up to," Blood Bones said, leading the way through the dense underbrush that separated the sugarcane fields from the beach.

Sesostris nodded, allowing Blood Bones to walk ahead. They walked quietly over the white sand, their approach masked by the soft earth below their feet.

Leah had her back to the woods and out of nowhere, a shadow appeared on the raft, startling her. She swung a hammer lightly, knocking in a nail, but at the last minute gasped in surprise and hit her fingers.

"Ow!" she yelled. "Damn!"

"Sorry to startle you!" Blood Bones said. He stood a few feet away from the raft, and all of the men around it turned toward him. "I just wanted to check on your progress."

Leah squeezed her fingers tightly. After a moment, she looked down. They had begun to swell, but there was no blood. "I am sorry for cursing, it just hurt so bad!"

Blood Bones bellowed in laughter. "Look around, my *dear* Luis—" His words lingered. "—you are amongst pirates. You *are* a pirate. Curse like one!"

Sesostris smiled and moved forward to contribute. "Bloody hell!" he yelled loudly.

Blood Bones smiled. "Yargh! You scalawag!" The group now stared at Blood Bones. "It's your turn, Luis. Give it your best shot!"

She thought for a moment. She had been raised as a proper lady: she had been trained on harpsichord from a young age, she was well-educated, had gentle mannerisms, wit, and feminine beauty. She hid the latter behind several layers of clothing, her blonde locks beneath a watch cap, and walked with a different gait from the ladylike form she had taken before. She had been very careful to keep her speech minimal, speaking only when spoken to, and even then, mostly in grunts and mumbles. Now she had been put on the spot. Blood Bones nodded, urging her to participate.

She closed her eyes, recalling a certain passage from her favorite William Shakespeare play. "Thou mewling, sheep-biting hugger mugger!" A giggle escaped her lips once the words rolled off her tongue.

Blood Bones laughed loudly. "Ah, it seems you are well-read! William Shakespeare is one of my favorite playwrights!"

Harris and Sal exchanged a sideways glance. Blood Bones was certainly a unique individual.

Blood Bones skirted the group and then touched the raft, running his fingers over the edge. He looked left and then right, gazing at the structure. He nodded, pleased with the construction.

"How much longer will it take?" He asked of no one in particular.

David stepped forward. "Just another hour or so." He looked up at the sky, gauging the amount of sunlight remaining. "I would like to conduct a trial before sunset."

Blood Bones nodded. "Excellent. If it is not too much trouble, could you find me prior to it? I would like to observe."

"Absolutely. Will you be in your quarters?" Captain Nelson said, representing the group.

"Yes, I have some things to attend to," Blood Bones said, looking at Sesostris. "I will see you all later."

Blood Bones signaled the wizard, and the two left, maneuvering along the beach to continue their walk. They checked on the other groups before returning back to his shack.

※※※

By the end of the day, the group of five stood in front of the raft. They held their tools in their hands and examined their work. It seemed they were all content, and all that remained was to place the raft into the water and see if she floated.

Blood Bones and Sesostris stood a dozen paces behind, watching the group. As the sun kissed the western horizon, the group carried the raft toward the water's edge. Leah led them while the four men had their hands on each corner. The central mast on the raft was eight feet high, but had a slide adjustment on it so it could be rigged to different heights. There was a spoke to hang a lantern on to replicate the running lights of a vessel underway. They placed the raft into the calm water and pushed it a few feet out. Once Captain Nelson and Sal were knee deep in the water, they let the raft float free from their grips.

Blood Bones and Sesostris joined Leah and Harris.

"Let's push it out a little farther," David said. He stood with one foot still on the beach, and one foot in the water. The raft was now floating in a few feet of water. His hands were on his hips as he studied its buoyancy. He looked at the freeboard, and did a quick calculation in his head. "It should be sturdy enough to hold one or two of us."

"I'm already wet," Sal said. He looked over to Captain Nelson. "Can you keep it steady while I climb on?"

Captain Nelson spread two hands wide, maintaining the raft's balance, and carefully, Sal climbed onto the raft, swinging his legs up. He reached for the mast and then squatted, keeping his weight low. David watched with curiosity, noticing the change in displacement as Sal's weight bore down upon the raft. It sunk a mere half inch. He nodded. "Excellent! Miguel, will you join Salvador on the raft?" David moved forward, steadying the raft while Captain Nelson maneuvered gracefully onto it.

Blood Bones watched happily as the craft held the two men easily. "Let's see how many it will hold!" he bellowed loudly, causing everyone in the group to glance back at the pirate. "Come on now! I don't have all day! There is much for us to do!"

Harris then stepped into the water, heeding the command. He climbed onto the raft gently, taking a spot beside Captain Nelson and Sal. Next, Leah climbed on, perching beside the huddled trio. David remained in the water, holding the raft. He looked back at Blood Bones and Sesostris on the shore, where the calm water gently lapped at their toes.

"Are you content, Blood Bones?" David asked.

Blood Bones smiled and shook his head. "No! I believe there is room for one more!"

David laughed and then pulled himself on, taking a position just beside Leah and Captain Nelson. David was just out of reach to have a hand on the mast, so he tried to balance himself by placing his hands on the raft's planks. With no one holding the raft steady, it began to drift away slightly. Blood Bones laughed into the wind, overjoyed with the display. "That will suffice!"

Blood Bones smiled, placing a hand on the wizard's shoulder. He whispered in his friend's ear. "Watch this!"

The pirate captain charged forward, splashing through the water. He lifted his knees and forced his way to the raft, and then gave it a hefty shove. David fell sideways and then began to swing his arms in an attempt to steady himself. Everyone watched as he teetered on the edge, then fell into the water with a large splash.

Once David stood up and wiped his face clean of water, he laughed loudly. He ran his hands over the crest of a wave with a cupped hand, splashing everyone within a ten-foot arc. That was the catalyst—then Sal charged forward, wrapping his arms around Harris. They fell into the water beside David, and began to wrestle.

Blood Bones watched his crew goof around, enjoying a few moments of relaxation. Once they calmed down, the head pirate stood with his arms at his sides. He was completely soaked; Captain Nelson had leapt from the raft and knocked him down playfully.

"Men, I am very excited with the raft! I want more! Dozens more!"

The group smiled. Eager to continue serving Blood Bones. Captain Nelson nodded. Bones had rewarded their good work with compliments, and even partook in several minutes of fun. *Being a pirate isn't half bad*, Nelson thought as they pulled the raft back onto the sandy beach.

22

March 3, 1763
Pirate Lair

At the morning meeting, Blood Bones met with the five remaining ship captains. José Silva, captain of the xebec *El Viento*, had left several days earlier to recruit for the upcoming mission and had yet to return. The men were seated around the table as usual, and they stared at their leader, who paced slowly back and forth.

"Men, I am quite content with our progress," Blood Bones said with his arms crossed in front of his chest. "The rafts are coming along nicely, and are even strong enough to hold five people. The design is simple, but sturdy."

"That is good!" another of the captains said.

"Yes. I believe the rafts to be capable of much more than we originally intended, but I am not sure for what purposes yet." He paused, turning over something in his mind. He would meet with Sesostris later to discuss his latest thoughts about the rafts. "We have inventoried the stores aboard ship, as well as the island's excess material. We have plenty of cannons to spare, which we will install on the northwestern beaches of Haiti and also on Tortuga. We'll have a ship anchored at the end of our trap, pointing an entire broadside at the enemy ships."

"This sounds like it will be a massacre!" a captain said.

"Aye! And make us quite rich!" another boomed with laughter.

Blood Bones smiled. "I would like to careen each vessel. We'll need each vessel to be as fast as she can be. She must dance on the waves. We must evade the escorts, and lead them into the trap. It is paramount to the success of our mission. I do not wish to have an all-out battle against their entire fleet."

"That can be done! We have the men! We have the time!" a man yelled.

Blood Bones nodded. "We have a few more weeks to prepare. I would like to move the cannons into position within the week. If you can all attend to the careening, that is my first priority at the moment."

He dismissed the captains, and then poured himself a glass of red wine. There was something still that needed to be addressed—the other use of the raft. He considered the issue for the rest of the day. And then the solution finally came to him.

✖✖✖

David and Captain Nelson stared at the half-completed raft. It was time for lunch and Harris and Sal had begun cleaning up the mess, picking up used tools and stowing them in a leather pouch. Leah kept busy cleaning the work area with a broom, sweeping shavings into a pile. It wasn't a necessary chore, but Captain Nelson had preached keeping a clean ship, so the group practiced similar beliefs. They would get half an hour to relax and eat.

"Good work, everybody," Captain Nelson said. He took out a leather pouch, drinking a long draught of water from it. "Constructing this latest raft is going much more quickly than those of the past few days. We should finish an hour or two before sunset at this pace."

"I noticed that, too. We are getting more systematic," David replied. He took a few steps forward, and then got sidetracked by what was going on in the anchorage. A vessel, a sloop by the look of her, had been run dangerously close to the shallows. High in her masts, lines were run to the shore. He could see Blood Bones coordinating the efforts.

Leah stood beside David and pointed. "What are they doing?"

"Careening," David said simply.

"It's quite a feat, truth be told," Captain Nelson said to the group. Harris and Sal had never seen this done, and were both looking with opened mouths.

"That's really cool!" Sal said. "What are they doing?"

Captain Nelson stared at David. "Do you want the honors? Or shall I give the lesson?"

David laughed, displaying a full set of white teeth. "I will take this one!" He looked between Sal, Harris, and Leah. "So, I'm sure you've all heard of barnacles?"

The group collectively nodded.

"Well, as a ship moves through the water, if there are barnacles that cling to the hull, she moves more slowly. It's good practice to scrape the barnacles off. It can make a difference in battle. Every knot the ship below your feet can do may decide whether or not you will survive the day, or be buried at sea."

Captain Nelson smiled at the young man's knowledge. Although only twenty-two, David showed the promise of a good officer, and had that fire in his eye that Nelson admired. "Well said. Let's pay a visit to Blood Bones."

The group of five walked past several other groups of pirates at their campfires. Some were working, others were napping. As on a ship, life at the pirate lair went twenty-four hours a day, seven days a week—everyone with a different schedule depending on the day.

※※※

Blood Bones stood alongside a long line of men, roughly twenty-five in all. Sesostris stood beside another line of the same amount. Together, the two groups heaved to a cadence. "One-two-three-pull!"

The sloop was tilted to roughly forty-five degrees, exposing her outboard side and planks. Men stood in long boats, scraping at her barnacles with files. It was difficult work—slow and tedious. The fifty men on the ropes held the boat in position for over an hour before they were given the command to pay out. Hand over hand, the men let several inches of line pass through their hands. The sloop regained its position, and then would have to be turned around so that its other side could be scraped.

Blood Bones wiped a sleeve on his brow, pleased with the manual labor. As any good leader, he was standing beside his men.

He had his back to the beach as the group of five approached. Even though there was a lot going on around about him, Blood Bones heard the crunch of sand and turned quickly.

"Miguel, David," he said. Then he smiled at the others, who stood several feet behind. "How is your day going?"

"We're on pace to finish earlier than over the past few days. The rafts are coming together quite nicely," Captain Nelson reported. He was proud of his group, and very content with their work.

"Excellent, Miguel." Blood Bones paused, thinking of his newly developed idea. "I am very pleased with the rafts, but I have thought more on the matters of their usage—"

"Yes?" Captain Nelson interrupted. "Anything you need, it is yours."

That brought a smile to his lips. Blood Bones continued. "Well, once waterborne, would it be possible to—perhaps—explode?"

David thought for a minute. "A timed fuse?"

Blood Bones closed his eyes, replaying the vision that had come to him earlier. "Something to that extent." He looked over to Captain Nelson. "Do you gentlemen think it possible?"

Captain Nelson glanced at David, and he nodded. "Anything is possible. We just need to put our heads together."

Blood Bones smiled, appreciating the man's demeanor and confidence. "Continue making the rafts as you have been doing, but I would like to modify one or two."

"Understood," Captain Nelson said. He made eye contact with

David, and then turned to Leah, Sal, and Harris. "We will take our leave then, Blood Bones. We have much to do."

✖✖✖

Captain Nelson bent over the half-finished raft. David stood beside him. Both were trying to figure out a way to fulfill the captain's request.

"If you all can continue with the raft, David and I will work on the new task assigned to us," Captain Nelson announced.

The trio went on with their work, and David stepped back a few steps to get out of the way. He sat in the sand, cross-legged, and took out a little notebook. He began sketching diagrams of a raft, and two kegs filled with gun powder. Next, he sketched a vertical tube. He added a lever, and then next, a striking mechanism that would shower a tar-sealed cloth.

Captain Nelson looked on and smiled, realizing what the young man had just designed. "So, once she is waterborne, the water shoots up the tube, moving the lever?"

David nodded. "I've done similar things before, using a float. The water pressure rises, causing the float to move with it. The lever would then move. We just need to figure out a way to create enough of a striking force to set the gun powder alight."

The two talked of details, and began experimenting with various methods, learning many ways of not succeeding. But, they only needed to succeed once and then to replicate it.

23

March 16, 1763
Pirate Lair

Harris and Sal were standing watch in the lookout tower when two sets of sails came into view. They gazed through their telescopes and saw the white canvas of *El Viento*. Several hundred feet behind there was a second vessel in its wake.

"It looks like José Silva recruited a ship and lots of men," Harris said. There were several dozen men in the riggings, and more walking about the decks. "Sal, go find Blood Bones and let him know that *El Viento* is back. They're about two miles out." He saw the white caps, and estimated the wind's speed. "Maybe like twenty minutes or so until they pass through into the hidden bay."

"Roger, I'll go now. See you soon, buddy." Sal moved around the open space of the lookout tower, and then lifted the trap door that led to a ladder below. He disappeared out of sight, and Harris continued looking through his telescope, watching the two vessels move closer to the shore with every passing second.

※※※

Blood Bones now had eight vessels at anchor in the secret lair, all willing participants in his venture. He smiled, walking before the seven other captains present for their meeting. "We are just about to set our plan into action. We now have more men and ships than previously anticipated, which will go a long way when the time comes. We are almost finished with our rafts, and we have something clever up our sleeves in the works. I would like to stage the cannons this week, so we will distribute our men and resources. The treasure fleet gets underway from Veracruz in just over two weeks."

The other pirate captains bellowed in laughter.

"Let us make fools of the Spaniards!" one yelled.

"And all those who cross our paths!" Blood Bones replied. He held his left hand high, and rotated the scarlet stone upon his finger. The stone glowed with life.

David finished installing the final product. This would be the first 'live fire' exercise. They had informed Blood Bones that they would commence the test at sunset. He gauged that the timing sequence would last a minute, which is not a lot of time in the heat of battle, but at the same time, a minute could seem like an eternity when blades and bullets are aimed at you.

He picked the worst-constructed raft, and Captain Nelson helped place the barrels of gunpowder on it. Sal and Harris secured the barrels off with several knots. Leah aligned the striking mechanism, which led to a piece of metal. Below it, a freshly tarred cloth sat, ready to catch the sparks.

"Are you all ready?" David looked around. They had positioned the raft on the edge of the shoreline, and once Blood Bones had signaled them to begin the demonstration, the group pushed the raft out into the water.

With haste, the group continued out into deeper water. They waded until it came to their chests, and with one last shove, let the currents of the bay welcome the raft. The float rose inside of the hollow pipe, causing a lever to sink, striking the metal, spraying the tarred cloth with hot sparks. Moments later, the sparks caught on an exposed trail of gunpowder.

The two casks caught fire, and exploded with a large concussion. The raft itself leapt up off the water several feet, breaking in half and sending pieces of wood in all directions. Wooden boards sailed over the heads of the retreating pirates, who were now only twenty feet away. They dove into the water, escaping the splinters that would have showered them.

Moments later, as they stood up from the water, Blood Bones was clapping his hands at the display. A large smile covered his face.

"Bravo!" the pirate said. "It looks like everything is falling into place!"

✖✖✖✖

David held the chicken thigh to his mouth and nibbled at the smoked meat. He took a sip of grog and wiped his face of the juices. "I am very pleased with how that went."

Captain Nelson nodded. "As am I." He stared off into the setting sun and then turned his attention back to the group. "You have earned my trust, David. I would like to share with you the true story behind my little group of misfits."

David glanced into the fire for a minute, and watched the flames dance on the wood burning inside the ring of stone. "Thank you. I would also like to share the tale of how I became a pirate."

"You go first," Captain Nelson said. He reached forward and placed another log on the fire. "Our collective stories are quite lengthy."

The group laughed, and then David began his tale.

"Well, as I've mentioned, I am from Connecticut. My sister is several years younger than I, and as she was walking home one afternoon from the market for a quick errand, several soldiers decided to—attempt to have their way with her."

Leah shuddered; memories of the very same kind clouded her eyes with tears.

"Luckily, I was splitting firewood nearby. I saw the soldiers make their advance, but I didn't think twice. I usually kept to myself. But then I saw my sister's face, and I could not let their assault go unchecked."

The group edged forward in their seats, intrigued by David's story. He would be a great addition to their band of ill-fated sailors. "Well, I approached the soldiers from behind and I attacked them violently. I knocked them to the ground one by one so my sister could escape, but then ran for it. I ran and ran, until I couldn't go on any farther. I fell asleep in the bordering woods and returned to my home the next morning. My father was not happy with my actions, and he commanded me to not voice my opinions about the British rule of our colonies, even thought the actions of those soldiers were deplorable. My father was very loyal to King and Country, and very stubborn. He pointed to the door, and I obliged."

"Wow," Sal said, stumbling for words of encouragement. "I respect that you stood up for what you believe in."

Silence lingered, and then Sal turned his gaze to Harris, as if prodding him to begin their own story. But where should they begin? They had gone through so much since discovering the cursed treasure of Captain Blood Bones.

Harris cleared his throat, and then spoke for nearly half an hour, telling David their true identities, of their adventures, and of the twists and turns that fate incessantly brought to them. By the end of the story, David stood from his seat and walked around the campfire with his hands on his head, overwhelmed. After several passes, he sat back on a log.

"I knew there was something different about you all. I just never thought it could be—that!"

24

April 11, 1763
At sea

The first row of Spanish sails came into view in the last rays of sunlight. The sun had just kissed the western horizon, and Blood Bones smiled, waiting to engage the Spanish fleet. He stood atop the uppermost crow's nest, allowing him to see farther than if he stayed on deck. Days earlier, they had arrived at their position. Their men had been distributed between the eight vessels, as well as at the cannons placed on the Haitian shores.

He climbed the tarred rat lines slowly, joining Captain Nelson by the windward railing. The wind carried the sea spray up to them, and he licked his lips, savoring the salty taste.

"Miguel, there is nothing better than the taste of the sea upon your lips, with the one exception of a bottle of red wine!" Blood Bones laughed into the wind. "Are the men ready for the engagement?"

Captain Nelson nodded. "Yes, we have been training with the timing sequence for our secret weapon. They know what to do."

"Good!" Blood Bones stared off into the distance. "We will parallel their course for the duration of this watch, and then move in for the kill."

The bow lookout of the lead Spanish escort scanned the horizon with his telescope, starting dead ahead and then moving slowly to starboard. Content all was clear on that side, he reset his gaze back to dead ahead, and then moved slowly to port. One point off the port bow, he saw something. A light. He continued scanning the horizon, seeing another one. And another. And another. Lights filled the entire port side, several miles off. It was hard to tell the distance, as the horizon had faded to nothingness. He rang the bell to give warning to his shipmates.

Moments later, the captain came on deck. The bow lookout pointed off into the distance. He stared through his own telescope, and his expression turned sour upon seeing the rows of lights spreading across the vast horizon. "*Zafarrancho de combate!*" Prepare stations to combat!

He shook his head, knowing that a fight loomed in his not-so-distant future. The lookout gripped the lanyard of the clapper and rapidly rang the ship's bell five times, at five second repeats. Men came out of the woodwork, securing the vessel for battle.

※※※

Blood Bones had his ships spread out, each with several rafts towing behind. Seven of the pirates' ships were this part of the plan, while one remained anchored at the end of *Canal de la Tortue*, finalizing their trap. Their vessels skirted just out of cannon range, but they remained visible. Sometimes, he knew, just making a presence was enough. As seen in the vision, the Spanish vessels sailed onward, altering their course to starboard slightly, heading toward the western spit of Haiti.

"Let's shoot a few warning shots, let them know we intend to make our move soon," Blood Bones said after a long silence. He heard the ship's bell toll the time, and smiled.

Captain Nelson nodded. "I will relay the message."

Blood Bones watched the man head below decks. Moments

later, he saw the muzzle flash of the cannons below his feet. The ship recoiled with the broadside, and off in the distance he could hear the splash of the balls hitting the water. They fell a mere fifty yards away from their targets.

He placed his telescope to his eye, and saw very little of the damage he inflicted. He could see the outline of the vessel slowly alter course again to starboard, aiming the bow toward *Canal de la Tortue*. It seemed that the Spanish had no intention to fight, only to run closer to land, and that brought a smile to his face. His visions were quickly becoming reality.

✖✖✖

Hours passed as the pirate vessels closed in, shooting a broadside here and there. Just as soon as they were within range, they would back off. Soon Blood Bones was ready to deploy the explosive rafts against the Spanish escorts. He sent men above, climbing the tarred ratlines into the vast expanse of sail.

"Put out every extra inch," Sesostris ordered with a loud voice. Men scattered to and fro, tending to the request. The wizard then moved beside Blood Bones. "For this to work and for us to remain unscathed, we need to sail perhaps another knot or two faster."

Blood Bones nodded. He held up his left hand and revealed the scarlet stone upon his pinky. He closed his eyes and then mumbled a prayer. As if God, himself, was listening, the wind picked up, causing the vessel below to surge forward.

Blood Bones stood beside the helmsman, and the man pointed the *Courtesy*'s bow in front of the lead Spanish escort. Though the vessel aimed its cannons at HMS *Courtesy*, the angle of its approach was too steep and the gun carriages could not hurl their ammunition effectively. Balls splashed here and there, but none hit home. He pressed his telescope to his eye, gauging angles and distances. He did some quick mental calculations and called for an adjusted course once again.

Thirty minutes later, his vessel had closed the gap to just a few hundred yards. The darkness masked most of what was going on around them, but several lanterns here and there enabled him to make out figures moving to and fro on the deck of the Spanish vessel.

There were several muzzle flashes and the retort as the Spanish fired. Bullets flew across the deck, finding home in the wood, but no one was hit. The *Courtesy* sailed forward, inching closer to the bow of the Spanish vessel. The large cannons below decks still could not hit them from their approach, but several swivel cannons had been repositioned. Moments later, a whizz of balls flew through the air. Blood Bones ducked just in time to avoid decapitation.

"It will take more than that to best me and my men!" he yelled, laughing into the wind.

✖✖✖

HMS *Courtesy* crossed the lead vessel's bow by just hundred feet or so. The Spanish continued shooting pistols, rifles, and swivel cannons at the ship, doing only minimal damage. They were too distracted by the fleeing pirate ship to realize a floating object lay in the water dead ahead, decreasing in range. With every passing moment, their ship bore down upon the raft.

Once waterborne, the raft's timing mechanism set off the chain reaction, and just a minute later, the burning trail spread to the two casks of gunpowder. The vessel's bow crashed directly into the raft just as the explosion occurred. The bowsprit flew upward, tearing sail and rigging. Men were hurled about from the initial explosion, but that was only the beginning. Planks ripped inwards, leaving a large hole, inviting the seas to enter the Spanish ship. The ship shuddered, and the captain ran across the deck to find out why.

As he made it to the bow, the deck slanted dangerously forward. The weight of the incoming water pulled the entire forward section of the ship down, placing stress on the wooden frames and timbers. There were several loud snaps below his feet; it was too late. His ship had just broken in half and quickly began to sink.

"To the boats! To the boats!" He fell to the deck and slid into the gunwale. His body cartwheeled over the side and vanished into the water below.

※※※

Blood Bones scanned the scene behind him as they sailed away to the starboard side of the Spanish fleet. "Helmsman, let's beat to starboard. I would like to cut off any possible escape. We are nearly in sight of the island of Tortuga."

Captain Nelson gazed at the battle unfolding behind them. Several pirate ships had moved in to engage the escorts, while some engaged the galleons. They exchanged broadside after broadside, aiming for the sails and rigging. The pirate ships did not want to risk damaging the large treasure hidden in the depths of each Spanish vessel. Their tactic urged the Spanish to escape toward the supposed safety of *Canal de la Tortue*.

"It looks like they are taking the bait!" Nelson yelled toward Blood Bones.

The wind suddenly shifted, and the ship lurched forward sluggishly as the helmsman fought with the wheel, forcing HMS *Courtesy* to turn back toward the oncoming Spanish ships. With the shift, they lost a few knots in speed. Captain Nelson looked up and saw the white sails fluttering.

Blood Bones saw this and smiled. "Not to worry!" As before, he revealed his scarlet stone, and it beamed, lighting up the deck like a beacon. Harris, Sal, and Leah were only a few paces away. The combination of the power of the cursed medallions around their necks and the crimson journal in Captain Nelson's pocket all merged together, creating a beautiful display of light. Blood Bones whispered something, and moments later, the wind seemed to shift again.

"Oh my!" Leah gasped softly.

Tortuga was now in sight, and the Spanish vessels sailed directly into the trap, thinking they would evade the pirates, but oh, were they wrong.

Gun crews from the Haitian beaches, from the island of Tortuga, and the anchored vessel at the eastern end of *Canal de la Tortue* now focused their cannons and aimed their fire at the one remaining escort ship. The remaining Spanish vessels followed the escort into the mile-wide gap between the mainland and Tortuga, and then realized there was no escape. The vessels now tried to tack back out to the safety of the sea, but suddenly, the wind died to near-nothingness.

Blood Bones laughed loudly, and his voice carried to the Spanish sailors across the way. It was over before it had even really started.

25

April 17, 1763
St. Augustine

Sixteen new ships sailed into port that morning. Blood Bones met with the members of the captured Spanish ships, and gave the men of those crews three options: to become slaves, to die, or to join him as pirates. As always, those loyal to their king or queen lost their lives by the blade, while others who were a bit more morally flexible joined their ranks. All in all, the pirates had lost very little; there had only been a handful of deaths and injuries from stray cannon balls.

It was now time to bury their immense treasure.

❈❈❈

Blood Bones called the cadence as the rowboat propelled forward toward the egg-shaped island. He stood tall and proud by the tiller, leading a fleet of rowboats laden with treasure as far as the eye could see. From the sixteen vessels he now commanded, they had utilized each and every available long boat for the effort.

Harris and Sal looked at each other in shock, as Roosevelt Island grew larger with every pull of the oars. This was now the second time their eyes had gazed upon the familiar beach in this time period. They had last seen the island just a few months ago, showing Blood Bones the cavern system that they had discovered back in modern times, at the beginning of their eventful adventure. This time, however, Benjamin Manry was not present. They pulled on the oars, knowing that once this part of their mission was done, they could cross the Atlantic Ocean and rescue Ben and the others at the gallows in London.

For the past few months, Captain Nelson, Leah, Harris, and Sal had worn disguises. Each moment of each day, they had performed the duties of fearless pirates, serving under Blood Bones. They had even convinced themselves that they were capable of such things, and in doing so, sparked a new type of thinking amongst themselves. The group had also met a young rebel named David Hawley. Their small and loyal group had taken to the twenty-two-year-old and his hatred toward the British.

"Let's go, men! We're almost there!" bellowed Blood Bones over the steady noise as each paddle broke the water's surface, moving the longboat ever closer to its destination. This time around, Blood Bones navigated them through the waterways that led from the port of St. Augustine to the island a few hours away.

The sun had just reached its zenith in the sky as they arrived on the beach of Roosevelt Island. Two boulders marked their landing, as if greeting them for the next leg of their journey.

Blood Bones jumped out of the boat. "Excellent! We made good time. It was a fair distance from the port, now let us begin!"

The groups pulled their longboats out of the water onto the beach. Boatload after boatload discharged; the pirates soon filled the beach.

Captain Nelson exchanged a glance with Harris, Sal, and Leah. He nodded, giving them each a little boost of encouragement for what would occur next.

The pirates hooted with excitement, eager for their own personal share, as well as for burying the treasures that had accumulated during their recent adventures.

Leah removed her watch cap, and ran a hand through her shaggy blonde locks. She missed her long hair, but not as much as she missed Benjamin Manry. She thought of him often enough, and the thought of saving him from the gallows in London kept her head held high. The transition into becoming a pirate had perhaps been the most difficult for her. Harris and Sal had seemed almost too eager at the prospect, and Nelson, being an English privateer with a Letter of Marque from the king, had already been given permission to plunder. Now he just did so for the personal gain of the pirates, rather than only commandeering the goods of enemies of the Crown.

Harris looked up at the protective canopy of the trees. He unsheathed a blade and followed the rest of the pirates as Blood Bones led his party into the thick vegetation. Some men were ordered to stay behind, guarding the boats and treasure, and to make a camp.

Thirteen pirates hacked wildly, slicing and dicing at the new undergrowth, making slow and steady progress toward the center of the island. They followed the remnants of the trail made several months before.

※※※

The entire afternoon passed before they emerged into a clearing. Just ahead, the opening of a menacing-looking cave lay before them. The group froze in place, jaws dropping as they scanned the ten-foot-high mouth of rock in the hillside. It was almost as if the rock face smiled in welcome.

"We shall camp here for the night," Blood Bones glanced at the diminishing sunlight above. "We will recommence in the morning. Gentlemen, good work. Until then, let's get a fire going and the tents set up."

Within a half hour, several strips of spare sailcloth had been stretched between tree trunks, creating rude shelters. A fire sparked as fresh wood popped and hissed.

Captain Nelson sat on a log beside his close friends, prodding at the fire with a stick. Jugs of grog and strips of salted meats were passed between the sailors, and soon enough, song and dance filled the small camp.

※※※

"I put my hand upon her toe. Yo ho! Yo ho! I put my hand upon her toe. Yo ho! Yo ho! I put my hand upon her toe she said hey sailor you're way too low, get in get out quit fucking about yo ho, yo ho, yo ho!" Sal bellowed the first stanza to the fabled sea shanty. The area around the fire was crowded with singing and dancing men, each member taking a stab at the song.

Leah had perfected a deep, raspy voice that fooled all those around. She joined in on the song and the crowd let out a booming cheer. She smiled at a ridiculous thought that filled her head: *I wonder if my parents, or even if Eve would have picked me out of this crowd to be the respectful Leah Highmore*. She shivered at the thought of that name, mentally scratching out the hated surname. *Leah Williamson? Hmm, how about Leah Manry?* She beamed a smile at the thought, so bright it would equal the light of a full moon at perigee. Harris saw her smile, and waved a friendly hello to her.

The stars soon seized control of the sky. Captain Nelson glanced skyward at the Big Dipper. He followed the pointer stars toward Polaris. He let out a large, content sigh. He then shook hands with Sal, Harris, David, and Leah before turning in for the night. Slowly, one by one, the members of the entourage followed suit until all was quiet about the camp.

※※※

Two men stayed awake, maintaining the fire and keeping a lookout. This watch rotated every four hours, until the camp slowly awoke as the sun rose the following morning. Breakfast was cooked quickly, with a portion of piping hot coffee or tea, mixed with a small portion of rum for each member of the party. The pirates filtered past the cook, Sesostris, at the fireplace to get their share. After half an hour, Blood Bones stood to address his men.

"Gentlemen, we have made good progress thus far. Today, I would like to venture on and explore the island and the cave system in more detail." The pirate leader glanced toward Sal and his friends. "Finish up breakfast; we enter the caverns in ten minutes."

The camp hurried about their business, readying for the day's adventure. Harris wound a strip of tarred cloth around a long stick. Sal followed suit, creating several torches for the expedition into the dark and musty caves.

Nelson and Leah gathered their meager belongings and joined the other two.

"Are you ready to do this again?" Harris asked Sal.

He shrugged his shoulders. "It's going to be weird, man!" Sal paused. "We're going to be burying the treasure we find back in modern day."

Harris laughed. "Yeah, tell me about it. I still can't comprehend this!" He paused. "All right, we've made a bunch of these torches. That should be good for now."

Captain Nelson nodded. "Good; how many have you made?"

Harris placed a hand over the pile, counting each wooden shaft. "Sal and I made three each. Six in total."

David looked up from a pile at his feet. "I also made three."

"Excellent! I'm sure Blood Bones will be pleased." Nelson reached down to help the group carry the torches to where the pirates were assembled outside of the cavern's entrance.

Off in the distance, Blood Bones stood with a large smile plastered across his face. As his hand reached across to stroke his goatee, he paused, catching a glimpse of the scarlet stone upon his pinky finger. Once all his men were present, he lit one of the handmade torches, and was the first to enter the first cavern. The remaining men quickly followed.

The flames from the torchlight pierced through the darkness. Ahead, the group could hear the gurgling of the water that carved through the cavern system. They inched slowly toward the edge, casting torchlight down toward the foaming waters below. On the other side, a faint outline of solid rock could be seen. Blood Bones squinted, using his nautical eye to gauge the distance.

He tossed the torch in his hand across the gap, and heard the sound of the wood bounce off the rock. The clatter caused his men to shift their gaze from the waters below to the rock opposite them. The flames illuminated the entrance to another cave system across the gap, and it dawned on them that they could not progress any farther.

"Men, we had to climb down, cross through the water, and then climb the opposite wall. It is just a temporary hindrance. Not to worry, we shall prevail, as we always do!"

A man raised a hand to volunteer. "Excellent. We'll need a length of line to start out with. After that initial line is set up, we will follow with three more. A simple wooden-board foundation and rope hand lines could be easily constructed. Let's get back to work!"

The men roared in approval. All were eager to call the cave system their hideout.

✖✖✖

The man who'd volunteered reached down to the edge of the rock platform. He turned his body around and then slid his feet down. The fall was roughly fifteen feet, and to just jump down would probably not be wise. He worked in dim lighting, for the torches cast only a shadow upon his hand and footholds, but it was enough to allow him to work slowly and methodically. The man then crossed through the still waters and climbed the opposite wall. With every step forward, another figure would pay out a coil of line.

Several minutes passed as all watched from across the gap. The pirate stood heroically, smiling at his shipmates.

"I made it! Toss me another torch so I can find a place to secure this rope."

At the request, a torch was hurled across the gap. After a few minutes, the end of the line was secured to a stalagmite. The pirates spent the remainder of the day constructing the bridge that would lead them further into the cave system of Roosevelt Island.

26

April 19, 1763
St. Augustine

Blood Bones stood before a group of men at the campfire. He walked back and forth with a large smile on his face.

"Men, excellent job yesterday. The rope bridge is sturdy, and will speed up our process as we continue farther into the cave system. Tomorrow morning, I would like a group of you to explore the water source. Find where it comes from, and see if we can make some rapids!"

Captain Nelson laughed and nodded. "I'll volunteer," he said, looking at his group of friends. Sal, Harris, Leah, and David all agreed consent. "We'll report back to you with our findings."

Blood Bones tended to some details about the campsite, leaving the rest to finish their breakfasts and gather their things before work started for the day.

"Yeah, when we first discovered the treasure, we had to cross over a pretty ridiculous river," Sal said, chewing a mouthful of salted meat and a biscuit. "There were spikes and whatnot sticking up from it."

"Yeah, there was even that impaled body!" Harris chipped in.

Leah shuddered at the imagery her friends were painting for her. Harris noticed this and shrugged. "Sorry."

Leah smiled. "Pirates—remember?"

The group shared a long laughed. As one, they stood, ready to continue work in the cave system.

※※※

Captain Nelson held a torch high above his head, casting a glow into the dark cavern.

The group trekked through various caves, following the water that trickled at their feet. For hours they walked, until they came to a large obstruction. It looked like there had been a cave-in. Boulders and smaller rocks filled the expanse, and through the gaps, water dripped in slowly, and then puddled up where they now stood.

"So, I guess this is the end of the—tunnel," Sal said with a serious voice.

Harris moved forward, placing a hand beside the miniature waterfall. He looked back the way they had come from, and noticed the gentle downward slope. "Yeah, this is definitely it."

"Blood Bones wants us to make a raging river," Captain Nelson said, looking between the group. Their flickering flames caused shadows to dance on the walls.

"I think we will need to remove this wall." David knelt down, looking at the various gaps of boulder and gravel. "It can be easily done. We'll need to have a measured explosion, unless we decide to dig."

"I think we should totally blow it up!" Sal laughed.

Harris playfully pushed his friend. "Of course you would."

"All right, let us return to Blood Bones with the news. I am sure he will be content with our findings." Captain Nelson's voice echoed off the walls, and then he led his expedition party back slowly through the various tunnels that made the cavern system.

※※※

Blood Bones nodded throughout Captain Nelson's report.

"Excellent, Miguel," he said. He stroked his goatee for a moment, deep in thought. "I would like to bring in all the treasure first, and set up all the booby traps." He closed his eyes, remembering a vision he had earlier. "Have Hector and Salvador create a map of the island. I would like David to be in charge of the measured explosion. Sesostris is working with a group of men on the trapdoor."

Blood Bones was referring to the black and white mosaic that would be created as the second phase of the booby-trapped cave.

"It looks like everything is falling into place!" Captain Nelson smiled.

"That it is!" The duo laughed; their voices carried through the tunnels.

27

May 21, 1763
St. Augustine

Just over a month passed as the pirates continued to make improvements to the secret lair of Roosevelt Island. The rope bridge now had two iron loops that had been driven deep into the stone. The ropes that held the bridge were secured to the metal loops, which Blood Bones had requested at the last minute. A mosaic with white and black tiles had been created, with the missing pieces strategically placed about the island, according to the map that Harris and Sal created. A geared door directly behind the mosaic was constructed, with the key to opening it being the missing tiles that were strewn about the island. Once the lettered tiles were inputted into the correct slots, the sequence of gears would shift the immense stone door that blocked off a narrow path, completely ending the treasure hunt.

After the booby traps were tested and deemed worthy, Blood Bones than orchestrated the massive effort to offload each longboat, and bring the treasure deep into the cavern system to the six smaller caves at the end of the tunnel. Treasure chests containing gold, silver, rubies, and various treasures from Central America, as well as colonial taxes filled the treasure rooms to the brink.

"Are you ready?" David said to Blood Bones and Captain Nelson. "I was able to create a delay of about fifteen minutes. It was tough to get one longer than that with the materials I had. We'll have to stage the fuse about fifty or so feet away. Once we light it, we need to get the hell out of the caves, at least to the rope bridge where we'll be out of the path for the water. It'll be cutting it close!"

Blood Bones smiled. "If we didn't cut things close from time to time, things would be uneventful, and life would be boring!"

Captain Nelson laughed, appreciating the pirate's humor. After having served the man for the past few months, he had grown to like and respect him. He now considered him a good friend. Each night, for the past several weeks, the two would talk long into the night of battles, strategies, and of the many *what could be's* of life.

"Ready when you are," Blood Bones said.

The group watched David work his magic. His fingers navigated through a series of checks, and then once content, he lit the fuse. Once it caught, he placed it lightly on the ground and for a moment, watched as it moved forward slowly.

In a gentle voice, which quickly progressed into a yell, he said: "I think it's time to RUN!"

The trio ran through a series of tunnels, entering larger lobbies, and hanging lefts and rights marked with torches showing them the correct path.

Captain Nelson had an excellent sense of the passing of time, and once his internal clock hit the mark, he looked back over of his shoulder. There was no sign of an explosion just yet, and he shrugged, unsure of whether something had befallen the timed fuse, or if his internal estimate was off. Just after his head returned forward, the reverberations of an explosion shook the walls around him. It had taken a few moments to catch up, but once it did, dust filled the space around them.

They ran as fast as they had ever run in their lives. Blood Bones held a torch in his hand, but the flames flickered to near-death as his arms pumped with his quick gait. Realizing the torch's purpose was now null and void, he tossed it aside. His eyes followed the arced path of his throw, and he realized that they truly were cutting it close.

What had only minutes ago been a gentle stream, maybe an inch or two deep, was now a roaring force of water to be reckoned with. The water level already rose up to their knees, and the trio continued forward, racing against fate.

※※※

"I wonder what's taking them so long." Harris wondered.

Sal and Leah leaned against the rope bridge. Sal scanned the well-lit cavern. Lanterns and torches hung here and there, splashing light around. All of a sudden, several torches danced with a forceful emanation of wind.

"What was that?" Leah gasped.

And then the deafening echo of the explosion reached their ears.

"Holy crap!" Sal yelled. There was now a loud gurgling sound that filled the tunnel that led to where they were.

Harris looked down, noticing the stream bed rising, slowly at first; but with each passing minute, it rose inch after inch.

Sal stared across the gap to the opposite ledge. From his vantage point, he could see the water rising against the black rock. The water level was now roughly four feet high, and he turned his attention back to the source of the disturbance.

Three figures bobbed as the water carried them into view. They were half-running, half-swimming, but totally at the whim of the powerful flow.

Harris instantly ran out onto the rope bridge and lay down, reaching down. "Reach for my arms!"

Their heads bobbed up and down as the water ripped through the tunnel, but the trio managed to center their advance and as a group, grabbed hold of Harris's extended hands.

Sal joined the effort and pulled Captain Nelson up first. Blood Bones fought against the current, holding one of the timbers that made the floor of the rope bridge. It took a few moments to pull them up, but David and Blood Bones made it to the safety of the rope bridge. They lay sprawled out beside Harris.

Blood Bones turned his head and with a sarcastic smile caught David's full gaze. "Well, that was certainly eventful!"

❈❈❈

Later that evening, Sesostris and Blood Bones navigated the depths of the tunnels into the last one. They placed a chair in the middle of the room. Inside this last room, there were only three chests. Two were fully laden with booty; the last was empty.

Blood Bones took a seat in the wooden chair, and allowed Sesostris to move about the room at his whim. "I am ready when you are," the pirate said to the wizard.

"Aye, just one more moment," Sesostris said. He had a satchel slung across his chest and removed his crystal ball. "I will no longer be needing this. I believe this is the end for me. I would like to take my earnings somewhere and just live out the rest of my days in peace and quiet."

Blood Bones smiled, nodding at his old friend. "So be it. You have earned it!"

"Thank you. Your words are kind, and you have been one of my closest friends for a very long time." Sesostris closed his eyes and placed both hands on the crystal ball, which lay amidst its pile of rags.

He hummed for a moment, and then spoke in a strange language. When his eyes opened, only the whites showed. His pupils hung back in his skull, which shook as a mysterious power radiated outward from the crystal ball.

Blood Bones remained in the chair, watching. He looked at his scarlet stone and saw that the glow was stronger than he had ever seen before.

Nearly ten minutes passed as Sesostris mumbled words of an ancient language. Without even looking, his fingers found a lone medallion, a crimson journal, and a magic staff with a glowing red stone-piece. His hands stretched outwards, and it seemed as though the power from the crystal ball flowed through space and time into his body. The energy filtered through the wizard's body, and then his eyes suddenly opened. The pupils vibrated violently, as light shone out of his hands. The light connected to the three objects lying on the floor and once it faded, Sesostris seemed normal again. He no longer mumbled, and he craned his neck, as if stretching out a kink in the muscles there.

"It is done," the wizard simply said.

Blood Bones stood from the wooden chair, and as he stepped away there remained in the seat what was almost a negative of him: a perfect replica of his body, though just a haze of colors and energy, appeared to sit quietly.

The curse of Blood Bones had finally been cast.

28

May 22, 1763
St. Augustine

The pirates retraced their path back to their ships at anchor in St. Augustine. They had followed a code of honor serving under Blood Bones: Although only a select group had been inside the cavern and knew of the trap's locations and the correct paths to avoid it, every man had a fully laden purse after their successes.

Captain Nelson stood before Sesostris and Blood Bones. He extended his hand. "Thank you again, for everything."

"I am sad to see you and your friends leave, but I know that it is important for you to do so." Blood Bones gripped the man's hand, and shook eagerly. "I have asked the captain of *El Viento*, José Silva to take you and your friends forward on your journey. He is at your complete and utter disposal."

Leah stepped forward, realizing that within the hour, they would be aboard the xebec sailing for London. That meant they were one long step away from saving Benjamin Manry at the gallows. They had just over a month to transit the ocean and get there in time. She extended her hand and gripped the man's weather-worn hand. The pirate smiled. "It was *my* pleasure."

The others exchanged polite farewells with Blood Bones and Sesostris. They had learned a lot from the two. Even though Captain Nelson had also always planned strategically prior to battle, and also drilled his men on routines, the pirates were more democratic in nature, and far surpassed any naval or army detachment their group had run into.

They boarded *El Viento* and waved one last good-bye toward the anchored ships in the harbor. *Castillo de San Marcos* faded from view as the sails caught the Gulf Stream, and the vessel propelled forward toward their destination across the Atlantic Ocean.

29

June 26, 1763
London, England

A man with a booming voice began to read out the death sentences before the large crowd. Leah pushed her way through the crowd even though her tears had already started to flow. From her viewpoint, it looked as if they were already too late. Several bodies swung limply as the clicks of gears brought the ill-fated sailors to meet their makers one by one.

❈❈❈

Ben closed his eyes—a slight prayer escaped his lips as he awaited his fate. It would be only a few moments until his very world would cease to exist; a life that yearned to be lived would end with the clicking of a gear below his feet.

Men and women from all over England had come to witness the demise of this certain group of heroes. Their fates had been sealed by order of the king, the very same king who had caused them to attempt the treasonous assassination in the first place.

❈❈❈

A journalist for a Spanish newspaper looked on from the crowded courtyard. He was translating the death sentences verbally while his assistant penned the deliverances.

"…como Las multitudes chillaron fuera, algunos oran que El perdón para los ocho hombres acerca de cuelgue para la traición. otros gritan fuera para sus muertes, una muerte lenta e inevitable. seguro, los pAgadores de impuesto son trastornados con las indulgencias recientes de primer ministro, pero quizás estos Hombres trataron de tomar cosas en propias las manos. cualquier su historia es, ellos no lO estarán compartiendo en comida nocturna, paRa las baterías empieza su golpe constAnte mas otra vez. sus autorizaciones y las oraciones son leídas, pero entonces hay un viento rápido que lleva a través de la plataforMa. las batas son erizadas como un rasgones deslumbradores de lA luz por la muLtitud. yo, yo mismo, me caí hacia atrás como tropecé en el temor. o trabajo de la magia o el Diablo que yo no puedo decIr, pero en ese destello de energía dos Cuerpos desaparecieron. seis quedado, columpiando sin vida como la multitud chilló EN la incredulidad en el espectáculo, lA naranja y desvanecer amarillo de resplandor lentamente en este día, 26 Junio, **1763**."

The hidden message, *"Le Ahora Maldicen a 1763"* carried to the ears of all those around. The first click of a gear sent a sailor on the far left to his slow, choking death.

✖✖✖

Leah continued her mad dash through the crowd as Harris and Sal followed on her heels. Captain Nelson was several yards back, trying to catch up. They were all dressed the same—in the cloth of the British Royal Marines. No one looked twice at them, as there were other soldiers throughout the crowded courtyard.

She heard another loud click as the man beside Ben fell; the noose tightened around the man's neck and she watched the sailor struggle with his last breath before his kicking legs fell limp. She saw Ben's eyes close one last time in silent prayer.

Several hundred feet away, Captain Richard Highmore's fiery

locks bounced when he nodded with approval. In a quick backward glance Leah saw her husband's wicked smile, as well as her very own blonde locks whipping in the breeze around her very own body. Her pace slowed down considerably. She quickly glanced away, filled with the weird sensation of being able to view herself standing there, but not.

As Leah focused solely on Ben the floor beneath him fell away and the noose around his neck tightened with a quick jerk.

※※※

Ben let out a yelp of pain as his body jarred from the drop. His pulse pounded intensely, sending a fresh rush of adrenaline throughout his body. This extra energy caused his dangling hands to move from his hips to the noose around his neck. He managed to slip a few fingers beneath the tight rope, allowing him to take one deep breath before his grip slipped. This intake of fresh air gave him an extra surge of hope. He heard the mixed approvals of the crowd as he struggled to survive.

A gaoler dressed in black stood. "Someone not accepting death, eh? Well, I will see about that," the man muttered as he moved down the platform to where Ben continued his fight for life. He kicked every few seconds, as if treading water. He was not ready to die.

The man brandished a sword, rearing it back, ready to take Ben's life. He swung the sword back and forth, putting on a show for the crowd as they cheered loudly. He tossed the sword from hand to hand, swinging the blade occasionally as Ben continued to struggle.

Ben's feet kicked back and forth wildly, struggling for each and every breath.

Leah was now within arm's length of the platform. She reached to her neck, feeling for Ben's golden medallion. She remembered every conversation she had had with Sal and Harris about their travels and about the medallions' part in them, and something deep inside her knew to remove Ben's from around her neck. She held it tightly in her right hand as her view of Ben disappeared when the black-robed gaoler stepped in front of him.

She crashed into the wooden platform, grimacing in pain at the sudden stop, and the necklace flew out of her hand. The medallion sailed though the air and bounced several times on the wooden platform, sliding past the feet of the gaoler by mere inches.

✖✖✖

The black-robed man had removed a foot-long stick from inside a deep pocket of his robe. His smile was hidden beneath his hood, but his eyes gleamed with blood lust. Highmore, his commander, had told him that Ben was a fighter and had foreseen the young sailor's unwillingness to succumb to the slow, choking death.

As the gaoler tossed the wooden stick up, his right hand quickly snapped the sword through the air, cutting the stick in half. The crowd screamed and cheered at the demonstration. The sharp blade glistened in the sunlight.

Ben's rapid kicks and desperate clawing at the noose slowly diminished in intensity as the moments trickled by. Strength was leaving him faster with every second that passed. It was only a matter of time before he succumbed.

But something caught his eye—a familiar metallic object slid toward his feet. He looked down and identified it instantly—it was the cursed golden medallion that had transported him back to the eighteenth century. His eyes quickly scanned the immediate area, and to his astonishment, he saw Leah. He saw her blonde hair just as the black-robed man shifted in his approach. The gaoler slowly brought the hilt of the sword sideways, ready to begin the swing toward Ben's midsection. The entire crowd seemed to cease breathing in their excitement for the final kill.

The medallion at his feet began to glow a bright orange, and he heard segmented words in Spanish carry to his ears.

"*Le ahora maldicen a 1763—*"

Three beams of spiraling orange and yellow light linked together, with a greenish mist emanating from the crimson journal that Harris, also now nearby, carried tightly in his hand. The lights from the objects blinded the crowd as they became one, sending a roaring wind throughout the crowd.

Ben added all the pieces together, knowing he had not a moment to lose as he watched the gaoler prepare for the arced swing with his sharp blade. Ben ceased his kicking and managed to lift and bring his feet together around the medallion, lifting the medallion up in an upward flick. The medallion floated high enough for Ben to reach out for it with one hand. Letting one hand away from the noose for this sent Ben struggling downward yet again, but he held out with all his strength as the fourth and final phase of the curse of Blood Bones took place.

The gaoler's blade whipped around as the crowd screamed anxiously, awaiting blood that would surely come. But just as the blade arrived at where Ben's midsection should have been, all that surrounded him disappeared. His world spun about, a kaleidoscope of bright colors and a network of unearthly energies.

30

Modern Day
Roosevelt Island

A squirrel sat atop a log with the day's harvest of acorns. The animal looked up as a bird began chirping a beautiful tune from high in the treetops. The island was peaceful as usual, but then as the bird's song came to an end, three figures warped through boundless time and space. A vortex of yellow and orange light and green radiating energy stirred up a violent wind outside the cave. The dirt and leaves surrounding the entrance to the subterranean maze swirled around as if a tornado was blowing through.

Ben, Harris, and Sal fell out of thin air, crashing into the bushes that bordered the cave's entrance. Ben's body slid to a halt. It took him a few moments to piece everything together. The last he remembered he had been holding a medallion firmly in his hand as a gaoler whipped around a blade, about to end his life. He reached down with his free hand to feel at his ribcage and was content to find no blood or any sign of injury. But upon further inspection, a blade had clearly cut through nearly all the material that hung loosely around his body. His shirt was literally ripped to shreds.

Sal stood beside Harris.

He grabbed at his shins, cursing loudly. "It's a shame we can't control our landings—I think I landed on a rock," he complained.

Sal slapped a hand on his friend's back. "Hey, there's a rumor going around town these days. Apparently girls really like boys with scars; hopefully you can finally get one!"

Ben ignored them. His brain was processing everything that had just happened. He looked around and took in the surroundings. "Whoa guys, look.," He pointed forward. Three pairs of eyes turned toward the mouthlike cave that stood awaiting them.

"Is that what I think it is?" Harris smiled, placing his outstretched arms on Ben and Sal's shoulders. "Are we back on Roosevelt Island?"

"Harris, Sal, I think it is. We might finally be home, back in our own time," Ben said, pausing as he realized that his past and future lifestyles were veering rapidly apart on two separate courses. He slipped the medallion into his pocket and felt for Leah's necklace around his neck. "At least I have had some great memories," he added in a whisper.

"Ben, do you remember how I was the one who was leading us into here the last time?" Harris paused, awaiting his younger brother's nod. "So, much has changed since then."

Sal and Ben both nodded. Their eyes met.

"It all began at this cursed island, it's all going to end here," Ben said as he moved to the edge of the dark cave. "Come on, guys, let's go. I've got a weird feeling that we should keep going. You know? We can't just turn around now."

Harris and Sal both nodded, signaling for Ben to once again take the lead.

Ben remained where he was. He closed his eyes, whispering a silent prayer. He wasn't afraid of what lay before him, but at the same time, he sensed something looming dangerously ahead. He took a deep breath and opened his eyes, trudging forward into the darkness with Sal and Harris quick on his heels.

After only a few paces, the group stopped. It was pitch-black inside the cavern. Harris bumped into Sal's back, causing the two to curse loudly. Ben turned around to look at his friends, but could barely see even his own outstretched hand.

"Come on guys, we've come so far already in our little—or

rather—our adventure. We can do this!" Ben said with a smile—that no one could see.

As Ben turned back, he caught something in his peripheral vision. From the distance he couldn't tell exactly what it was, but as he moved closer he could feel his jaw drop with the recognition of what hung on the cave's wall.

His fingers moved through the pitch-black space and he gently grazed the patterned glass, the flint-wheel, and the clever design of a lantern that had been designed by Leah's brother.

Ben removed the lantern from its hook. He held the base lightly in his hand, stunned by the irony of the situation.

"How did this get here?"

Two figures emerged from behind and stared at the object.

"What's that?" Sal asked.

Ben paused, waiting for something to formulate, and the words eventually came. "Um, well. Okay, I've seen this before—I've even touched it. Leah's brother made this!"

Harris interrupted his brother. "Wait, what? Really?"

Ben nodded and continued. "Yes. Here, let's see if it works. We could really use some light. I can't see anything in here."

Ben felt for the string that connected to the flint-wheel. Studying the contraption he opened the glass slightly and pulled down on the string. The flint-wheel struck the steel striker and the tarred cloth caught several sparks. Instantly the wick lit and the lantern emitted enough light for everyone to see Ben blink away several tears of happy memories.

"Are you okay, bro?" Harris clapped him on the shoulder.

Ben sniffed a few times, clearing his head. Soon he was ready to continue their adventure. "Yeah, I'm fine. Just reliving old memories, you know?"

"I hear you, bro," Harris said.

With renewed vigor, they moved quickly through the sloped tunnels. The lantern cast enough light for the group to comfortably move through the cave system. Up ahead, they heard a familiar gurgling sound. Ben moved through a corridor and paused at the edge of the underwater river system. Three pairs of eyes readjusted to the new scenery, and to their astonishment the rope bridge that they had once crossed was no longer there. Instead a wooden structure spanned the raging rapids below. In the dim lighting they could make out the sharpened poles impaled corpses.

"Whoa, a wooden bridge!" Sal laughed with delight. "This wasn't here the first or second time we were here!"

Ben looked at his friend with confused eyes. "Wait, what second time?"

Sal turned to Harris then back to Ben. "Do you want the honors?" he directed the question to the older brother.

"Well, I don't really know where to start to be honest," Harris began, waiting for something remotely sensible to come into his mind. "You died, man, and Leah had your medallion. Remember when we were all captured in Sherwood Forest by Leah's husband and his men? Well, I managed to escape without being seen. Leah was a spectator at the execution. I ran through the crowd to try and save you and the others, but the curse was set before I could get to the gallows. I guess you could call it the second phase. Anyways, as I was saying, you died."

Ben looked confused. "I don't get it. I am alive now. This is so weird," he said. He closed his eyes, trying to comprehend how the curse actually worked. Back in time, and now forward in time? Did he miss out on another back and forth that Sal and Harris, and apparently Leah, had gone on?

Harris reached into his pocket and extracted the crimson journal, the cursed book that held the countless secrets of Blood Bones.

"Yeah, it's all in here—Nelson had this and we read through it a few times to figure out how the curse worked. So, since Leah had your medallion, Sal and I had ours, and Captain Nelson had the journal, we were all sent forward in time while you dangled from the noose."

Ben stared at his brother. "Obviously you came back then, so that was the third phase, correct?"

Harris nodded. "Yes, I guess. So, as we figured out how the curse worked, we managed to go back to 1763, but we ended up being sent to *La Monzón*, too early to go right back to you, and across the ocean."

Ben closed his eyes for a moment, calculating a convergence of times, events and ideas.

"Okay, so you're saying the four of you lived among Blood Bones? How did he not catch you?"

Sal put a hand on Ben's shoulders, giving Harris a break from the long explanation. "Well, to be honest, I think he kind of knew why we were there. He would always look at his ring and smile. He never threatened us or anything. It was kind of weird, but awesome at the same time." He paused for a moment, collecting his thoughts. "He was sort of the coolest pirate I've ever met. Leah cut her hair off, wore several layers of clothes, and barely ever talked. We went completely under pirate-cover."

The thought made Ben chuckle. As if he were looking through a kaleidoscope, he envisioned scenes mingling with friends and foes. "Okay, so then you came back to the island sometime after?"

Harris nodded, "Yeah, we actually were standing beside Blood Bones as he commandeered the HMS *Courtesy* out of Boston Harbor. We sailed to their lair, stayed there for a bit and had this epic battle versus a Spanish treasure fleet. It was crazy!"

"So, that must have been when we were shipwrecked the last time on the uncharted island with the Iraja and Hetra?" Ben asked with a puzzled look on his face. He thought of the friends he had made there. Those warriors had been brave and fearless. He looked back at his friends.

"Yeah, at least on a calendar." Sal shrugged.

"Okay, I guess you guys can tell me everything later. Let's continue," said Ben as he held the lantern in front of him. He moved forward, leading the way over the wooden bridge.

Through several more tunnels the adventurers traveled, following the walls until they emerged into a central cavern. As before, there was the mosaic of a skull and bones set into the ground below their feet. It seemed as though the mosaic was nearly complete, with only four empty spaces. Three of them were only a few inches in circumference, slightly larger than a coin; the fourth missing slot was rectangular, the size of a small book.

"Is anybody getting that weird feeling again?" Ben asked. They all looked at each other, completely confused.

"Someone's obviously been here since we buried the treasure—" Sal's words drifted into nothing.

A wicked smile began to form as Ben slipped a hand in his pocket, removing the golden medallion. He bent over and placed his cursed prize into an empty slot, and the gold metal glowed orange and yellow. Harris and Sal moved to the two remaining circular slots and inserted their medallions. Once done, they looked at Ben, watching as the leader of the group placed the crimson journal in the fourth and final slot. A mist of green colorful light hovered over the mosaic. The yellow and orange light slowly began to rotate as the energy emitted began to recede to the far wall.

They stared at each other before speaking.

"Wow, this is just, wow," Sal managed as his jaw dropped.

"Ben, what are you thinking?" Harris nudged. "Should we take the items with us?"

The younger Manry sighed. "I don't really know! I mean the door or opening might close. We know we have that one last obstacle left. I mean this last one and the bridge practically are the same, just more advanced. You know?"

Sal and Harris nodded. "Better to be safe." They all grabbed at their medallions.

"Okay, you're right. Let's go!" Ben said, moving toward the gap in the wall. His friends followed closely as Ben made his way to the next obstacle. As before, a tunnel ended abruptly in a rough circular area. Ben yelled at the top of his lungs and the echo radiated upwards through the vertical shaft.

"Great, we just need to find the way up," Ben started to shrug as Sal nudged him on the shoulder.

"Already found it. Take a look," Sal said with one hand gripping a rope ladder that hung against the rock surface in front of them.

"Too bad this stuff wasn't here the first time." Harris smiled.

Ben then had another slightly odd feeling. *Maybe it was here all along*, he thought. He shook off the recurring *déjà vu* and gripped the rope ladder at about shoulder height. He put his foot on the second rung and began the climb.

"Come on guys, we're almost there." He heard shuffling below as he swung his body over the edge of the rock wall several moments later.

Ben awaited the arrival of his friends, and as he shifted his weight anxiously he brushed a hand against an old wooden desk. As before, there was a message pinned to it by a sharp knife. Beside the note, there was another lantern with the same design as earlier. Ben moved forward and lit the lantern. The group inched closer to the desk, eager to read the message.

The penmanship looked very familiar.

Ben tilted his head for a closer look, and something about the way the i's were dotted, and how the t's were crossed jumped off the page at him.

"Are you okay, bro?" Harris asked.

"Yeah, I'm fine. It's just, weird I guess. You know—how all this panned out and all?"

Sal and Harris both placed comforting hands on their awestruck friend.

"All right, come on, let's keep going," Ben sighed.

They followed Ben again and slowly emerged into the tunnel that led to the treasure rooms. The three adventurers paused at the opening of the first cave.

"Do you think all the treasure's going to be gone?" Sal stared into the darkness that loomed ahead.

Ben looked at Sal and deeply sighed. He shook his head in utter confusion. "Yeah. I mean, someone's obviously been here since our first expedition and your second trip here. You know?"

Harris nodded, casting a shadow onto the wall from the light of the flickering flame held by his brother.

"I guess it wouldn't hurt to look, right?" Sal shrugged. "Who knows, maybe we'll become millionaires and never have to go back to high school!"

The brothers smiled, appreciating Sal's humor even through the ups and downs of their adventures. They made their way into the first treasure room. This time there was nothing but a layer of dust on the cavern floor. They exited the first room, and made the rounds of the next four.

"You were right, Miss Cleo Manry," Sal laughed, teasing Ben.

Harris boomed with laughter, slapping his brother on the back. "So, what's your prediction for the sixth and final room?"

Ben closed his eyes. Technically, he was looking into the future, predicting what would happen when they walked into that final cavern. But, as they had been here before, at least their combined memories survived.

"I don't know, but everything we've been through was because of this last room. It all started there, and I think everything will end there. Come on, let's go," Ben stated, itching with anticipation.

He held the lantern high in his hand, walking forward behind the protection of light that it emitted. A chair remained in the center of the room. From this angle, the young adventurers could only see tattered old clothing on a long-dead body.

The three figures moved forward, angling their path around three chests that lay at the feet of the skeleton of Blood Bones. The scarlet stone upon the famous pirate's left pinky finger glowed with eternal life. It sparkled as Ben passed the lantern before the skeleton for a closer look.

"Yeah, that's Blood Bones all right, and exactly where we first met him," Ben said as he heard his brother clear his throat from behind.

"Hey, remember there was only one chest the first time?" Harris called as he bent over to examine the chest at his feet.

Sal began to do the same, leaving Ben to check the last one for himself.

"Okay, three chests, three of us, one skeleton," Ben mocked their situation, causing his friends to laugh.

"Wait, look in the center of this forward edge. It's where a lock should be, but there is none. It's—" he paused in confusion, "—it looks the same size as the medallions!" Ben said as all three closely examined their respective chests.

"Holy shit. This keeps getting weirder and weirder," Sal chipped in.

"You're telling me," Ben replied. "All right. Let's see what's inside." He placed his medallion into the slot in the wooden encasement. He heard a metallic click inside the chest, and then watched as the lid sprung open.

Before he'd even glanced in, he heard two more clicks and the excited yelps of Sal and Harris as they dug their hands in, each finding themselves elbow-deep in a chest laden with treasures. They pulled out strings of pearls, crowned rubies, and gold coins. Ben saw the excitement on his brother's and best friend's faces.

Finally, he concentrated on the chest at his feet. Oddly he was actually not surprised at all to find it barren of any treasure. Inside sat a lone medallion, a crimson journal, and a staff with a glowing red head-piece. As his hands touched the objects, he sensed a powerful aura radiating from each item. He looked up and noticed Harris and Sal at his side.

"Well, we can share our treasure with you." Sal smiled, placing a coin against Ben's chest.

Ben laughed, grabbing the coin from his friend's hand. "I definitely did not see this one coming at all!"

Harris chuckled, "The better question would be—did you see any of this coming?"

The three laughed for what seemed an eternity, but then they stopped as a sudden chill emerged into the room. A slight breeze ruffled the hair atop each young man's head. The glow of that familiar energy circulated through the room as all four parts of the curse began to feed off each other. The scarlet stone upon the skeleton's hand burned a bright red. Ben could feel the energy emitted from the head stone atop the magical staff flow through the open space. He looked down at the crimson journal and was not surprised to see that it, too, seemed to have an energy to it that flowed as if the cover was made of a thick and deep red liquid. All three components hinted to one thing, and that one thing alone. As Ben grabbed the medallion and placed it around his neck, he heard a moan that made him shiver. It was an unearthly howl, and the hairs on his neck stood on end. His gaze shifted from his brother to Sal.

And then it came, an unexpected, loud boom of laughter as the skeleton slowly came to life. Blood Bones's fleshless mouth moved, as if crunching on empty air, and somehow the lungless creature produced howls of laughter that seemed to shake the very walls.

Their gazes remained glued to the figure sitting before them. Its milk-white bones began to disappear, giving way to sinews, muscles, and veins that grew out of thin air. The room about them spun wildly as the ethereal display of lights and energy reformed the being that was, and now became, Blood Bones. A long lock of dark hair appeared from beneath the hat that covered the tanned skin of the Spaniard. His twisted smile set the three adventures stumbling back in shock. A goatee formed around his mouth. It was as if nothing had changed about the man's physical presence since the last time they had seen him.

"Do not be afraid, my friends. I will not hurt you!" Blood Bones laughed. "Why would I hurt you, for you three are my saviors? You have saved me from a lifeless life, and now you have given me a deathless existence—immortality. The curse that I had created so long ago has now at last worked."

Ben moved forward. "But, I've seen you die. You perished before our eyes by the noose in Boston." Blood Bones smiled, enjoying the forward movement in Ben's step.

"Just as you also died, Ben. You are as much a part of my curse as I am. We now have grand powers, the powers of the Gods, if you will. I, the power of eternal life, and you—the power to freely travel through time at your whim. You have a destiny to fulfill, but alas, you will figure that out for yourself soon enough. Keep what is in each chest—," he said, looking at Sal and Harris, "—as a reward for your loyal service." Blood Bones winked at them. He stood and stretched over two hundred years' worth of cracks from his ancient bones. After a smile, the cursed pirate turned and began to walk out of the room. "I bid you gentlemen farewell. Perhaps our destinies will cross paths once again, maybe in this world or in the next, at some other time and place." He took a large bow, spreading his arms wide and leaning forward with a smile on his face. "But until then."

He snapped back to his full height and swept a hand through the air in a large and overdramatic wave. The group stood motionless in the center of the cave. As Blood Bones stared at the trio, he removed the ring from his left pinky and flicked it up. The scarlet stone radiated a glow as it flipped and somersaulted through the air.

Ben watched as it spiraled toward him slowly. He reached a hand out, and the ring found a home on his finger effortlessly. A sudden surge of power swept through his body, causing him to stand to his full height. His chest stuck out with great pride. Throughout his body he felt each strand of muscle grow just a little bit more. Each contraction of his heart pushed fresh blood filled with oxygen throughout his body. He felt stronger, more alive than any time he could ever remember. He felt like a god, no longer a mere mortal.

The figure of a laughing Blood Bones glittered off the scarlet stone as one of the two destined ring bearers vanished into the darkness.

Harris bent down toward the lantern that sat between the chests. He picked it up and then moved beside his brother. Ben stood there, eyes transfixed by some distant point in space or time. With a nudge from his brother, Ben shook out the cobwebs of thought from his mind. The lantern cast a loom of light as the brothers watched Sal move to his treasure chest.

"So, what now?" Sal smiled as he extracted a diamond the size of his fist.

Ben remained silent, unsure of how to react or even what to say. He couldn't accurately describe how he felt. He just knew that he felt completely different in every way possible. He stared down at the scarlet stone and his eyes noticed the mirror-imaged B's of the setting that held the precious jewel. The ring fit far too well for it to be purely coincidental. The pirate's last comment about Ben being as much a part of the curse sent a wave of shock through his body.

Harris nudged his brother again. "Come on, buddy, what's wrong?"

Ben remained standing there, looking at the back wall. Then he made a decision. "I need to get out of here. Now. I need some fresh air."

Sal placed the lantern atop his treasure chest and began to walk through the entrance slowly. Harris picked up his chest and followed quickly at Sal's heels. As the two figures left the dark space, Ben moved to the remaining chest and reached in, hurriedly grabbing the remaining three objects.

He followed his friends out and with one last look back, noticed an odd and eerie mist lingered in the cavern.

☠☠☠

Margie Manry sat perched like a queen atop her wicker chair on the porch. She was deeply content, reading the book in her hands. Her husband was in the living room watching Saturday college football, while her son Harris and his best friend Sal had gone off on a weekend canoeing trip to Roosevelt Island. She sipped from her iced tea and allowed the refreshing liquid to tingle her lips before looking back down at the book in her lap. Before she could begin reading again, she heard the excited ramblings of three figures coming up the driveway.

They were carrying the canoe up the path as she called out, "Harris, honey! Is anything wrong? I thought you'd be back tomorrow afternoon!"

Harris hesitated, not sure of what to say. As his eyes drifted from his mom on the porch to Ben and Sal in front of him, he suddenly realized they were still dressed in garb from the eighteenth century.

Ben carried the canoe while backpedalling up the familiar path. He had walked down that driveway countless times. He called over his shoulder to answer his mother's voice.

"We rowed into a submerged tree. We think we did some damage to the canoe," Ben answered quickly, explaining their early return.

"Oh, hello, Sal," Margie Manry called out as Ben shifted to the side, allowing his mother a view of Harris and Sal. "Oh, Harris, who's your friend? I thought just you and Sal went on the trip."

Ben turned his head, surprised that his mother failed to recognize him in his untidy attire.

"Hello there! I'm Margie, Harris's mother. What's your name?"

"Uh," Ben paused in his footsteps, causing Harris and Sal to almost drop their end of the canoe.

Harris saw his brother's blank expression. "His name is Ben. Where's Pops?"

Ben heard his mother's voice over his shoulder again as she answered her son. "Pleased to meet you, Ben." She looked at Harris with a smile. "*Your* father is inside watching the football game. Why don't you put that heavy canoe down by the shed and come on inside for some lemonade and some sandwiches!" she paused, carefully studying her son and his friends. "What on Earth are you all wearing?"

They looked at each other rapidly before Sal broke the silence. "Oh, it's some new fishing gear—you know, state of the art, so fish don't see us."

Margie Manry smiled, buying Sal's frantic excuse. The three exhaled with relief as they moved around the house toward the shed.

"Sal, don't try that excuse on *my* dad," Harris laughed.

Harris paused, noticing something was wrong. He gazed at Ben, aware that something was bothering him.

"Mom—didn't recognize *me*," Ben said slowly.

"Maybe she just didn't see *your* face clearly?" Harris replied.

Ben shook his head. "I don't know, bro. It's like I don't exist."

Sal nudged them forward. "Come on, guys, this canoe is heavy. It feels like we've been carrying it *forever*."

✖✖✖

After covering the canoe with a tarp to hide the treasure chests, they ran into the house through the back door and up the staircase that led to the second floor. As Ben passed each picture frame on the way up, he noticed only there were now only three figures happily posing in the pictorial timeline of the Manry family—John, Margie, and Harris. His image was nowhere to be found. It was as if he had been completely erased from each picture.

Maybe they're playing a prank on me, Ben thought to himself as he rounded the second-story platform, nearly stopping in his tracks as a familiar painting came into view. It was *George Washington Crossing the Delaware* by Emanuel Gottlieb Leutze.

Harris and Sal were already in the computer room when Ben stumbled in. As he went to sit beside Sal on the futon, Ben took a glance into the mirror hanging beside the office work desk. His face was pale and ghastly, as if he'd just seen a ghost, and he felt as if he were looking at someone from a far off distant place, almost as if it was his long-dead face in the mirror staring back.

He took a seat and closed his eyes, breathing in slowly to clear his mind. He massaged his temples. In this meditative state he heard a voice calling from afar, but he recognized it as Leah's, now only a distant memory. Ben sighed as he grabbed at the necklace around his neck. He felt two pairs of eyes on him as he whispered a comforting prayer, holding his precious keepsake of a former life. He stared down at his hands and noticed the scarlet stone, mocking him.

Harris leaned back in his leather chair, glancing up at the skylight overhead. It was only noon, on the same exact Saturday that they had first departed for Roosevelt Island, but they all had almost a year's worth of living memories from the eighteenth century—battling pirates, sailing around the Atlantic, and serving under the brave privateer Captain Arthur F. Nelson.

Sal looked over—Ben's eyes were closed and Harris's eyes wide open. The brothers could be so different from each other at times, but throughout their endeavors, he had noticed many similarities between them. Sal twisted in his seat and the sound of his movement startled Ben.

"So, what do you guys want to do?" Harris called over his shoulder. Ben and Sal looked up from the futon.

"Eat. I'm starving," Sal said with a smile.

"Shower," Ben said quietly. He was still adjusting to everything, while it seemed as if the other two had never left the room.

Harris let out a hearty laugh. "Yeah, we need to get out of these clothes. We're lucky *my* dad didn't see us wearing this. He'd have a heart attack. He'd literally die laughing."

Ben looked away. Something was definitely awry.

※※※

Ben walked down the hall to the room he had lived in his entire life. He pushed open the door and stood there, appalled. He was stunned, completely befuddled.

It looked like a museum—almost as if it had not been touched or lived in for centuries. Where posters of his favorite sport teams used to be were now paintings of battlefields and ships; where his paintball gun and mask used to rest, there now lay an antique cutlass and pistol. It seemed as though the only thing that hadn't changed was the writing desk beside an ancient-looking bed. As he looked into the historical time capsule, he failed to notice a detailed painting. In it, three figures stood before a newly constructed house on the grounds of the very same twenty-five acre estate where he currently stood. A gold plaque dated 1778 was attached to the frame.

※※※

"Ah, the gloriousness that is modern plumbing," Ben whispered as the shower head above dumped a fast flow of extremely hot water over his skin. For almost a year now, all he'd had were streams in the wild and washbasins inside his stateroom to cleanse his body. Of course, he had quickly adapted to the change in lifestyle, but as the memories remained, thoughts of his two different lives continued to perplex him.

The water rinsed off the filth and grime of a life lived in the eighteenth century. He looked down at Leah's keepsake around his neck and the cursed ring on his left pinky. These two objects were facets of happy times and he smiled as he finished bathing. He turned off the shower and reached for a towel. Ben stepped out and stood before the mirror over the sink, watching the steam on the glass slowly fade away as the fan above cooled the room. A grizzled face stared back. His brown hair hung well past his eyes now, and he had the beginnings of a bright orange goatee clinging to his chin.

Ben took a step forward and opened the cabinet inside the mirror. His fingers grazed past several bars of soap, capsules of expired medicine, and finally settled on a can of shaving cream and a fresh razor. He had begun lathering his face when he heard a knock on the door.

"Come in," Ben called out.

The door edged open and John Manry peered in.

Ben shivered violently as he began to add the puzzle pieces together. He began hatching a conclusion. *Not only did my parents not recognize me, but there seems to be no evidence of me living here anymore. Harris kept saying* my *and not* our. *It doesn't make any sense. Not any of it.*

"Hello, Ben. Welcome to my home." He paused, staring in a friendly way into Ben's eyes. "The guys said you're new to town. Anyways, lunch will be ready in a few." The razor drew blood as he rounded his straight jawline with the blade.

"Damn!" Ben paused. "Okay, I'll be down shortly."

"Great. I brought some of *his* clothes. They should fit you. I laid them outside in the hall for when you're ready to get dressed."

"Thanks—," Ben replied sullenly.

As John Manry closed the door, Ben once again stared deeply into the mirror, unsure of how this new path of life would pan out.

"Damn it! It's like I don't belong here!"

Frustrated, Ben cursed loudly and slammed a fist into the sink's countertop. The sudden movement caused a drop of blood from his chin to fall into the sink below. Ben's deep blue eyes looked down as blood, water, and shaving cream mingled in its descent to the drain.

※※※

Margie Manry danced in the kitchen, waiting for the timer to go off. After a moment's tango, she moved to the stove and stared down into a pot of boiling rice. She picked up a wooden spoon that rested on a paper towel and stirred. Inside the oven, a pot roast was nearly done. She took a few long sniffs, and the aroma caused her to smile. She then moved to the countertop to toss the salad. Everything was nearly ready. She was excited to meet and talk to Ben in more detail.

"Come on, boys! Five minutes!"

※※※

Ben sat beside Harris and Sal on a couch in the living room. John Manry had his feet up on the leather Ottoman. He was sipping a beer from the bottle.

Ben was there physically, but his mind was elsewhere. He completely ignored the football game on the television, while the three others were on the edges of their seats, eagerly watching the game.

This was just too much to handle. He blinked his eyes for a minute, and his brain calculated dates and times. He tried to piece together fragments of his life. Memories glued themselves together but now only completed a slipshod timeline. What had actually happened? What had not?

Margie Manry entered and cleared her throat to get their attention. "Come on, guys. Dinner is ready."

As she flicked on the lights in the dining room, Ben caught a reflection in the scarlet stone upon his left finger. It looked like a face. He moved his hand closer to his eyes, and now he saw a crowded courtyard. There were cobblestones, showing between the bodies of a bustling populace. He saw the red hair of Captain Richard Highmore, and then his chest began to pound heavily. He saw Leah's blonde hair. She pushed aside a lock of hair that covered her eyes, revealing her face.

And then it hit him. He knew what he had to do.

✺✺✺✺

Dinner could have been summed up in one word—awkward.

Ben stood on the pier looking off into the gentle river that cut through the Manry estate. There were a few plastic canoes, a dinghy, and even a small powerboat tied to the wooden pier. Harris and Sal stood a few feet behind him, giving their best friend some much needed space.

Silence was their remedy for the time being. It was a temporary solution for what might just be a permanent problem.

Six eyes stared off into the distance, each of them thinking of the previous year they had lived through in the eighteenth century. There had been countless ups and downs, twists and turns in their shared roller coaster-like adventure.

When Ben was finally ready, he broke the silence. "Guys, I don't even know what to think."

Harris looked at Sal. They remained quiet.

Ben had mulled it over ever since they had returned from the cave. There was literally no evidence of the existence of Benjamin Manry in the present; however, there was plenty that supported his unique existence during the eighteenth century. That was why he was having such a difficult time accepting the fate that had been thrown his way.

Ben sat down, stretching his legs out in front of him. He leaned forward and untied his shoes, slipping them off. He peeled back his socks, then dipped his feet into the cool water below. It seemed to calm his nerves for the moment.

He palmed the edge of the pier as he swung his feet back and forth, his toes gliding through the water. The last rays of the day's sunlight caught the scarlet stone upon his left pinky. It sparkled, and he somehow knew it was a sign. Everything had turned out to be some sort of sign, supernatural occurrences that helped guide him. The locket around his neck seemed to grow warm. One face seemed etched into the back of his mind. It was a face he'd never forget—Leah Williamson's.

Of course, her surname was now Highmore, he remembered. He shook with thoughts of her marriage to Captain Richard Highmore, with memories of the man's deceit, and his undermining, behind-the-back attacks upon Ben and his friends. This was the one man who tried, and succeeded, in separating Ben and Leah for good.

Or had he?

Ben stared at the scarlet stone again. He smiled, remembering what Blood Bones had said inside the cave system.

He couldn't take his eyes off it. It glowed. It sparkled. It yielded a supernatural power—the power to travel freely through time at his whim.

His mind was made up.

He cleared his throat as he remained seated. Harris and Sal took the cue, and followed suit. They both removed their shoes, and their socks, and took a seat beside Ben.

"Guys, I'm going back for Leah." He removed three objects out of a large hiking pack he'd borrowed from Harris. He placed them on the dock beside them.

Harris and Sal smiled. "Aw, you're in love!"

"Yes. Yes, I am," Ben laughed. "She's the one I'm destined to be with. I am sure about it."

"So, what are you going to do?" Harris asked.

"I'm not sure exactly, but I guess I can go back to a specific point in time and live the remainder of my life there."

"What's your first move?" Sal kicked his toes in the water.

"Probably back to the day of the hanging. Rescue all our friends. Run away with Leah. Start a life together." Ben's eyes were closed as he laid out the plan.

Ben reached down for each item he had just brought out. The crimson journal contained countless stories and tales that Blood

Bones had written. Inside, he would learn of the man's style of leadership, which Sal and Harris had witnessed firsthand. His gaze then shifted to the medallion. He placed it around his neck. The trio stared down at the last remaining relic.

"Are you ready?" Harris asked.

Ben nodded. "Yeah, I think so." He slid his finger down the shaft of the magic staff, and felt for the pressure point. He slid the latch forward, and unlocked the stone's headpiece. Inside were several documents.

"Whoa, what is that?" As Sal peered over, his shadow blocked the sunlight from hitting the parchment below.

"I'm not sure; can you move a little?" Ben said. He held up what looked like a map of the Atlantic Ocean. The right side was jagged, as if it had been ripped from a larger document.

"The details are amazing!" Harris said. "That's awesome."

"Wait, this wasn't in here before when we first found it. It's like— Blood Bones left this for me."

Sal and Harris looked at each other, and then smiled at Ben.

Harris laughed. "It looks like you have another mission, besides rescuing Captain Nelson and the others."

"And finding Leah!" Sal added.

"It looks like I do," Ben said with a smile growing on his lips.

What he would soon find out was that he held a document called the Piri Re'is map. It had been constructed by a Turkish admiral and it was made using various charts, maps, and publications from the Library of Alexandria. It was rumored to be a map that led to lost city of Atlantis.

"I guess I should get a move on." Ben placed the journal back in the pack. He then rolled the map up and replaced it into the hollow tube of the scepter.

The magic staff had originally been given to Sir Francis Drake by Queen Elizabeth. Using the secret compartment, she had once exchanged documents with Drake and various other members of High Society. Blood Bones had obtained the scepter when he sacked *El Morro*.

And now, it was in the possession of the brave and fearless, Benjamin Manry.

The trio stood. They exchanged hugs and handshakes in silence. It was painful knowing they'd never see each other again, but deep down they each knew this was what had to be done.

It was written.

It was Benjamin Manry's fate.

Epilogue

ST. AUGUSTINE HIGH SCHOOL, FLORIDA
MONDAY, MODERN DAY

Harris Manry stirred from a deep sleep as he heard an alarm clock go off in a nearby room. He thought of all the night's dreams and nightmares before swinging his legs out of the bed. He yawned and cracked his back but was unaware of what time or even what day it was. The days of the past year had sort of all blended into one long dream, or nightmare. He wasn't sure which one. There were too many highs and lows throughout it all.

As he got out of bed, he yawned and scratched at an itch in his boxers. A knock on the door startled him.

"Come on Harris, you're going to be late for school," his mother's voice called from behind the closed door.

"What? Oh yeah," Harris paused, suddenly aware that the entire weekend had passed as if it had actually never really happened.

For almost the last year, Harris, his brother Ben and their best friend Sal had traipsed through the eighteenth century. But it was a Monday now, and on the calendar behind the teacher, no time had passed. He had seen things no senior in high school could even dream of.

The fact that he was back in modern day startled him. It was like it had all been a dream—a very awesome dream. He still cringed, knowing his brother was now traipsing through the eighteenth century.

※※※

"Sal Draben," the teacher called from behind her desk.

Sal rotated a coffee cup on his desk as he looked up. "Here."

The teacher marked him present, continuing down the list. A minute later, she was up to the letter M.

"Sally Madison," the teacher called out, reading the name off the attendance sheet. Sally responded with a "present."

Sitting at the desk beside Sal, Harris fidgeted anxiously—the pencil in his tight grip quivered impatiently as he waited for his name to be called.

Throughout the night, Harris had dreamt of the many adventures from his old life, of serving beside a lot of brave and daring men.

"Harris Manry," she called out.

"Here!" he called, eager to get through class so he could meet up with Sal at lunch and discuss the crazy adventures from their "extended" weekend.

A few more names were called and then the teacher paused.

"Hello all, I'm glad you are all present and all look like you had a pleasant weekend." She looked down at the course curriculum and smiled. "We'll continue with poetry from the previous class, but as a reminder I hope you all thought about the paper and presentation that's due at the end of the month." She stopped to look at a desk calendar. "As I look ahead at our schedule, next class we'll be doing a split segment with the U.S. History class." She paused for a moment while a few students laughed. There were also some deep and annoyed sighs of discontent. "Oh, class, it will be exciting! Since we are nearly done with the poetry of the early Americas, I wanted to give you all a sneak peak at U.S. History at that time, too."

She looked at her watch and then continued her speech as if she'd planned it the entire weekend. "Well, we will watch a video about the beginning of the Revolutionary War, the causes and some of the many theories behind them, as well as look at some key battles. There's a few interesting segments on the heroes of the war and of our early nation, of course. Come on, class, let's name some of the founding fathers of our great nation."

The class sighed as a whole. It was eight in the morning on a Monday. No one in their right mind wanted to be inside of that classroom, but slowly students began reciting the common knowledge.

"Benjamin…Franklin," one student called out.

The familiar first name caused Harris to shift in his seat, but then he heard the surname attached.

"Thomas Jefferson," another shouted.

"Good," the teacher said, eyeing the class to encourage more participation.

"Of course, George Washington," a girl hiding behind a textbook said from the back of the room.

"Yes, of course. He was the first President of the United States," the teacher smiled. There was a long delay then as the teacher prodded the class with her unflinching gaze. "Come on, there's another name on the list that we should all recognize. His estate isn't too far from the school, actually."

The class remained silent. Finally, one student called out a name that made Harris snap the pencil between his fingers. "Benjamin… Manry."

Another student added, "All we hear is Benjamin Manry this and Benjamin Manry that. What's so important about him?"

The teacher sighed with impatience. "Class, he was one of the founders of the United States Navy and Marine Corps, as well as being famous for personally saving George Washington's life in the crossing of the Delaware River. If it wasn't for that brave young man—who knows where our country would be today! We might even be speaking British English, and we'd all enjoy cups of tea and crumpets on our lunch break. You could say that he single handedly changed the fate of our country."

The class erupted in laughter at the absurd picture she painted.

Some of the teenagers nodded as the familiar story popped into conversation among the crowd.

Harris closed his eyes, remembering the date the Manry estate was built, the famous painting of the previously mentioned river crossing, and of the memories that he had shared with his brother and their best friend on their adventures traveling through the perils of time.

He opened his eyes and let out a laugh. Just the day before, he had said good-bye to Ben, and today, he was learning about him in the classroom.

✺✺✺

Leah's lower body was pinned to the edge of the platform as the crowd around her pushed forward to get a better view. Just as the gaoler had been about to put the blade to flesh, intending to end the unfortunate young man's frantic struggle, a display of colored lights and a howling wind had sent a wave of energy throughout the crowded courtyard.

And then Ben was gone—a blinding light momentarily flashed as whirlwinds of energy and light converged. She was hysterically crying as she pushed her way through the crowd to escape the event's reality.

✺✺✺

Ben was gone from her life yet again, and this time it seemed for good. It wasn't as if he was just going back to sea or even on another mission; this time Sal and Harris had also been sent to another place, but more importantly, another time.

As tears clouded her view, a figure rounded a corner and his large hands wrapped around her petite frame. The abrupt movement made Leah jump back, but Captain Richard Highmore held on tightly to his recent bride.

"I could have you arrested, do you know that?" he sneered with utter hatred for the young woman in front of him. He looked her up and down, pondering her wardrobe and vastly differently appearance from just moments before. She stood dressed as a British Royal Marine.

She was overwhelmed with emotion, and her tears continued to flow as if a dam had been broken.

A crowd formed around them, watching the spectacle. Confusion was on everyone's faces as a woman was wearing a man's uniform.

"Stop crying, you little whore! He's gone, this time for good! Just like you will be if you continue on like this," Highmore said, extremely irate. "We are leaving now for Southdowns. All our things are packed and ready. Come along quietly or I will make you."

Leah tugged away, attempting escape only to meet with a backhand from her husband. Her eyes welled with a fresh wave of tears as a trickle of blood from her split lip smeared her chin. Highmore continued pulling hard on his relenting wife, and finally the two emerged into an empty street that paralleled the courtyard. As if on cue, a horse carriage moved from a hundred paces down the alley and stopped at the curb before them.

"I despise you!" Leah cried out as she struggled against the man's brute force.

He threw her against the carriage door, and held her there for a moment.

"You may despise me now, my beautiful bride, but someday you will learn to love me." He gave her an evil smile. "It may take quite some time."

Leah spit into his face. "I could never love an animal like you!" She slapped him repeatedly, but he continued to push her against the carriage door. She managed to hit him several times in the face, causing a fit of laughter in her husband.

"You think you can fight me? I may just have have my way with you now right her and now, and whenever I deem it necessary. After all, you are just a common whore!" He sneered his insult.

Leah felt the hilt of a small blade on her hip, and realized she still had it on her.

"I can, and I will."

In one fluid motion, she pushed against him hard, allowing her right hand to free itself from the carriage door. He stumbled back a foot, but it was enough for Leah to draw the short blade, and quickly slice at her husband's face.

The blade dug in, right across the eyebrow and sliced through his left eyeball. He fell instantly to his knees, howling in pain. It was not a fatal strike, but he would carry the scar until he was six feet under. It would forever mark him as a coward.

"If you were half the man Benjamin *was*, I may have thought of marrying you on my own accord!" Leah yelled. Something inside her flipped upside-down. Whether it was the training she had from serving under Blood Bones, or finally being able to speak her mind, something gave. And she embraced every ounce of the newfound strength and energy that surged through her body.

The crowd cheered at the dispute, but the attention now warranted guards and other military to investigate.

She was surrounded on all three sides by men with swords drawn and pikes raised. She stood tall and proud, with her back to the carriage door, ready to fight to the death if needed. *I have already lost Benjamin, there is not much else to live for*, she thought. She held the short blade high, swinging it around to keep her distance from the approaching mob.

And then out of nowhere, a horseman atop a beautiful white stallion barreled through the crowd. Men and women were knocked to the side, and as Benjamin Manry had promised her, he had at last come to her rescue. He reached down, and pulled her onto the saddle. She held onto him tightly, and a tear of joy escaped her eyes as Ben raced away towards the seaport. He had a ship to catch.

*F*ifteen years later, Benjamin Arthur Manry walked beside his father and mother as the trio stood before their newly constructed home. The vibrant six-year-old smiled as he quickly grabbed at his father's right hand.

"Poppa! Poppa! Build me one next!"

Leah Manry chuckled, slipping a hand into Ben's empty left. Her fingertips grazed the scarlet stone that shone brightly on his left pinky. The two looked at each other before staring at their two-story home. It was large and beautiful, set on twenty-five acres of land, with a stream running through the center of the estate.

"Benjamin, it looks magnificent!" Captain Arthur F. Nelson said as he approached from the dirt road that led into the town of St. Augustine. He had been like a father to Ben since they had met back in 1763.

"I hereby concur!" Charles Marconi added, also newly arriving to the group.

"Aye, well done, lad. The three of you will have a long and happy life together in this house," Nate Brodkin chipped in.

David Hawley and Jacob Hughson stood several feet behind with a group of Irajan warriors that had served Captain Arthur F. Nelson throughout the American Revolution.

Even America's first president, George Washington, was in attendance for the celebration. They let out a cheerful laugh. The sun was setting, and its rays cast a brilliant reflection off the stream that bordered the house. At the edge of the steam, several poles stuck out of the mud for Ben's next project—a dock.

He had promised his young and adventurous son he would soon take him to the secret caves on Roosevelt Island. The caves were rumored to have the buried treasure of Atlantis hidden deep within.

CPSIA information can be obtained at www.ICGtesting.com
Printed in the USA
BVOW040810270313

316533BV00002B/59/P